What Is Left
the
Daughter

**Center Point
Large Print**

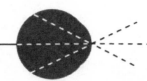

**This Large Print Book carries the
Seal of Approval of N.A.V.H.**

What Is Left
the
Daughter

HOWARD NORMAN

CENTER POINT PUBLISHING
THORNDIKE, MAINE

This Center Point Large Print edition
is published in the year 2010 by arrangement with
Houghton Mifflin Harcourt Publishing Company.

The text of this Large Print edition is unabridged.
In other aspects, this book may vary
from the original edition.
Printed in the United States of America
on permanent paper.
Set in 16-point Times New Roman type.

ISBN: 978-1-60285-897-8

Library of Congress Cataloging-in-Publication Data

Norman, Howard A.
  What is left the daughter / Howard Norman.
    p. cm.
  ISBN 978-1-60285-897-8 (library binding : alk. paper)
  1. Life change events—Fiction. 2. Germans—Canada—Fiction.
  3. World War, 1939–1945—Canada—Fiction. 4. Nova Scotia—Fiction.
  5. Large type books. I. Title.
  PR9199.3.N564W47 2010b
  813′.54—dc22
                                                    2010024059

FOR EMMA

I can't swim at all, and it is dangerous to converse with an unaccustomed Element.
—ERASMUS

What Is Left the Daughter

M ARLAIS, today is March 27, 1967, your twenty-first birthday. I'm writing because I refuse any longer to have my life defined by what I haven't told you. I've waited until now to relate the terrible incident that I took part in on October 16, 1942, when I was nineteen.

Your mother, Tilda Hillyer, frequently consulted *The Highland Book of Platitudes*, which had 411 pages. She had it practically memorized. She found instruction and solace in that book, even the solution to certain puzzles about life. But I thought all those platitudes put together avoided the fact that life is unpredictable. For instance, after moving hotel to hotel here in Halifax for many years, I've finally returned to my childhood house at 58 Robie Street, which I never thought I'd set foot in again.

In fact, it's now three A.M.—I scarcely sleep anyway—and I'm writing at my kitchen table.

Two Sundays ago, I stopped in at Harbor Methodist Church. On occasion I do that. More out of nostalgia than present faith, to say the least. Anyway, when I entered the church Reverend Lundrigan was recounting some ancient parable or other in which an elderly woman listens to her son hold forth about how much heartbreak, sour luck and spiritual depletion can be packed into a life. But talk as he might, the man from the parable fails to address the one thing his mother is most curious about. "What of your daughter?" she asks. "Have you seen her? How is her life? Do not doubt that wonderment may be found when you find her again." Turns out, the man hasn't seen his own daughter in ages. "Rain, wind, hunger, thirst, joy and sorrow have visited her all along," the woman says. "Yet her father has not." She listens more, all the while experiencing a deeper and deeper sadness, until finally she says, "And what is left the daughter?" She doesn't mean heirloom objects. She doesn't mean money. She doesn't care about anything like those. She says, "I think you have a secret untold that keeps a distance between you and her and the life you were given."

Well, Marlais, you know how people talked in biblical times. Still, when I left the church, I thought, Strange how you can't predict during which happenstance you might take something to heart. And right then and there I understood that all I had to leave you, really, is what I'm writing here. I've read some of the English poet John Keats, and he said something to the effect that memory shouldn't be confused with knowledge. Of course, I have no way of knowing if, after you've read a paragraph or two, any curiosity you might've had will abruptly sour to disgust, or worse. Yet I hope you'll see these pages through. And that whatever else you may think, whatever judgments you come to, please at least accept the knowledge that I've always loved you, without cease.

How Your Father Became an Apprentice in Sleds and Toboggans in the Village of Middle Economy, Nova Scotia

In *The Highland Book of Platitudes*, Marlais, there's an entry that reads, "Not all ghosts earn our memory in equal measure." I think about this sometimes. I think especially about the word "earn," because it implies an ongoing willful effort on the part of the dead, so that if you believe the platitude, you have to believe in the afterlife, don't you? Following that line of thought, there seem to be certain people—call them ghosts—with the ability to insinuate themselves into your life with more belligerence and exactitude than others—it's their employment and expertise.

My parents are such people. How else to describe it? Let me try. Last evening, for instance, I sat at the table. It was lightly raining. I was having a cup of tea, listening to a Beethoven quartet (Quartet No. 9 in C Major, my favorite) on the nightly classical radio program, when suddenly the broadcast was interrupted by static. Maybe I take things with the radio too personally, but I got the uneasy feeling—I've felt this many times—the static was really my mother's and father's indecipherable tidings from the afterlife. Were they trying to tell me something? What was the message?

I imagine that your mother informed you of this—maybe she didn't—but let me say it directly. My own mother, Katherine, and my father, Joseph, leapt from separate bridges in Halifax on the same evening. I was seventeen. Oh, it was quite the scandal. It made for bold headlines in the *Halifax Mail* (page two the day after it happened, page four the following day; the war was on, so most of the front page was reserved for Allied victories and setbacks, and Axis atrocities). So there I was, a spectacle for every Haligonian to pity, victim of a SORDID LOVE TRIANGLE, orphaned all of a single hour, on August 27, 1941, between six and seven o'clock, not quite dusk at that time of year, but almost. Odd as it might sound, the first thing I experienced, past the initial shock, was embarrassment. And when I returned to school the day after the funerals, I could hardly breathe for the shame and embarrassment of it all. That may not reflect well on me, but it's the truth. Of course, at night the weird sadness found me, and everything familiar to my life, absolutely everything, had suddenly become unfamiliar.

It's been twenty-six years, then, since my father leapt from the Halifax-Dartmouth Toll Bridge, connecting Highway 111 to the Bedford Highway, my mother from the toll bridge connecting North Street to Windmill Road. Rough waters that day under all bridges, Bedford Basin to Halifax Harbor, wild dark skies and gulls more catapulted and buffeted than flying here to there, all of which I could see from my high school on Barrington Street. Anyway, I keep the clippings in a mintwood box. Among their headlines are UNUSUAL LOVE NEST RESULTS IN TWIN SUICIDES and MYSTERY WOMAN CAUSES FAMILY TRAGEDY.

Have you ever read the poet Emily Dickinson? She says that to travel all you need to do is close your eyes. Here at 58 Robie some nights, I close my eyes and I'm back on August 27, 1941, sitting on the porch when the first of two police cars pulls up in front of our house. Imagine, only ten or fifteen minutes before, I'd gotten a phone call telling me what'd happened. And here I'd been complaining to myself: Where is everybody? Am I going to have to make my own supper?

First page to last, *The Highland Book of Platitudes*, originally published in Scotland, does not contain a platitude that addresses a woman falling in love with a woman, and a man falling in love with the same woman. Yet that was the situation with my parents—and this included our next-door neighbor Reese Mac Isaac. In 1941 Reese Mac Isaac was thirty-five years old. Her hair was the color of dark honey, she was slim and dressed smart, and was, to my mind, as lovely and mysterious as any woman you'd see in an advertisement for perfume in the *Saturday Evening Post*. My family didn't have a subscription, but you could find copies in the lobby of the Lord Nelson Hotel, on Spring Garden Road across from the Public Gardens.

In fact, Reese was employed as a switchboard operator at the hotel. Also, she'd taken acting lessons, and in 1937 had appeared in *Widow's Walk*. It was a picture about a woman whose husband's fishing boat capsizes in a storm on the same night she'd been dallying with the handsome village doctor. Out of guilt and remorse, the woman goes mad and spends the rest of her nights in a widow's walk atop her house. For the few months that it was being filmed, *Widow's Walk* was all the gossip. Referred to as "an all-Canadian production," most of it was shot near Port Medway—they'd even built a temporary lighthouse.

In the heart of winter the following year, *Widow's Walk* played in Halifax and I went to see it with my parents. Just after the opening credits, Reese Mac Isaac appeared on screen. She played a hotel switchboard operator! "Hold on, please," she said, and listened through an earpiece. "I'm sorry, your party is not answering. Try again later, please." This scene took all of thirty seconds. Still, I was impressed, and though *Widow's Walk* had no true movie stars in it and box-office-wise it fell short of popularity, I imagined all sorts of associations. I wondered, Had Reese met Loretta Young? Had she met Tyrone Power? Had she met Jean Harlow? When the meager audience filed out of the theater, I said, "Pretty lucky of them to find someone with firsthand experience with switchboards like Reese has!"

Right there on the sidewalk my parents fell apart laughing. My mother said, "Darling, I hate to point out the obvious, but Reese Mac Isaac's cameo took place in the switchboard cubby she actually works in, six A.M. to three P.M. every day but Sunday."

"Hardly a big stretch," my father said.

"I don't care," I said. "She did well with what she was given."

A week after the funerals, as I lay on the sofa drinking whiskey to try and help me sleep, I realized that I didn't begrudge my father that he loved Reese Mac Isaac. The same went for my mother, all received morality notwithstanding, for which I didn't give a good goddamn, not in the least. I knew that my parents no longer loved each other. Since I was eight or nine I knew it, even earlier. Civility had become their mainstay. Civility bowed and curtsied—"Good night, dear"—as they went to separate bedrooms.

I suppose that I was happy enough that we all

still lived under the same roof. Besides, in high school I was captain of the fencing team, and fencing, in 1941, had most of my attention. I'd placed well in tournaments as far-flung as St. John's, Newfoundland. (I quit fencing after my parents died, just somehow lost the connection to it.) And though I'd been quite friendly with Reese Mac Isaac, had even paid the price of a ticket to see her play a handmaiden in a stage production of *Romeo and Juliet*, I can't say that I knew much about her. However, one summer night when I was fifteen, I caught sight of Reese dressed in a nightgown—it looked silky—with a pattern of outsized lilies, exotic nightwear for Halifax, I thought. She was watering the three plants on her kitchen sill with an eyedropper. My thought was, That's being frugal, though it might be stinginess.

Truth be told, after my parents' suicides, for days on end my emotions roughed me up, and I went from seething anger to stupefying bewilderment to sadness that put me to bed at odd hours. What's certain is that it was during this period my sleepless nights began. My parents are buried in Camp Hill Cemetery. Their funerals were an hour apart, each officiated by Reverend Carmichael, then at Harbor Methodist, the church with which my parents had a hit-or-miss affiliation.

Chapter and verse, Reverend Carmichael's

services were standard. The fencing team attended. My mother had been an accountant at HMC Dockyard, and many of her colleagues paid their respects. My father owned a stationery and typewriter repair shop on Grafton Street, and I can recall his business partner, Mr. Amoury, at the graveside, along with Mrs. Amoury and their two daughters. When he and I shook hands, I noticed that Mr. Amoury had typewriter ribbon smudges on his fingers.

When all was said and done, I handed Reverend Carmichael fifty dollars in an envelope. He looked inside and shook his head and said, "You know, I usually charge fifty dollars each, but this was"—and he couldn't find the next word. Then he left. During both services it had been drizzling, but afterward people held their umbrellas closed. As they milled about, I didn't have a single direct conversation. Instead, I walked around half in a daze, mostly eavesdropping, I think. For instance, there was Oliver Tapper, who wrote the "Canadians at the Front" column for the *Sunday Mail.* Oliver, who had published a collection of patriotic poems, was a regular customer at my father's shop, often in a panic, claiming some emergency deadline. On the wet grass of the cemetery he said, "Look, there's poor Katherine not ten feet away, and there's, right in front of us, poor Joseph. All this good air to breathe and guess who gets to breathe it, none other than that—harlot! That wretched failed actress!"

"What are you saying, Oliver?" Mrs. Tapper said. "You want fairness? You want her punished for sordid immoralities? Well, those were *shared,* don't forget. And besides, we're at a funeral. Please mind your language."

Oh, I almost forgot, the most peculiar newspaper headline was accompanied by a photograph of me, the one taken for the high school yearbook: LOCAL BOY ORPHANED BY BRIDGES. As if I weren't already seventeen, hardly a boy. As if it were the bridges' fault, not human nature's.

You only live the life right in front of you. All day at school on August 27, which was just the fifth day of classes in the autumn 1941 term, I had no idea how my parents' fates were being determined. We'd all had breakfast together. My father had been chatty; my mother wasn't sullen. Later, though, I pieced a few things together from the newspaper accounts and from conversations—call them that—I had with the police officers who'd been sent out to the bridges.

Officer Dhomnaill, who was born in Ireland and still retained the accent, told me about my mother. "I tried talking her down," he said. "You try and make the person in distress confide what makes them happy in life. You try and work with that if at all possible. See what I mean? And I'm sorry I failed. Very sorry in the end I failed." I could see that Officer Dhomnaill was honestly shaken.

"Didn't she at least say goodbye to me?" I asked. "Because she didn't leave a note."

"Being so fraught as your mother was," he said, "and what with the wind high on that bridge making it so difficult to catch every last word. But I think she said, 'I suppose this will be all over the radio. No matter. I have nothing to be ashamed about.' "

"Okay. All right, then. Thank you."

"My job's hardly all peaches and cream," Dhomnaill said. "Your mother was my first jumper. Some police never get one. Don't please let that word offend you. It's just a police word."

"I understand."

"I'm sorry for what happened."

I'm afraid I shut the door in his face.

When it came to my father, an Officer Padgett delivered the report. He knocked, and I stepped out on the porch again. We shook hands and he said, "I know Officer Dhomnaill stopped by earlier."

"Yes, he did."

"So I am speaking to Mr. Wyatt Hillyer, then. Correct?"

"Correct."

"Wyatt, just let me say my piece. Officially say it. So I can get back to the station house, and say

I said it, and do my paperwork. Leave you with your private thoughts, eh?"

"Fine."

He consulted his notebook. "I arrived to the bridge at six-fifteen P.M.," he said. "I climbed up close as possible to your father. He looked tired. To me he looked tired. He said, 'For a long time I've had this private joke. So private I never told my wife. It's what I want on my gravestone. What I want on my gravestone is: *I just knew this would happen!*'" He checked his notes again. "And your father said, 'Both women were damn interesting, each in their own way. There it is. Tell my son, Wyatt, to forgive me, please. Ask him to at least try.' I asked him what's his name, and he said Joseph Hillyer. So I said, 'Joseph, do you like the steaks at Halloran's?' Since in our training we're taught to try and persuade a person back into normal daily life. You mention a pop-ular restaurant. Or you ask which church they attend. But your father let go of the bridge."

I stepped back inside and shut the door and watched through the window as Officer Padgett got into his car. There seemed no apparent reason, but he kept his siren on the whole way down the block.

Naturally, my aunt Constance Bates-Hillyer and my uncle Donald Hillyer drove in from Middle Economy to attend the funerals. They also stayed on to help me get things in order, settle my parents' estate, so called. It consisted of 58 Robie Street, completely paid for, a modest life insurance settlement, $1,334 in a savings account, and my mother's collection of radios. "I have absolutely no idea of the worth of these radios or how to find out," my uncle said. "We can look into that later."

All told, my mother had fifty-eight radios. The sound of radio voices or music had almost nightly drifted into my bedroom, the volume turned up when my parents wanted to deafen me to their quarreling. Among her collection was a 1938 International Kadette, a white Silvertone, four different Bakelite models, and a Philco Transitone. She had two Fada radios, a 1939 RCA from the Golden Gate International Exposition in San Francisco (she didn't attend), a Zenith Model 835 and other wood-frame sets. She had a Crosley chrome radio, an RCA Victor La Siesta, which featured a colorful painting of a man in a sombrero sitting near a tall saguaro cactus with mountains and clouds in the distance. She had a Kadette Topper, an Emerson Snow White model that had an inlaid design of Snow White and the Seven Dwarfs (they were creepy), and three Detrola Pee Wee models, red and white, black, and blue and white. There were three small molded-plastic radios made by the F.A.D. Andrea Corporation, RCA and Crosley. She had a Bendix with a fake mottled mahogany casing, and that one had standard broadcast and shortwave bands and could operate on both AC and DC power. In the last three years of her life, my mother preferred novelty sets adorned with popular celebrities. For instance, there was a Stewart Warner set with a decal of the famous Dionne quintuplets, who'd been taken away from their parents but kept together in a foster home. My mother followed that story religiously. "Heartbreaking," she said. "It's really too much to bear." On the decal, the Dionne quints appeared to be about three years old. They were standing together, all hope and smiles.

On September 15, my aunt and uncle and I took a walk down to the harbor. We each held a paper cup of coffee and stood looking at the ferries, tugs, freighters and ocean liners. The steamer *Victoria* was boarding. We were close enough to see the passengers walking up the gangway, and suddenly I thought I saw Reese Mac Isaac. It was unseasonably cold, and she was wearing a camel-hair coat and black scarf, holding a suitcase, though I imagine her wardrobe trunk was already on board ship. At one point she turned as if to gaze back at Halifax, and I saw her face in full. It was Reese all right. I must've let out a gasp or made some other involuntary sound, because my aunt said, "What's the matter, dear?"

"Nothing," I said. "Nothing at all. Except I was just thinking how grateful I am for all you've done. I haven't been much of a nephew to you. I hardly ever visit."

"That's all right, dear," my aunt said. "When you have visited, we always had a lovely time."

"Wyatt," my uncle said, "the way you've been looking at those passengers makes me think you'd like to be on that steamer to New York. I've noticed some handsome women getting on board."

"Donald, it sounds like it's *you* wishes that for yourself," my aunt said.

Small laughter all around. "I've really only traveled anywhere with my fencing team," I said. "I'd like to see New York someday, though."

"You're going to need a trade, Nephew," my uncle said. "Constance and I talked this over. Would you consider sleds and toboggans? I can use an apprentice. Someday I might leave the business to you, say it's still thriving as it's been lately. In fact, I've got orders backed up from three provinces, plus Maine and Vermont in the States."

"Don't forget that family from Sweden who stopped to ask directions and admired your handiwork," my aunt said.

"They spent a good hour with us," he said.

"Well, people from those countries—Sweden, Denmark, Norway and the like—appreciate snow toboggans, even in summer," my aunt said.

"Lord help us, I've just had a sorry thought,"

my uncle said. "What if that Swedish family wants to pay me in Swedish money?"

"I'd deal with the problem right away," my aunt said. "Discuss it in a letter ahead of time. Then just hope the war lets a letter get to Sweden."

"Sound advice, Constance," he said. "I'll want to set their minds at ease that our provincial banks know how to handle such a transaction."

The *Victoria* pulled in its gangway. "Should I sell the house, do you think?" I said. "I mean, if I take you up on your generous offer."

"I wouldn't sell just yet," my aunt said.

"No—ask rent," my uncle said. "What with the view of the park, it shouldn't be difficult. No, I'd hang on to the house, Wyatt. Hang on to your mother's radios, too. If you decide yes, drive on out to Middle Economy when you're ready. Or you could leave the house unoccupied. You might want to stay in it now and then. You're a young man. There's far more entertainment in the city. Movie houses, pubs, young ladies and so forth."

"That's not saying much," my aunt said, "considering our entertainment at home's watching gulls bicker on the trawlers."

"Anyway, Wyatt, you're resourceful," my uncle said. "And besides, you'll have Joe's car, right? You can drive into Halifax any time you like."

I slept on it, and the next morning I accepted the apprenticeship. The fact was, I didn't want to spend another minute alone in the house, deploring my circumstances. I decided to leave 58 Robie empty. My aunt and uncle went home. Several days later I stopped by my high school and filled out an official form that declared I wasn't intending to graduate. "Good luck to you, then, Wyatt," Mrs. Cornish, the assistant principal, said. "Have you said goodbye to your friends yet?"

"I've told who I wanted to tell," I said.

"I hear it's nice along the Bay of Fundy," she said. "Fifty-three years in Nova Scotia and I've never been."

Directly from the school, I drove my father's black DeSoto four-door—badly in need of repairs, but they could wait—to Middle Economy, smoking Chesterfield cigarettes one after the next. Nowadays it's paralleled by Highway 102, but in 1941 you could only take Route 2 north to Truro, at the center of the province. Between the roadside villages of Beaver Bank, Home Settlement, Shubenacadie, Alton, Stewiacke, Hilden and Millbrook were long stretches of woods and fields. In Truro I stopped for a sandwich at Canaan's Restaurant and took considerable time in a shop choosing a box of chocolates for my aunt. From Truro I traveled west on Route 2, the blue-gray expanse of the Minas Basin on my left, rain clouds building on the horizon. Through the villages of Central

Onslow, Glenholme, Great Village, Portapique, Bass River, Upper Economy, then into Middle Economy. Because of the condition of the DeSoto I had to drive slowly. The entire trip took about four and a half hours.

My aunt and uncle's house was half a mile inland from the Minas Basin, along Cove Road. I moved into the spare bedroom. That first year I went back to visit Halifax five or six weekends, but never once slept at 58 Robie, didn't even drive past. Instead I stayed at the Baptist Spa, on Morris and Barrington, $1.25 a night. Shared washroom down the hall. Breakfast served in a small dining room on the street level.

But the evening before I'd left Halifax, my next-door neighbor on the side opposite Reese Mac Isaac's house, elderly Mr. Lessard, said he'd be willing to look after things, mow the lawn, clip the shrubbery, forward any mail—there was little mail—leave a few lights on at night, that sort of thing. "Part of the booming nightlife of Halifax of late's been break-ins," he said.

"I'm not too worried," I said.

"Well, I liked Katherine and Joe," he said. "Besides, it's hardly putting me out, now, is it? I don't take my morning constitutional to the harbor and back anymore. But I'm still capable of walking next door."

"I appreciate it."

"One thing, and I'd need your permission," he

said. "I'd like to have all your mother's radios on at the same time, just during *Classical Hour* out of Buffalo, as it might be the closest I'll ever get to hearing a full orchestra in person. Reese Mac Isaac's gone to New York City, anyone's guess for how long. So the radios won't disturb her. I haven't figured out yet how to plug them all in and not blow every fuse in the house, but somebody at Metcalf's Electric will advise."

"It's all fine with me," I said.

"I'll do this only once," Mr. Lessard said. "It'd be a Sunday night, since that's when *Classical Hour* comes on. I'll make my decision which Sunday by checking the programming schedule in the newspaper. I won't stand for any godforsaken Vivaldi. You don't have to worry about that. Beethoven, Johann Sebastian Bach and a bunch of others—they're allowed. Would you care to be told on which Sunday I had all the radios on at once?"

"Not necessary," I said.

"All right, then, Wyatt," he said. "Good luck to you. I'll look after your house. Vivaldi won't break in. Not on my watch."

Are You Sure You Took Down What the Radio Said Word for Word?

MIDDLE ECONOMY SITS between Upper Economy and Lower Economy. Upper Economy is farthest west. Locally the joke was, if you were traveling west to east along the Minas Basin, your financial prospects got worse by the mile, until finally you ended up in Lower Economy. I never once heard the logic of that joke reversed: if you traveled from east to west, you'd get rich. I suppose it just wasn't the disposition of people born and raised in that part of Nova Scotia to tell it that way.

I hadn't set eyes on Tilda in close to four years, since the summer of 1937, when she would have been going into ninth form. On that occasion, Tilda had come to Halifax with my aunt and uncle because Constance needed to have a tooth pulled, and they all spent the night at my family's house. Despite my aunt's being in pain, we had a nice family reunion. Though I do recall my father and uncle sitting in the parlor after supper discussing in somber tones Hitler and Germany, commenting on radio broadcasts made by Winston Churchill. My mother sat on the porch, providing my aunt with powdered aspirin and commiserating with her over her throbbing tooth. At one point Tilda and I were playing a spirited game of checkers at the dining room table when we heard my aunt call out the word "Groan!" which extended into an actual groan. That made us laugh, though sympathetically. Also, we couldn't help but eavesdrop on my father and uncle. "My dad's got more opinions about current events than the Smith Brothers have cough drops," Tilda said.

I think I was five or six when I first met Tilda. I remember how my mother put it: "You're about to have a very special surprise, darling. Aunt Constance and Uncle Donald couldn't have children of their own. God saw to that—no, no, I mean God has graced their lives with a new little girl. They've named her Tilda. They're all coming to visit this afternoon."

Tilda's real parents had lived in Glenholme, which is fairly close to the Economys. There was no immediate family, or none willing to take Tilda, age two, when her parents died within three months of each other. The only word about that I ever heard was "wasting disease."

Anyway, my aunt's dentist appointment was at nine the next morning. While Tilda sat in the waiting room, my uncle took the opportunity to ship out two sleds directly from the train station. I'd gone along. "My very first customers from British Columbia," he said. "You just can't get any further away in Canada than that, can you? Excepting Eskimo territories, and I'd be God's biggest fool to think Eskimos would need one of my sleds." By one o'clock they were back on the road. I can still see them driving off. My aunt sat in the middle, her face swollen, still groggy from laughing gas. She leaned against Tilda's shoulder. When my uncle's truck got five or six houses down the block, Tilda, without turning to look back, stretched her arm out the window and waved goodbye. It's my self-generated theory that Tilda assumed I'd be watching from the porch, not wanting her to leave—that she somehow knew, far in advance of me, that I already loved her, even though we'd spent virtually no time alone and had made only small talk.

Two habits were set early on in my life in Middle Economy. One was set by my uncle, the other was set by me. Starting the first day of my apprenticeship, my uncle insisted that I join him every workday morning for breakfast in the kitchen at six A.M., allowing us to be in the work shed by six-forty-five sharp. Then, with his permission, at ten I'd drive my DeSoto over to the bakery owned and operated by Mrs. Cornelia Tell and spend my half-hour break over a coffee.

The bakery was in the center of town. On one side was MAUD'S SEWING (Maud Dunne sat in the window working her sewing machine), on the other BAIT AND TACKLE. Early on, I'd got a sample of how Cornelia Tell questioned all motives for politeness. I'd sat down and said, "Would it be too much trouble if I got a scone with my coffee?" Cornelia Tell shot back, "Even if it does cause me trouble, do you still want a scone?" I never put it that way again, believe me. I just said, "I'd like a scone." That same morning, while I sat eating a cranberry scone and drinking my coffee, Cornelia Tell was behind the counter, swirling frosting on cupcakes. "Today being Tuesday," she said, "do you know who you're going to meet back home at lunch?"

"I have no idea," I said.

"You'll be sitting down for lunch with Lenore Teachout. She's originally from Great Village, not too far down the road. Her parents still live there."

"And why would Lenore Teachout be at our house today?"

"Because every Tuesday, Wednesday, Thursday and Friday—except earlier this week she had a cold—Lenore carries a box of pencils, a pencil sharpener, a notebook and an exercise book called *Shorthand Self-Taught* over to your house. She knocks on your door and your aunt lets her inside and serves tea. Then Lenore listens to your radio. She writes down what people on the radio say. She practices stenography—do you know what stenography is, Wyatt?"

"There's a stenographer in Magistrate's Court, right?"

"Right as rain. And that's the employment Lenore Teachout aspires to. And it's very sensible of her. Because Lenore potentially could find work in any Canadian city where there's a busy courthouse."

"Why does she practice stenography in our house, though?"

"Because she doesn't own a radio."

"You seem to know a lot about her."

"Your aunt Constance and I are dear, dear friends, Wyatt. True, even the dearest of friends keep things from each other, but they don't keep everything from each other. Your aunt keeps very little about Lenore Teachout from me."

"Does Lenore know that?"

"Maybe, maybe not. Anyway, you'll notice how tall Lenore is. She was always tall for her age. Wait here, I'll show you something."

Cornelia Tell went out the door onto the street, then back in an adjacent door that led up a flight of stairs to her rooms. She'd lived above her bakery since her husband, Llewyn, a fisherman, had drowned at sea twenty-three years earlier. When she returned to the bakery she set down a copy of the Great Village Elementary School yearbook for 1914 and paged through the grainy individual portraits of administrators, the school nurse, teachers and students, and a photograph of all the students taken near the flagpole. "Aha!" she said, "found it!" She placed her finger on a quarter-page photograph of a Christmas pageant. "This girl, right here, is Lenore Teachout, age ten. Your aunt Constance brought this to my attention." I bent close and saw that Lenore was costumed up as a camel, on all fours, men's shoes for hooves, a bale of hay on her back, posed next to the Magi and a crèche. "They made her a camel," Mrs. Tell said, "because she was tall for her age, eh?"

"She doesn't look too happy there," I said.

"Unhappiness followed Lenore all the way up to her adult life," Cornelia Tell said, "though lately she seems less unhappy, which bodes well. Anyway, who in their right mind would ever say a person was *supposed* to be happy? In your life happiness is either cut to your length or isn't."

"Thanks, Cornelia, for all the this-and-that about Lenore Teachout, whom I'm about to share lunch with," I said.

"You're very welcome." She noticed that I had a few bites of scone and half a cup of coffee left. "Let's see, what else?" she said. "Well, Lenore had a year at Dalhousie University. The first in her family to go to college. Too bad Halifax proved to be all distractions. Lenore made a whirlwind marriage to a fellow student, then just as whirlwind a divorce. Have to hand it to her, though, she fit a lot into that month of February! I remember Lenore saying, 'True, I failed my academic course work. But I kept my ears open and got highly educated in the thoughts of men and women.' According to rumor—I suspect a rumor started by Lenore herself—during her time in Halifax she kept over a thousand pages of a journal full of conversations. I don't know where she got the moxie, but she didn't merely eavesdrop, she actually wrote down what she'd overheard!"

"A thousand pages," I said. "That's impressive."

"I once asked her, 'Lenore, don't you annoy people, writing down their every word like that?' And do you know, she got all huffy and said, 'Well, Cornelia, aren't you grateful someone took down all those actual conversations found in the Bible? What if nobody had bothered? Where would we all be then?'"

"I'll have to think about that one," I said.

"You do that," Cornelia Tell said.

I paid for my scone and coffee, stepped outside the bakery, smoked a Chesterfield and then drove back to the house. In the shed, while my uncle measured and cut crosspieces, I sanded planks for an hour or so, trying not to respond to his sidelong glances or deep sighs, which were judgments of my work. It didn't much bother me. Finally, he said, "You go on in, Wyatt. I'm skipping lunch today, I'm pretty sure. Aggravated stomach. Maybe bring out a thermos of tea when you come back, okay?"

"Sure thing, Uncle Donald."

"You're doing fine, by the way. Honestly, better than I expected."

"Damning with faint praise, but thanks."

When I entered the house through the back door, I heard Tilda talking to someone in the kitchen. Taking off my work shoes, I listened in.

"—what with Wyatt sleeping in the room next to mine, I don't feel nearly as comfortable walking around in my birthday suit, eh? Not that he can see through walls or anything. It's just that I like to be—how's Mom say it? 'Elegant in my dailiness.' It just wouldn't feel right somehow. From now on I'll have to change directly from clothes to nightshirt, no lingering in between. Hardly a sacrifice, is it, considering how grateful Wyatt must be to have a home with relatives, employment, not having to go it alone in Halifax. Wouldn't you agree, Lenore?"

"Fully agree with everything," Lenore said.

"Did you catch every last word?" Tilda asked.

"I think so," Lenore said.

"Read it back to me, then."

Lenore began, " 'You know, Lenore, what with Wyatt sleeping in the room next to mine—' " But I shuffled loudly, on purpose, into the kitchen. Tilda turned toward me, holding a tray, which held two cups of tea, a porcelain hippopotamus full of sugar, two cloth napkins and a spoon. "Oh, Wyatt!" she said. "Speak of the devil."

I looked away. Tilda must've thought it was out of embarrassment.

Then I glanced at Lenore. Factoring in her ten-year-old self from the yearbook, I thought, Yes, she appears to be about thirty-seven or thirty-eight. She had a lovely face, including deep worry lines, cascading brown hair. She was wearing the same sorts of clothes that Tilda wore, dungarees, sensible shoes, flannel shirt. But Lenore wore eyeglasses. Tilda set the tray on the table. "Wyatt," she said, "I'd like you to meet our friend and neighbor Lenore Teachout. She's here quite often to practice her stenography. Or the stenographic art. Didn't you once call it that, Lenore, the stenographic art?"

"Just the word 'stenography' does the trick," Lenore said. "Glad to meet you, Wyatt."

"Take a close look, Wyatt," Tilda said. "You'll see authentic shorthand, which at first might look like children's squiggles and doodles, but it's a method." I leaned over to inspect Lenore's note-book. "Is this your first opportunity to see short-hand?"

"Yes, it is," I said.

I stared at Tilda, and she stared right back and held her stare. She looked ravishing. (I'll later tell you why I used that word.) Tilda was about an inch taller than me, "shapely and mostly modest about it," as my aunt later said. Tilda had green eyes, the only student who did in her elementary and high school career. A lovely mouth, slightly tilted smile, only slightly, though. "Rambunctious, with a mind of its own" is how she described her thick black hair. Mornings before school she'd attempt to discipline her hair with a hundred strokes of a brush, tightly combed and organized it with no fewer than eight bobby pins and two barrettes, yet still there'd be unruly precincts. At table, Tilda always sat like a marionette held stiffly upright on a string. At age eleven, she'd injured her back in a spill off one of my uncle's sleds. A patch of ice hidden under the snow had spun her every which way and finally into a tree. Once out of hospital, she'd been trussed up and assigned to bed for several weeks. She had to see a specialist in Halifax. He prescribed exercises to keep her limber, one of which was to sit as upright as possible at each meal, let alone at her desk in school. "At first she cried and cried, the pain worse for sitting up so straight," my aunt had said. "But our Tilda impressed us all, what with the diligent work it took to hold her posture."

My aunt walked in carrying a Grundig-Majestic radio, which she placed on the kitchen table, stretched the cord and plugged it into the outlet near the sink. When she looked at us, Tilda's and my eyes were still locked. "Great glory's sake, Wyatt," she said, "cat got your tongue?"

I snapped out of whatever I was in. "Oh, hello,

Aunt Constance," I said. "I just came in out of the cold rain into this warm kitchen." No doubt, I'd obviously just described how I'd felt while looking at Tilda. But it must've sounded loony.

"Interesting, since it's not raining out," my aunt said.

I tried to regain some balance and said, "Uncle Donald's not feeling well enough to eat. He'd like tea later, though."

"Well, sit yourself down, then," my aunt said. "How's my husband treating you out there, anyway?"

"I'm learning a lot," I said.

I noticed Lenore writing away, taking down everything she heard.

"Don't let him bend over your work and hurry you," my aunt said. "You're not a sewing machine."

"No, I won't."

I sat down opposite Lenore. Once she had served carrot soup and bread, my aunt sat opposite Tilda. I ate too fast, which my aunt noticed. "Wyatt," she said, "in this house, if a meal's not satisfying, you want it over with fast, one way or the other."

Tilda and Lenore exchanged glances, and I said, "No, no, the soup's delicious. I think I just need some air. The shed's close quarters, Aunt Constance, that's all. I think I'll take a short walk down the road and back."

"It's a nice day for a walk," my aunt said.

"The soup was delicious," I said.

"You've said that twice. The second time convinced me less, but thank you," my aunt said.

I stood up from the table and started toward the front door. "You don't have any shoes on," Tilda said.

"Maybe in Halifax they take walks in stocking feet," Lenore said.

"Don't trip on the dog porch," Tilda said.

See, Marlais, in local parlance "dog porch" meant the floor. So by saying I shouldn't trip on the dog porch, Tilda was declaring how I could hardly handle the simplest thing—a conversation—which was true enough. Though more to the point, it was the sudden new import of Tilda's loveliness that had got me so tongue-tied.

Then, for some reason, I sat down at the table again. "Is there enough for seconds?" I asked.

"Seconds, thirds and fourths," my aunt said.

"I'll serve myself, thanks," I said. I went to the stove and ladled more soup into my bowl. I sat down and ate at a deliberately slow pace. My uncle came in and said, "My poor stomach's making me call it quits for the day, I'm afraid. Say, Wyatt, why'd you take your shoes off? I nearly killed myself stumbling over them."

"Do you want a bromide?" my aunt asked.

"Maybe later," he said. "I'll just sit here for a while and have some tea. Then I'll go in and lie down. Probably a nap."

"Well, you were up to all hours with those radio bulletins, Donald," my aunt said.

"I have to keep up with the war," my uncle said. "Some choose not to."

My aunt poured him a cup of tea. My uncle turned on the radio. As he fiddled with the tuner dial, he said, "No European war news on yet, but let's see what's what anyway, shall we?" As he jumped from station to station, he said, "Lenore, if I catch you using your stenography on our small talk, I'm going to have to ask you to put on a dunce cap and finish your soup in the parlor."

It seemed to me that my uncle was teasing, but Lenore was stung and quickly set her notebook and pencil aside. My uncle finally found a program out of Halifax in which people called in items they wanted to get rid of—from sofas to pigs, firewood to egg beaters, fishing rods to dolls, hay to hay wagons—for an hour it ran the gamut. The program was called *Bargain Basement* and was hosted by a man named Arthur Bunting. "I've always found it dishonest of Arthur Bunting," my uncle said, "to speak of every item, no matter what, with equal excitement. I mean, how can you compare a dog collar to a freestanding generator? On the air he'd peddle lint out of a pocket if someone called in to declare said lint was no longer wanted and would take fifty cents for it."

"Admit it, Donald," my aunt said, "you're still

angry at Arthur Bunting, despite the fact it's been two years since he offended you."

My aunt then spoke directly to me, probably because everyone else already knew the story. "Roughly two years ago," she said, "we were listening to *Bargain Basement* when all of a sudden Graham Hejinian—I've sat in the same pew in church with his family, before they moved to Advocate Harbor—Mr. Hejinian called in to say he had one of Donald's toboggans for sale, at a very cheap price. Kristin, the Hejinians' daughter, was already married and living in Kentville. And their son Charles was in the RCN—and the Royal Canadian Navy isn't going to allow a toboggan on a Navy vessel, now, is it? So it made perfect sense that their toboggan was no longer needed. But couldn't Graham have simply stored it in the attic or basement? Let it wait there for a grandchild."

"Seems to me the blame sits with Graham Hejinian," Lenore said, "not Arthur Bunting."

"Well, Donald considers them partners in crime, you see," my aunt said.

My uncle got the tuning just right, static close on either side on the dial. The first caller was a woman who had a love seat on offer. She said it was only a month old. She was asking ten dollars.

My uncle sipped his tea and remarked, "Let's see, today is September 23, so that means it only took since August 23 for love not to work out anymore on that seat, eh? If my calculations are correct."

"People do have sudden debts," my aunt said. She was clearing the dishes, except for teacups. "Perhaps the caller had an unexpected debt."

"I should've jotted down that woman's telephone number," Lenore said, "because I'm interested in that love seat. Even though I live alone."

"What about Denholme Mont?" my aunt said at the sink, rinsing the dishes.

"Postal worker from Truro?" Lenore asked.

"The very same," my aunt said, setting plates on the wooden drying rack.

"What about him?" Lenore said.

"Well, I believe we were talking about love seats and living alone," my aunt said.

"If you must know," Lenore said, "since last April, Denholme Mont and I have lived together, but for only a few hours of a given evening."

"At a *go,* you mean," my uncle said. "But maybe if you had a love seat, he'd begin to stay upward of twenty-four hours. Weekdays and holidays, at least. Him being a postal worker."

"I have no intention of learning how to cook breakfast for two," Lenore said.

"Come on, Lenore," my aunt said. "It's just doubling the amount of eggs, toast and whatnot."

"If only that was all there was to it," Lenore said.

That ended the conversation. My uncle went

into the master bedroom and I started back for the shed. But as I put on my shoes, I heard Lenore say, "Ladies, in my notebook, here, I have a conversation. Hundreds of words Denholme Mont and I said to each other. Saturday last."

"Did you take down every word, do you think?" my aunt asked.

"Denholme fell asleep right after," Lenore said. "So I quickly took up my pencil. I think I got most of it."

"Practice makes perfect," Tilda said.

"Would you like to hear it?" Lenore said.

"Not if I'm going to need smelling salts and a fainting couch," my aunt said.

"Probably not, Constance," Lenore said. "Unfortunately."

"Go right ahead, then," my aunt said.

I quietly closed the door behind me.

Truth be told, during lunch that day, it was I who practically needed smelling salts. I'd never thought of myself as particularly romantic, or romantically available, or romantically interesting, though in high school I'd taken girls to dances. Also, some had refused me dances. The previous winter, however, I had what might be called a dedicated romance with Mavis Joubert, a French Canadian, and I stayed miserably dedicated months after she broke it off. During our courtship, Mavis was twenty and waitressed at a fish-and-chips place near the bottom of Duke

Street. Her two-room apartment in a house on Gerrish Street spilled over with books. After our breakup she got involved with a professor of art history at Dalhousie, who took her on a tour of museums in Italy, though she returned by herself. Yet once my wounds had mended, I realized I was grateful Mavis and I had had nighttime experiences together, of the sort my mother preferred to call "not casual."

Marlais, it's important for me to tell you why I looked away from Tilda in the kitchen. It's related to memories of a teacher I had in tenth form in Halifax. Her name was Mrs. Francine Woods. The thing is, my grades were only average, but I felt above average at paying attention, especially when it came to history and English literature. For instance, I'd paid very close attention when Mrs. Woods—I'm amazed now to think that she was probably no more than your age, or perhaps a year or two older—spoke passionately and learnedly about the English poet John Keats. She recited his sonnets and read us some of his letters. Keats was her favorite writer of all time, and she said as much, more than once.

Now, you may well ask, how does this pertain to my turning away from Tilda? It pertains because I can definitely say without hesitation that stepping into the kitchen and watching her prepare tea was the moment I fell in love with her. Completely gone, smitten, whatever other words you might find in the dictionary. She was *too much beauty,* and I had to turn away.

You see, at some point during a full week devoted to Keats, Mrs. Woods provided an anecdote. One day John Keats and a friend were walking in the English countryside, which they often did. They trekked up a hill and took in the broad vista below. The sun was behind some clouds and the pale moon could still be seen in the sky. Mist hung low over a pond, swans gliding in and out of view. The big elm trees looked magnificently intelligent (I think "magnificently intelligent" were Mrs. Woods's words, not Keats's). And according to Mrs. Woods, the sight was suddenly too much for John Keats. "Too much beauty—he had to look away," she said. "Class, can you understand this?"

Despite the fact that your father is whatever is the opposite of a poet, there in the kitchen, when I looked at Tilda, when I really took her in, too much beauty is why I looked away. I'm certain you can understand this.

We had a nice birthday party for Tilda that autumn. Her eighteenth birthday, November 4. (My eighteenth was October 11 and passed without me telling anyone.) It was attended by three of her high school friends, Constance, Donald, Cornelia Tell and me. Cornelia provided the cake. There was gramophone and radio music all evening. I had one dance with Tilda and one

46

with my aunt. No one else asked me, and I didn't ask anyone else.

My apprenticeship in sleds and toboggans went methodically. One week my uncle instructed me in how to test the pliability and strength of plywood, how to measure and cut it. The next week I learned to construct a cargo box and fit iron runners. The following week we went step by step in completing a seven-foot-long trapper's sled, including the metal and leather dog harness. The days were given over to the use of steel bridges, brackets, hitch crosspieces, clevis bolts, various types of sandpaper, the application of glues and linseed oil, and so on. I also learned about the clerical aspects of the business, invoices, correspondence, bills to pay.

A month or so after I started in the business, my uncle allowed me to work solo on a three-board toboggan with wrappers and hitch, along with a cargo box and standard handles. It had been ordered by a man living in Heart's Desire, Newfoundland. "I sold him a sled last year," my uncle said. "He's expecting quality work again. My reputation's based on quality work, Wyatt." In order to give my fullest attention to this toboggan—that is, to prevent Uncle Donald from giving me pointers every minute—I decided to work on it after supper and late into the night, and kept it under a tarpaulin outside the shed during the day. Difficult as it may have been for him, my uncle, much to his credit, took the hint. I finished the toboggan in two weeks, and I mean fourteen full days, because I worked on Sundays, too.

At seven A.M. the following Monday, I unveiled my toboggan. I stood there while my uncle inspected it top to bottom, testing every joint, running his hands over the wood to detect splinters or rough spots of any sort, tilting it to examine more closely the linseed flush and how evenly the shellac had been applied. "Yesterday," he finally said, "I saw some children sledding in back of the church. Snow's always nicely packed on the slope there. I'll take this toboggan over there right now and try it out, eh? If it can hold me, who's practically a walrus compared to those boys, how bad can the world be? But if it splits and I fly through the air and crack open my skull, Wyatt, you're to look after your aunt Constance, understand?"

"I understand," I said.

"I don't have a last will and testament," he said, "except what I've told my wife in pillow talk, and that's not open to discussion."

I waited a good hour and a half in the shed, mostly smoking cigarettes and listening to the radio kept on a high shelf, and when my uncle returned, he said, "It's fine." We went directly back to work on two sleds ordered by a family from MacLeod Settlement in Nova Scotia. Their letter had mentioned that there were twin girls, age seven, so could Mr. Hillyer please somehow differentiate the sleds in some way that didn't interfere with his design, "to avoid the girls' bickering"? The letter suggested that my uncle paint a board on one sled black or red. After an hour or so of working on these sleds, my uncle slid a log into the woodstove and said, "Wyatt, I've been wanting to ask you something."

"Go right ahead, Uncle Donald."

"At the time you left Halifax, what was the mood in the city? About the war, I mean. Your aunt complains that I'm becoming more and more agitated by the day. Truth is, she only knows the half of just how agitated I am."

I looked at a few of the headlines from the *Halifax Mail* that were tacked on the wall over the workbench:

UNHAPPY CHRISTMAS DAY
FOR GERMAN TROOPS

TIDE OF BATTLE TURNS HEAVILY
AGAINST HITLER

IN ALL-NIGHT BATTLE,
ALLIED TROOPS FIGHT FOR THEIR LIVES

AXIS U-BOAT "WOLF PACK"
ATTACK CONVOY; 11 SHIPS LOST

"There's a restaurant, the Green Lantern," I said. "People like to call it the Green Latrine. It's along a block of brothels, and nearby's the Orpheum Theatre. Every night the place is crowded as a pigeon coop. Lots of military. Lots of music and dancing. Anyway, there's this fellow named H. B. Jefferson—have you heard of him?"

"The newspaperman," my uncle said, "who was appointed wartime press censor."

"That's him. That's H. B. Jefferson. His voice is very recognizable. He's always on the radio using that American slogan 'Loose lips sink ships.' Warning there might be German spies listening in all the time, so if you have a husband or wife in the military, you shouldn't repeat anything they've told you, you know, just daily on the street corner."

"Sure, sure," my uncle said.

"Well, one night H. B. Jefferson steps out with his wife, Lennie, to the Green Lantern. People are shouting and laughing and drinking and dancing, the place is jumping. I was there that night with some friends of mine. In fact, we had a table right next to H. B. Jefferson's, and some sailors and their wives or girlfriends had a table on the other side of H. B. Jefferson's. Suddenly a sailor recognizes Jefferson's voice—his radio voice. And this sailor'd had quite a bit to drink, that wasn't hard to tell. And he stands up on his chair and busts a beer bottle on the table and points at H. B. Jefferson and shouts, 'Hey—hey, everyone! That right there's Mr. H. B. Jefferson—right there! Say, Mr. H. B. Jefferson, what do you know that you're not telling all these fine people in this fine establishment?' Then some other sailors got that fellow right out the door."

"What's the point, Wyatt?"

"On the one hand, maybe more than ever, the war's made people let off steam, drinking, dancing. Brothels. Over to Rigolo's Pub. The Green Lantern. The Night Owl. Drink and dance and get crazy every night they possibly can."

"On the other hand?" my uncle said. He had stopped working and was listening closely.

"On the other hand, the whole time people have their stomachs twisted in knots worrying that there's some terrible news they don't yet know about. Like there's a terrible secret about to be told them. And see, at the Green Lantern that night? There was a moment where I really thought some of those sailors were going to drag H. B. Jefferson into an alley and kick him senseless till he told them what he knew and they didn't know yet."

"You couldn't really blame them if they did, eh?" my uncle said.

"No, not really, I guess not," I said. "But H. B. Jefferson's got a tough job, I'd say."

"Certainly he does," my uncle said. "But don't forget, there's human nature. I remember being in an English village during the last war. My buddies and I were beat to hell and hadn't slept in days. We were put up in a farmhouse. The farmer told us that his neighbors had shot a collaborator of some sort. He didn't go into detail. But in a nutshell, he was talking about how suspicion got cranked up so high, his very own neighbors, some he'd known his whole life, were all at wits' end. And I'll never forget what he said. He said, 'My neighbors, they got wind of a saboteur in their midst and started to look at everybody in a different light, for all I know even their cows and sheep.' What I'm saying is, as a wartime censor, H. B. Jefferson's walking a fine line."

"A fine line between—?"

"Between both slogans I hear are posted all over Halifax: 'Keep a smile on your face, hopes alive' and 'Loose lips sink ships.' You've got to feel for the man, though. Knowing what secrets he knows, he can't be but a light sleeper."

"Yeah, I bet his telephone rings in the middle of the night," I said.

"I bet every night it does."

As my uncle stared at the newspaper headlines on the shed wall, I could almost see his sympathy for H. B. Jefferson draining like color from his cheeks. "But I don't need H. B. Jefferson's secret information to know that things are getting worse by the hour," he said. "Wars always get worse by the hour. That's their nature. Then they end. And the average person's stunned shitless when a war ends. Why? Because up to the last minute things are still getting worse."

Just before supper there was a knock on the shed door. What happened next, to my mind, went hand in hand with my uncle's brief lecture on war. He opened the door, stepped back and said, "Lenore, what brings you so far from the house?"

Lenore held up a piece of paper. "I used my stenography and took down a bulletin from the radio a short while ago, Donald," she said. "An auxiliary Navy vessel called *Lady Quintanna* was sunk. Yesterday, November 19. Thirty-seven people lost."

My uncle sat right down on the floor. "Isn't there one living, breathing soul—where's Adolf Hitler live? It's in Berlin, isn't it?" he said. "Isn't there one person in all of goddamn Berlin, Germany, with enough goddamn sense and gumption to shoot Hitler in the head?"

Lenore looked pensive. "My father," she said, "when I was about five, he put a bullet into our dog because the veterinarian said our dog had a fever in the brain. Not curable."

"Point well taken," my uncle said. "All right, then, Wyatt, let's close up shop for the day. We're in for supper. Probably you're eating with us, Lenore."

"I've been invited, yes," Lenore said.

She shut the door. My uncle and I tidied things up a bit and went into the house. When we washed our hands in the sink and sat at the kitchen table, my aunt said, "I've put the radio in the bedroom, Donald. I don't want to listen to it while we eat."

"I'll tune in after supper," my uncle said. "Immediately after."

Aunt Constance served us chicken and potatoes. The conversation hopped subject to subject, and that was good, because it kept things lively, though the lack of continuity in conversations often put my aunt on edge, and she'd say, "Can we please keep the needle in the groove, *please?*" But this time she left well enough alone. When Tilda had cleared the dishes, Uncle Donald took from his shirt pocket the radio bulletin Lenore had copied out in shorthand, and said, "Lenore, would you kindly translate this into English for me?"

"Mr. Hillyer," Lenore said, "it's common knowledge I'm training to be a *professional* stenographer."

"Of course," my uncle said. "Well, once you've completed the task, make out a receipt and I'll be happy to sign it and pay you on the spot."

"May I use your parlor?" Lenore said.

"Yes, Lenore, use the parlor," Tilda said.

Lenore took about half an hour. She then wrote

out a receipt on a page torn from her notebook. My uncle read it. "This amount's being professional, all right," he said. "It's steep, but so be it." He went ahead and signed it. He then handed Lenore three dollars and the receipt.

"Should we have tea in the parlor or at the table?" my aunt asked.

"At the table," Tilda said.

But first my uncle sat in the parlor and read what Lenore had translated. He then came to the kitchen table and started reading all five pages, about the sinking of the *Lady Somers*, out loud. My aunt and Lenore were sitting at the table. I was standing at the counter. Tilda was in the doorway to the bedrooms. Tea hadn't been served yet. When my uncle finished reading, you could hear a pin drop.

"Now, Lenore," he finally said, "are you sure you took down what the radio said word for word?"

Lenore looked confident. "I'm satisfied that I did," she said.

My uncle said, "Then this bulletin isn't your average keepsake."

The First Time I Saw the German Student Hans Mohring

BY THE SPRING OF 1942, my uncle had dele-gated to me five new customers, all in Quebec province. I wrote them letters and three of them agreed to let me build their toboggans, whereas two said they'd prefer Donald's work, and who could blame them? They'd said it nicely. Of course, my uncle and I continued to work together as well.

Tilda was often on my mind. Or I might better say, she rarely was not. Yet I felt I still knew very little about her. So every new discovery, every fact of her upbringing and nature, was a revelation. For instance, on August 25, 1942, Tilda kept an appointment with a mesmerist, Dr. Everett Sewell, of 27 Ingus Street in Halifax. Donald and Constance hoped that Dr. Sewell, using the techniques of hypnotism, might get Tilda to "talk in her waking sleep," as Donald put it, and reveal why she hardly thought of much else but mourning the deaths of people she'd never met, some of whose names she found in the obituary pages of Halifax newspapers. Up until this time, I had only a general understanding of this. I knew that she could recite certain obituaries like

56

Scripture, a practice begun when she was fifteen. By age seventeen she'd invented her own obituaries, which she'd write down. Fictions. Eventually she let me read some. On page after page I recognized Tilda's writerly talents. I don't know how the wider world would've judged this, but to my mind Tilda wrote like a dream. She didn't scrimp on imagination, I thought. Anyone would be honored to have her write their obituary. It's an art if a true artist is at work.

Yet when Tilda announced her intention of being a professional mourner (in Nova Scotia, only two other people were legally registered as such), Donald and Constance were thrown into a tizzy. I was present, but Tilda wasn't, when Reverend Witt, of Bayside Methodist Church of Middle Economy, took tea in our kitchen and suggested that Tilda see a mesmerist. Witt was acquainted with Dr. Sewell and provided Tilda a letter of introduction. "It's not that her wanting to be a mourner is on the whole undignified," Witt said. "Families estranged from the deceased person, say. Or say a person's ostracized from society for some moral trespass. Or say the deceased simply outlived anyone who knew him. There's any number of possibilities for why a person has nobody to mourn for him. Indeed, a mourner provides a useful service, perhaps even a spiritual one."

"So what's the problem, then?" my uncle said.

"It's just that the other day," Reverend Witt said, "when I'd officiated graveside at Great Village Cemetery over Mary Albright's internment—and I know you didn't know the Albrights—I happened to look over and see your Tilda throwing herself on the ground in front of a gravestone near the picket fence. Tilda was wailing, too. The sound carried."

"Are you saying my daughter shouldn't have a trade?" my uncle asked.

"No, that'd be independent of her, and that's pride and that's good," Reverend Witt said. "From what you've told me, she's not for university. True, there's a tradition—professional mourners have been in Nova Scotia a long time. But since you asked for advice, I'm merely saying that it's a somewhat morbid choice for such a beautiful young woman, so alive, so full of the appetite for life, as anyone can see. What's more, I understand she's sewn two black dresses in advance of starting this employment."

"She's a fine seamstress," my aunt said. "I take responsibility for that."

My uncle picked up Reverend Witt's teacup before he'd finished his tea. Looking out the window over the sink, my uncle said, "If Tilda chooses to publicly demonstrate she's got that much additional sadness to give away—plus there's the wages, however modest. I have to trust what you saw in Great Village was Tilda practicing her craft, so to speak. So to speak, and right while you were practicing yours, by the way, on Mary Albright's behalf."

"But seeing this Dr. Sewell probably can't hurt," my aunt said.

"It can hurt twenty-five dollars," my uncle said. "The appointment costs twenty-five dollars, according to Reverend Witt here."

After Reverend Witt left our house, my aunt said, "Wyatt, what do you think?"

Well, I secretly loved Tilda so much, I could only answer as if she was in the room, as if she was right there judging me. "Why not just put it directly to Tilda?"

"Fair enough," my uncle said. He scrubbed out Reverend Witt's teacup.

That evening at supper, Donald broached the subject. He quoted Reverend Witt at length. Tilda was all serious ears, and she nodded thoughtfully throughout. When my uncle finished talking, he looked to my aunt, indicating it was her turn, but she deferred to Tilda.

"First, as for my carrying on in Great Village," Tilda said, "and what Reverend Witt saw? I'd say I was in top form that day. And as for this Dr. Sewell, I'm steamed at you for suggesting that my thoughts have become all higgledy-piggledy—isn't that how Cornelia Tell refers to a mind being muddled? So steamed, in fact, I'm going to pack my bags, get on the Acadian Line bus and see to it that you spend hard-earned dollars for me to get hypnotized. I'm interested in getting hypnotized, actually. I imagine I'll be the first in Middle Economy to do so. I haven't been to Halifax in two years anyway. You know how much I like it there. The bus out and back, the stop for sandwiches in Truro. All the sights along the way, thank you very much."

"I hope you're not too angry at us," my aunt said. "We only had your best interests at heart."

"My heart's my best interest, Mom," Tilda said. "And it tells me I've got a good opportunity here. Plus, think of the practicalities, eh? Let's say I'm asked to mourn somebody in Kentville, or all the way up to Prince Edward Island. I could come back and finally be able to contribute to my room and board, until I move away."

"She's got a point there," my uncle said.

"Know what?" Tilda said. "Just now I've lost my appetite. But before I go to my room, let me tell you something. Mother, Father—you too, Wyatt. I like mourning and I've got a natural talent for it. And I can hardly wait until I get my first commission. In fact, when in Halifax, I'll stay at the Baptist Spa there, which is just a block from the office where I submit my application. And I expect, and you should expect, that it will be approved."

My aunt had asked me to meet Tilda's return bus. So at about six o'clock in the evening, August

27, I was waiting in front of the Esso station in Great Village. That was the stop nearest Middle Economy. I sat in my car for ten or so minutes, then saw the bus in the rearview mirror. The blue-and-white Acadian Line had silver panels on the sides, a sloped rear end and straight-down vertical front, two wide front windows with windshield wipers fixed below each window, and a wide curved silver front bumper. As it approached, I doused my Chesterfield in a cup of coffee, mostly dregs. I had expected Tilda to get off the bus on her own. But she was followed out by Hans Mohring. (Of course, I didn't know his name yet.) They were chatting away, and Tilda was not—rare sight—carrying her Dutch book satchel, Hans Mohring was. Well, there's something, I thought.

I took in Hans Mohring. My best estimation, he looked to be a couple years older than Tilda and me. I made another comparison: he was taller than me (I am five feet nine inches in bare feet). He had on brown corduroy trousers, held up by a belt that didn't pass through the trouser loops but was just fastened around his waist. I had seen this only once before, on a drunken piss-pants fellow on Barrington Street in Halifax, but Hans Mohring definitely hadn't fixed his belt absent-mindedly. And he wore a white shirt buttoned at the neck, very formal for a bus ride, and a black raincoat, for warmth, obviously, as it was a clear evening.

When Tilda steered Hans Mohring in my direction, I saw that he had a somewhat narrow, handsome face, pronounced crow's-feet at his eyes. He had thick brown hair, collar-length in back, neatly combed and parted neither left nor right, more slightly disheveled or windblown, not vainly. And he had a very open, in fact a wonderful smile (this irked me, as I had pronouncedly crooked front teeth, and had from about age five developed a tight-lipped smile to try and hide them), and whatever they had been laughing about, they continued to laugh about as the bus left Great Village.

When they got to the car, Tilda said, "Wyatt, this is Hans Mohring. I met him on the bus. He's from Germany and he's a student at Dalhousie. He's studying to be a philologist."

"Oh, a philologist," I said.

He could no doubt tell I had no idea what a philologist was. He offered his hand and I shook it.

"Yes, yes, philology," he said. "I can explain it to you later, philology, if you wish. Tilda comprehended everything about philology immediately, but not everyone can." His accent was more than noticeable; the word that came to mind to describe his English pronunciation was "punctual." I realized right away I meant "punctuated." Something in his tone got me to imagine that he was capable of saying very unfriendly things in a

companionable way, obviously just an unedu-
cated guess. One thing for sure, I could see Tilda
and Hans liked each other, and I didn't like that.
In fact, I said something next that put Tilda's
teeth on edge and made her corkscrew her
thumbs in her ears, as if she couldn't possibly
have heard what she had clearly heard. It was her
gesture of high annoyance.

"I don't make wishes," I said. "So I won't *wish*
for you to tell me about philology."

"All right, maybe later you'd like me to explain
it to you," Hans said.

"Where were you heading on the bus,
anyway?" I said.

"I wanted to take in the sights," Hans said,
"that's all. I was feeling—*cooped up*. At
Dalhousie. In my room. I simply went to the station and bought a ticket. I have a map. I thought
I'd go all the way around Nova Scotia. But now
it seems Tilda was meant to be my destination."

"Is that how you see it?" I said to Tilda.

"I see Hans and I talked and talked on the bus,"
she said. "And when he suggested he stop here, I
didn't say no. Those two things are how I see it.
No more, no less. Is that okay with you,
Detective Hillyer?"

"Wyatt, are you an excellent driver?" Hans
asked. "Because I'm an excellent driver, and I
can drive us to your village if you'd like to sit in
back."

"We can all three fit in front," I said.

"Hans is going to stay awhile," Tilda said. "I thought the rooms above the bakery might work."

"I'll drop him off," I said. "We have to pass by there anyway."

"Cornelia Tell can use the revenue, I bet," Tilda said. "Hans, do you have any money?"

"I have some Canadian money, yes," Hans said.

"Canadian's all that will work in Middle Economy, Hans," Tilda said. "Maybe since the bakery's got late hours tonight, after dinner we can have an éclair. Wyatt, you can chaperone me, eh?"

"If you need a chaperone just to have an éclair in the bakery, all right, sure," I said.

"On the bus we talked about my getting hypnotized," Tilda said. "Actually, Hans has been hypnotized, isn't that right, Hans?"

"Nine times," Hans said.

"For me, once was enough," Tilda said. "Enough to know it worked."

"How do you mean?" I said.

"Well, Mom and Dad wanted the mesmerist to talk me out of being a professional mourner, right? But when I snapped out of the hypnotism, I looked right at Dr. Sewell and said, 'I've just had the most clear, vivid and wonderful dream that I'd done a great job at a cemetery up in Northport, on the Northumberland shore. And the woman who'd paid me said she would recommend me in the wink of an eye.' Fact is, the second she said 'wink of an eye' is when I'd snapped out of my trance. Dr. Sewell didn't snap me out of it. I did it on my own. So, you see, twenty-five dollars was spent to reassure me I'm doing the right thing."

"I'm sure Reverend Witt had a different result in mind," I said.

"I'm sure he did," she said. "But aren't you happy for me?"

"Productive visit to the city, sounds like," I said.

I drove the three of us to the bakery. Cornelia was all too pleased to have a tenant. She and Hans quickly settled on a price. I was irritated to see Hans Mohring pay for a whole week in advance. "You're my first German to rent," Cornelia said. "I've let my rooms be occupied by—let's see. There's been a Dutch family of four. Then there was that Swedish man and wife who admired Donald's sleds. I recall the Swedish husband said he couldn't fall asleep without a strong cup of coffee. It took me a while to realize it was a joke—I'm pretty sure. And there's been a number of French speakers from Quebec. The rooms above my bakery are a regular tourist trap, eh? Anyway, Hans, as for any European cuisine you may be used to, you're out of luck. My pastries have a reputation, however. I don't serve dinner, but I'll fix you a sandwich, meat and cheese, if you like. Tomato slices included."

"I'd be honored," Hans said.

"Honored, well! My sandwiches aren't war medals, Hans," Cornelia said. "They're just sandwiches."

"Hans is a student of philology," Tilda said. "He's careful with words. If he said honored, he meant honored, is my guess."

"I must've had the war on my mind," Cornelia said. "What with those German wolf packs turned our coast into a shooting gallery. Right, Hans?"

"I can understand your not wishing me to stay above your bakery," Hans said.

"Oh, I know you're just a student, Hans," Cornelia said. "Probably you aren't communicating shore-to-ship with U-boats."

"Please understand," Hans said. "Your government willing, I'll become a citizen of Canada. My parents, too, wish this for themselves. And my sister. They live in Denmark."

"Somehow you're not a German sailor or soldier, are you, Hans? And I wonder, how'd that happen? How did you finagle out of conscription as such? Do you come from an influential family, Hans?"

"Influential, no," Hans said. "Modest of income."

"There's Canadian citizens at the bottom of the sea off our province, yet you're welcome to stay long as you want, Hans Mohring. But you should know that every time I look at you, I might think of the bottom of the sea. That's not because of anything you yourself did, mind you."

"I'm not in the military because we left Germany," Hans said.

"Enough of this tug of war," Cornelia said. "Your rooms are nice and clean, Hans. I did the sheets yesterday, in fact. My private room is directly below your rooms, Hans, so if you have any questions, knock, and if I'm not in my nightgown, I'll meet you in the hallway and tell you what's what."

"What are the house rules?" Hans asked.

"The only house rules I've got," Cornelia said, "is that you just now paid the rent. Look, I'm sorry. It's just this war's got me so off kilter. For instance, if I'm listening to war bulletins on the radio, I can scarcely bake at all."

"I'm coming back later to have éclairs with Hans," Tilda said.

"Want me to chaperone?" Cornelia said.

"Wyatt said he would," Tilda said.

"You don't see me behind the counter, come right in anyway," Cornelia said.

"All right, then," Tilda said. "See you in a couple of hours, Hans."

Hans shook hands with me, Tilda and Cornelia Tell, in that order. "How do I get to my rooms?" he asked.

"Step out the door, turn right, you'll see another door," Cornelia said. "The door handle's painted black. You can't miss it."

Carrying his backpack and satchel, Hans left the bakery.

"You aren't still under hypnosis, are you, Tilda?" Cornelia asked. "I heard that some people never snap out of it, even though they appear to have."

"No, Cornelia," Tilda said. "I asked Hans to stay in Middle Economy with my thoughts very much my own, if that's what you meant."

"I put him through the wringer, I suppose," Cornelia said.

"Along the chin, if you look closely, and down his neck and shoulders, it's discolored," Tilda said. "Bruised up. He's taken a few beatings in downtown Halifax. The collar covers that up a little. On the bus, he saw me notice, so he buttoned up his collar like that. Still, once we got to talking, he told me about the bruises straight out. Germans aren't much in favor in Halifax these days."

"Haligonians might wonder does Hans, there, have siblings working on a U-boat," Cornelia said.

"Cornelia, sit down a moment, will you?" Tilda said.

Cornelia sat at the nearest table.

"Hans has got some sort of heart condition," Tilda said.

"Well, now, who doesn't?" Cornelia said.

"His is medically diagnosed," Tilda said. "Now and then he blacks out. I'm talking out of school here, but he blacked out right on the bus—keeled over, just like that. I'd been wondering why he hadn't sat next to me. Fetching as I am. When he blacked out, I realized, it was out of specific politeness. He wanted, just in case, to avoid falling against my shoulder or whatnot, impolite and too forward. Mr. Harrison, the bus driver, saw Hans slump over in the rearview, pulled to the side of the road, came back and propped Hans up and took his pulse. Hans wasn't completely out. Said 'Sorry sorry sorry' to everyone on the bus, which happened to be just me and Mr. Harrison, but still. It was an eventful bus trip home. But we talked and talked. What's more, Cornelia? I've some money left over and would've paid out of my own pocket for you letting him the rooms, and I mean without a second thought."

Tilda and I drove home in complete silence. She looked out the window the whole way.

The Sooner You Might Declare Yourself to Tilda

I ALWAYS WONDERED what Hans Mohring thought of there being no books in my aunt and uncle's house. He couldn't help but notice this, him being a philology student. Me, I always felt a house that contains books (not only a Bible) has a concealed spirituality, and maybe I thought that because so few people in Middle Economy left their books in plain sight. Reading was a private enterprise, when it occurred, especially of novels. Come to think of it, Marlais, most of your mother's reading took place in the three-room Middle Economy Library, the only stone building in the village, located a short walk from the bakery. I recall Tilda shaking off the winter cold by the woodstove at home and saying, "This afternoon I've read straight through a collection by Katherine Mansfield. It's called *In a German Pension*. Katherine Mansfield is from New Zealand. Her stories are too excellent to summarize."

I shouldn't say no books were in the house, because Tilda signed out *The Highland Book of Platitudes* on her eighteenth birthday. How do I know that she never returned it? Because I'm looking at it right now. It's on my kitchen table. It's possible she considered *The Highland Book of Platitudes*, despite all propriety, as a kind of birthday gift to herself. As far as I know, the librarian at the time, Mrs. Bethany Oleander, born and raised in Newport Station, didn't get after her about it. Then again, I doubt that *The Highland Book of Platitudes* was in great demand. The book has a frayed red leather-bound cover. Your mother's brown leather bookmark, mail-ordered from Halifax, embossed with the initials *TH,* remains where she'd last placed it, between pages 112 and 113.

Yet the book was in demand nightly by Tilda. She kept it by her bedside. Late some nights I'd hear her read from it aloud, never bothering to whisper. I'm jumping ahead a little here, but I remember the first time Hans Mohring came to dinner at our house, she boldly said, "Come see my library, Hans," took him by the hand and led him into her bedroom, door kept open, naturally. I chaperoned from the hallway. She said, "Take a look at this book, Hans. It's called *The Highland Book of Platitudes*. It's inspirational." My aunt served tea in the parlor. We were all there, my uncle, aunt, Tilda, Hans and me. Hans took apart and put back together the word "platitude" as the rest of us listened. "It's not that platitudes can't say important things," Hans said. "But in the dictionary meaning—I won't be exact here—'platitude' is a statement that's basically dull or trite, but spoken as though it's brand-new. The way many politicians present their ideas, for instance—you understand."

"I don't find the platitudes in my book in the least dull," Tilda said. "Not a single one." With that, I was immediately alerted to two things. First, the fact that Tilda was not pleased. Second, maybe Hans had just fallen from grace a little. That was my hope, at least.

"Well, thank you, Hans. I've learned a lot," my aunt said. "We're in for supper now."

Remember my mentioning those éclairs? Well, back on the evening that Hans Mohring had arrived by bus, the three of us did meet up for éclairs. Cornelia sat in the corner, and I knew she'd noticed, though she didn't comment, that Hans held his fork, prongs curved downward, in his left hand and lifted pieces of éclair, neatly cut, to his mouth without transferring the fork to his right hand, which I learned was the European style. The next day, Tilda introduced Hans to Donald and Constance, but Tilda spirited him away quickly. "I'm going to tour Hans through Middle Economy," Tilda said. "All the sights there are to see. That'll be done in half an hour, then we'll sit at the wharf and reminisce about the tour for three or four hours. The thing itself; the memory of the thing, which gives it the longer life." I knew, with that last sentence, Tilda had quoted *The Highland Book of Platitudes*, though I don't know if Donald or Constance realized it. Off they went. A week later, Tilda announced, "I've invited Hans Mohring to supper."

"What's the hurry?" my aunt said.

"The invitation's made," Tilda said.

"Which evening?" my aunt asked.

"Tomorrow evening."

"I'll get out my recipes."

"It'll be nice for Hans," Tilda said. "He's only been eating Cornelia's sandwiches."

"I hope he's shared them with you," my aunt said.

"Is that your way of saying you haven't seen me for supper lately?"

The next evening at about six-thirty, Aunt Constance had the table set with her best china and Christmas cloth napkins. No tablecloth, but she had polished the wood. Hans was seated next to Tilda. I occupied the one chair opposite them, my place setting noticeably centered alone on that side of the table. Of course, my aunt and uncle sat at either end. My aunt served baked salmon, boiled potatoes, bread and—rare at our table—white wine, and there was a pitcher of water, too. She said a prayer. Hans dug right in, wielding his fork in that different fashion. "Well, won't you look at that!" my aunt said, and we all turned to the dining room window. Half a dozen children had their faces pressed to the glass.

"Cornelia Tell must've said something to some-body," Tilda said.

"You're giving those kids quite the lesson in German etiquette," my uncle said, moving his fork from his right to left hand, spearing a piece of salmon and eating it. Hans caught on directly.

"After dinner, perhaps I'll sit on the porch and tell them a Grimm's tale," Hans said.

"How grim?" my aunt asked. "They're our neighbors' children, after all."

"No, no," Hans said. "The Brothers Grimm. They are famous German storytellers. Long dead now—very important. You know 'Hansel and Gretel'?"

"I read it to Tilda when she was a little girl," my aunt said.

"Originally, that's a story told by the Brothers Grimm," Hans said.

"Those Grimms brothers," my uncle said, "did they tell any truly heart-stopping tales? If you know one of those, Hans, go right ahead and scare hell out of those little rabble-rousers out there. Maybe toss in a few German words to boot."

"You don't mean to tell me Hansel and Gretel were German children," my aunt said.

"Also 'Rapunzel' and 'Rumpelstiltskin'—both of them," Hans said.

"Not 'Rumpelstiltskin'!" my aunt said.

"I'm afraid so," Hans said.

"Well, live and learn."

Tilda wore a dress of her own design and her own making. It was ankle length, made of cotton material so dark a blue it was almost black. I'd seen her sewing it, but I'd never seen her wearing it. Hans Mohring coming to dinner apparently was the occasion she was waiting for. The dress had a high collar, and Tilda had pinned an ivory cameo to it. So, what with Hans wearing his same white shirt buttoned to the neck, they reminded me of a portrait of a stuffy Victorian British couple that used to hang above the card catalogue in Mrs. Oleander's library. I now realize my making that connection of Hans and Tilda with the portrait meant I had a sudden concern about them becoming an old married couple. Who knows? Maybe they'd become well-to-do, maybe they'd end up living in England. I didn't like the thought, but you can't help where your mind goes, can you?

Supper was pleasant enough, all "Please pass the bread" and "What is life like at university, Hans?" But I could see that Hans thought Tilda was the cat's pajamas—also, they'd been seen together in public, at Cornelia's bakery, Parrsboro Wharf, walking hand in hand along the horseshoe-shaped beach. Apparently Cornelia had even called them "lovebirds." And when Reverend Witt suggested Tilda bring Hans as a guest to church, according to Witt she said, "I have a different rendezvous in mind this Sunday." I knew they spent hours on end in the library, actually more hours than were officially posted as OPEN, because Mrs. Oleander had given Tilda a key. Separate arrangement, just so Tilda and Hans could discuss God knows which words, plus have privileged access to the big *Webster's* dictionary.

At supper, no subject caused a dustup, but then again, my uncle hadn't referred to U-boats or the war in general, and Hans didn't lecture us on philology. He took seconds on the potatoes, so did I, so did my uncle. There were two or three awkward silences. However, none felt like an outside presence had hushed all human voices. Because had such a silence occurred, my aunt predictably would have said, "An angel is passing." All well and good. Yet when Tilda stole, in plain sight, a spoonful of Hans's dessert of vanilla ice cream (he'd refused the maple syrup), the playfulness of it made me blurt out, "Hans, why would a person in their right mind get hypnotized nine times, anyway?"

Tilda corkscrewed her ears. Not only was I reckless in referring to the reason Reverend Witt had suggested that Tilda visit a mesmerist—that was a sore subject in our house—but, in the same breath, I'd more or less suggested that Hans, too, wasn't right in the head.

"Hans, my family—including Wyatt here—

doesn't have much experience with hypnotism," Tilda said. "Wyatt didn't mean anything by it."

"Yes, but for the sake of argument," Hans said, "let us say that Wyatt honestly did mean something. I can educate him—"

"I fell short of graduating high school by only a year," I said.

"—*educate* in the sense of why I needed hypnotism so many times," Hans said.

"Why not educate all of us, then?" my uncle said.

"But why not educate us in the parlor?" my aunt said. "Tilda, dear, please clear the dishes. Wyatt, fetch my gray sweater from its peg. I'm feeling the evening air." Once we were situated—Tilda in the rocking chair, Donald and Hans on ladder-back chairs brought from the kitchen, me on the sofa—Donald said, "Full speed ahead, Hans. Give us your reason for those nine hypnotisms."

My aunt carried in a tray and distributed tea and cookies all around, then sat next to me. Hans took a bite of cookie, leaned forward and said, "You see, I walked in my sleep. I was most prolific at this, you might say. It started at age ten. We lived in a small village. Larger than yours, yes, but not large by standards of German farm villages. It wasn't far from Munich. We had a small house. My parents are good people, you see. And they had, with me, I think you say, a handful. They had a handful. At night, I was walking long distances in my sleep. Usually I was found out on the road. Once I was about to swim in a pond. A number of times I was found in a neighbor's garden."

"Ever ride your bicycle asleep?" my uncle asked. "I always wondered, could a person do that?"

"No, I never rode a bicycle, Mr. Hillyer," Hans said. "At least nobody reported that I had. Most often my mother or father would discover me simply sitting at our kitchen table, sometimes eating food I'd taken from the icebox while asleep. Eventually my father had to purchase inside locks, and he locked the doors and windows. Still, I walked all over the house. I might visit every room. By morning I'd be exhausted. I could hardly stay awake in school. A hypnotist in Munich was recommended. I went to him nine times, as I mentioned to Tilda. Yet hypnotism didn't work. I walked in my sleep for several years. In Denmark it stopped. I never walked in my sleep in Denmark."

"Denmark?" my uncle said.

"We had to leave Germany. My uncle—my mother's brother—previously was living in Denmark. He has funds. In fact, he is sponsoring me at Dalhousie University."

"Germany to Denmark to Canada," my aunt said. "My goodness. I've never been further than Newfoundland."

"We escaped to Denmark in 1935. Adolf Hitler is not the travel agent you'd wish on your worst enemy—this was my father's joke," Hans said. "My father always tries to bring a little light to the darkness. My mother is quite different. She always thinks the darkness is about to get even darker. That is their different natures."

"Tilda mentioned you have a heart malady," my aunt said. "Forgive my prying."

"Yes, I was born with it," Hans said. "I'm used to it by now. It's simply part of life for me."

"Well, don't black out before you have another of those cookies," I said.

"I'll do my best to take that advice," Hans said, and picked up a cookie from the plate.

"Tilda," my aunt said, "why not get out the Criss Cross set and you three sit down and play it? Donald and I need to leave you young people to yourselves."

"Criss Cross?" Hans said.

"We're the only ones in Middle Economy owns a set," my uncle said.

"True for now," my aunt said, "but Reverend Witt's got one on order. He's going to try to incorporate it into his children's Bible class somehow."

"See, Hans," my uncle said, "back in 1931 a man named Alfred M. Butts invented this board game. He was an architect and he planned it out in detail and then pasted a model of it onto folding checkerboards. It's something like a crossword puzzle—not exactly, though. You connect words on the vertical and on the horizontal, and these words all have to reside in your head already. Because during play you're not allowed to consult a dictionary. We don't keep one in the house, anyway."

"I'll go over the rules with Hans, okay, Pop?" Tilda said.

"Anyway, Constance was visiting her childhood friend in St. John's, Newfoundland," my uncle said. "In fact, she's got another visit coming up. Isn't that right, Constance?"

"Happily," my aunt said.

"Her friend's Zoe Fielding," my uncle said. "Zoe received a Criss Cross set for Christmas, from an American. Zoe taught the game to Constance last visit, and Constance put one on order the minute she got home. And that's how Criss Cross arrived to our humble little part of Nova Scotia."

"Hans, believe me," Tilda said, "you'll take to this game like a fish to water."

"My goodness, that's true, isn't it," my aunt said. "Criss Cross is all but custom made for a philologist."

"Myself, I'm no good at it," I said.

"Maybe Hans'll make us both better," Tilda said.

"Remember, Hans, you can't use German

words," my uncle said. "That's breaking the law." My uncle was pacing the room now. I hadn't seen him do that except when he heard terrible war bulletins on the radio.

"I see," Hans said.

"For example, you can't use Germaniawerft," my uncle said, "the operation which builds a lot of U-boats. Germaniawerft—never mind my pronunciation, Hans."

"Donald, *please,*" my aunt said.

"Or Deutsche Werft, which built *U-553*, the one that sunk the *Nicoya* off the Gaspé," my uncle said. "And you can't use its goddamn son-of-a-bitch shithole commander's name, Karl Thurmann."

"I understand," Hans said.

"Come to think of it, don't try and get away with 'Rapunzel' or 'Rumpelstiltskin,' either."

Tilda took the Criss Cross set down from a shelf. My aunt washed and racked the dishes, and my uncle went outside to cool down with a cigarette. Tilda got all the little wooden Criss Cross letters lined up neatly. "You always have exactly ten letters to work with, Hans," she said.

"So, 'Rumpelstiltskin' wouldn't be allowed anyway," Hans said.

"Each turn, you spell out a word, then choose replacement letters. We play until all the letters run out," Tilda said, unfolding the board on the dining room table. Donald stepped back into the house. He and Constance said good night and repaired to their bedroom. Tilda, Hans and I sat at the table.

Tilda went through the few remaining rules, ending with "—each letter is worth a different amount. In the end, the player who's got the most points wins the game."

"It's mainly a spelling competition, I think," Hans said.

"Look at their values, Hans. Short words can be worth quite a lot," Tilda said. "The main thing is, you have to join your word to someone else's word." She formed a cross with her two pointer fingers. "Like an intersection on the road. The words *crisscross*."

"I'm prepared to start," Hans said.

We played for an hour, then we had seconds of ice cream. Tilda made coffee, which we took into the parlor. Back at the table, it was Hans's turn. He set down "ravishing."

"That's a lot of points," Tilda said.

"Do you know this word, Wyatt? Ravishing?" Hans asked. "Its definition is—well, basically, it's Tilda. Don't you agree?"

Quitting the game, I left the house and walked to the wharf. Stood there hangdog, only in shirt-sleeves. Roiled up. See, what had caught up with me, standing there in the cold fog of the wharf, was the stark belief that I was illiterate in matters of the heart. That is, I felt Tilda *was* ravishing, but I hadn't known to use that perfect word. I stood there for quite a while. Finally, my uncle's truck appeared and I walked toward it. My aunt was on the passenger side. They were both dressed properly for the weather. "You'll catch your death, Wyatt," my uncle said. I got in beside my aunt in the front seat. But my uncle opened his door and got out. He walked to the end of the dock and smoked a cigarette.

"Tilda said you might be down here," my aunt said.

"Where's Tilda now?" I said.

"She's not at home."

"I've a mind to go over to the bakery."

"And do what? You'd get to the bakery and do what?"

"Let's just get Uncle Donald and drive back to the house, then."

"Donald won't smoke the whole cigarette, so with what time we've got, please listen."

"All right."

"First off, I took to heart your undignified behavior, Wyatt. I mean at supper, and later on when I eavesdropped on your game of Criss Cross. And just so you know, Donald and I are quite aware of Tilda and this German boy's fawning over each other right from the start. Make no mistake about it, Hans Mohring has a genuine courtship in progress."

"I know that," I said.

"We need to keep our distance from it, Donald and I. Tilda's allowed her young woman's discoveries, eh? On the other hand, and Lord knows I'm no great student of people, but when you and Tilda are in the same room, you should just see how you light up. And how often in a lifetime do you have to hear 'All's fair in love and war' for it to become useful?"

"Really, you see me as being in love with Tilda, Aunt Constance?"

"Yes I do. Yes I do. How do you see yourself, Wyatt?"

"The same way."

"Wyatt, here's my two cents' worth of advice: the longer Hans Mohring lives over the bakery, the sooner you might declare yourself to Tilda. Give yourself a fighting chance, young man!"

"But—and I don't quite know how to ask—is there anything in the Bible, or in Nova Scotia law, that speaks to cousins?"

"Tilda's merely *called* your cousin, but her being adopted, she's not blood relations, family-tree-wise she's not. I consulted Reverend Witt, and he said—grudgingly, but still—he said even the church recognizes this. Besides, Donald and I might as well be from Mongolia, considering how little Tilda resembles us. Hard not to notice, our features are a world apart."

"I see you've put a lot of thought into this, Aunt Constance."

"What I mean is, ethically, if you have feelings for Tilda, there's leeway. I hadn't felt the urgency to discuss this with you before, Wyatt. Neither had Donald, out in the shed. But now there it is."

"Well, thanks for coming out here, Aunt Constance. Some rescue mission."

"With Tilda, you might also try a divination. Some people believe in them. If a divination doesn't work, nothing happens. If it does work, life changes for the better."

"What'd be a proper divination?"

"Start with something simple. Name your bedposts after the one you love."

"Name my bedposts *Tilda Hillyer*, is that what you're suggesting?"

"I'm suggesting it can't hurt."

When I looked over, I saw my uncle douse his cigarette by holding it above his head and wagging it a few times in the fog-drenched air. He tossed the butt onto the dock, not into the sea. My uncle wasn't much given to superstition, but he'd warned more than once: never sully the sea, or someday it'll come back at you hard, tenfold.

In Tilda's Own Hand

ON INTO AUTUMN OF 1942, there was, to my mind, a nagging sense of life being off kilter. Temperament-wise, my uncle sported a shorter and shorter fuse, and flare-ups, small and not so small, occurred between us at work, yet most of the time I couldn't figure out the provocation. Still, sleds and toboggans somehow got completed, deadlines were met, paperwork got done. There was, however, a new distance between Uncle Donald and me. Hard to say it right, but it seemed as if my uncle's closest human connection was now with the radio. For example—and this was a complete shock to my aunt and me—Donald didn't join us for dinner two, three or four evenings in a row. Some nights he'd come in so late, Constance would already be asleep. He wouldn't bother to heat up his food. Some nights I'd hear the radio and look in on him. He'd have his ear pressed to the speaker like a safecracker at a lock, except of course it was the tuning dial he turned in the tiniest calibrations.

Not wanting to act the lovesick village idiot anymore, especially in front of Tilda, I tried as best I could to avoid her and Hans. For the most part, this simply meant staying close to home. It helped that I was working such long hours, pretty much dawn to dusk, fairly collapsing after supper. What's more, when I listened to the rest of the house from my bed, I no longer heard the murmur of Tilda's reading from *The Highland Book of Platitudes* or *In a German Pension* or any other book. And one night, to my disturbing surprise, I realized I wasn't hearing my uncle's gramophone records, either.

I had to face facts: Tilda was in love with Hans. My aunt's phrase, "her young woman's discoveries," had loud nighttime echoes. Yet I never thought I'd see the day when my uncle stopped listening to Beethoven. I'm sure Constance could've told me where Donald's love for this composer had come from, and why it had persisted, but I had failed to ask her. I have to admit, Quartet No. 9 in C Major and Quartet No. 10 in E-flat Major were my favorites, and all the major symphonies. For Aunt Constance, the absence of gramophone music made her feel bereft. Then one night—and I mean at three A.M.—I heard my aunt's voice, louder than I'd ever heard it or could ever have imagined it. This time it had lost all decorum. It was as if she'd hired a total stranger to shout on her behalf: "You are allowing into our house the *wrong Germans* out of history, Donald! You're letting the wrong ones into our house!"

"What are you trying to say?" my uncle replied.

"I'm saying, listen to all the war bulletins you want to in your shed. But in the house? Donald, those war broadcasts are all murder, aren't they? All Hitler and death and ships lost at sea. I'm saying Beethoven's not those things."

But my uncle made up his mind differently, and one cold, windy, rainy morning in early October, all of his gramophone records were nowhere to be seen. Not just the Beethoven but his entire collection. "I've looked high and low," my aunt said in great distress. "They're gone." After that, it was exclusively radio programs—standard broadcasts and shortwave—that kept me awake until I couldn't keep my eyes open anymore. Bulletins, updates, casualty tolls, even stories of individual Canadian soldiers. Bleak news, that is, with the occasional reprieve of less bleak news. Static, static, static. My uncle puttering around in the kitchen. My aunt would call him to bed, often with reproach, and he'd respond, "Not yet, there's some news coming in from France," or something along those lines. I'd hear the tea kettle whistling or the coffeepot percolating, the thud of a whiskey bottle set down too hard on the table.

"God forgive me—and keep this to yourself," my aunt said. "Lately it's as if my beloved Donald's become a stranger to me, and we're married thirty-seven years! When I look in on him in the kitchen, often the lights are off. No candles, either. And he's blowing on those glowing radio tubes, when for years Donald has maintained that blowing on those tubes doesn't help the reception one bit."

In the last week of September and up to October 3, my uncle and I completed two sleds and a toboggan. The weather was all lowered clouds, rain threatened, threats realized, the Minas Basin wildly tossing and turning. Here is a sentence from the biographical notes printed on the back of the record album of Beethoven's First and Second symphonies: "During this period he was all too judiciously attended by insomnia." I knew what that meant. And so there we were, Constance, Donald and myself, absent Tilda. No books, no gramophone music. The radio in the shed, the radio on the kitchen table. My uncle listened to the radio in the bedroom too.

At seven A.M., October 5, Donald made a remark about my method of sanding a toboggan plank (it was one of my best skills) that was too critical for me to tolerate, so I drove, three hours earlier than usual, to the bakery to have coffee and a scone. Tilda was there, but not Hans, and I sat with her at a table near the window. "I see you're sitting here alone, without a book to read," I said.

"Hans is upstairs writing his supervising professor a letter," she said. "He keeps tearing it up and starting over. Obviously he hasn't been in classes. He's asking for next semester away from Dalhousie, too. It's called a leave of absence. Problem is, he doesn't want to upset his uncle, whose been so generous. That'll take a separate letter to Denmark. If letters still get there. Hans isn't so sure. He hasn't received one in months."

"And he can't tell this professor the real reason he doesn't want to come back, can he?" I said. "That reason being Tilda Hillyer."

"That's true," Tilda said. "It wouldn't wash."

"Well, if it doesn't work out the way he wants, you could always visit him in Halifax," I said.

"You mean the way *we* want," Tilda said. "Me and Hans, the way *we* want it to work out."

"I didn't mean that," I said. "I didn't mean that on purpose."

"Well, you should mean it," she said. "For my sake."

"Nonetheless," I said, "you could visit Halifax."

"Or I could *move* to Halifax," she said.

Naturally, that little exchange was a far cry from what my aunt had meant by declaring myself to Tilda. Stilted conversation along with no coffee, no scone—that was my breakfast with her. Except that as I was about to leave the bakery, Tilda said, "Wyatt, sit down again, will you?" So of course I sat right down and she cupped my hands in hers. "I need to ask you something. Please try to put aside your feelings toward Hans—or at least try to include my feelings for him—in how you listen to what I've got to say."

"All right, Tilda," I said. "Ask your question."

"Did you know that my father left broken pieces of all his gramophone records on our bed? Right upstairs from where we're sitting now. My own father trespassed in like a burglar or something. It had to be my dad. Nobody else would dare touch those records. Honestly, now, did you know he did that? Were you aware of it? Why would Pop do that? Because it was the most upsetting thing. Hans fixed an inside lock to the door of our rooms, can you imagine?"

"Aunt Constance and me couldn't find the records, Tilda," I said. "But I didn't know what happened to them. And that's God's truth."

"I believe you, Wyatt."

"I know Aunt Constance's been to see you."

"A number of times," Tilda said. "She didn't ask me to move back home. She said she's worried about Dad in all sorts of regards. You know what? Mom asked Cornelia, did my living out of wedlock with Hans above her bakery make her uncomfortable?"

"What'd Cornelia say to that?"

"She said, 'Constance, I lived with my husband Llewyn, rest in peace, two years before we got married. I'm no hypocrite.' "

"Sounds like Cornelia, all right," I said.

"Out of wedlock or no," Tilda said, "I'm getting sick of her sandwiches."

"Yesterday we had stew from the French cookbook," I said. "It was just me and Aunt Constance at table, though. Uncle Donald's appetite, what's left of it, hasn't been kicking in till later in the evening, you might say."

"Well, I'm not going home for supper, Wyatt," Tilda said. "But I am wanting to confide in you, because you're the most dignified man I know. Though not so dignified of late, eh?"

"I wouldn't call me dignified of late, no."

"Can I show you something?"

"All right."

Tilda reached into her Dutch school bag and took out a sheaf of papers held together by a paper clip. She set them in front of me and said, "I wrote this. Well, Hans talked to me and I took dictation. I'm hardly as capable as Lenore Teachout, but I did a pretty good job."

"What is it, anyway?"

"It's Hans's obituary. He provided a lot of facts, and I added some flourishes, you might say. Hans has the original, and he's writing one in German, too. For his parents."

"This kind of gives me the creeps, Tilda," I said. "Why'd Hans want you to write his obituary? He's only twenty years old."

"Twenty-one," Tilda said. "As to your question,

maybe the best way to put it is, Hans doesn't take life for granted. Not like many people take it for granted. That's the big lesson out of history he's learned. Don't take any single day for granted. At any rate, it's how he thinks. And it's a way of thinking he's earned, believe me. You read this obituary, you'll understand. He said I could just keep adding to it after we'd set up house and such together, eh? As the years go by."

"Maybe I'll get a coffee now." I poured a cup of coffee from the pot on the electric ring behind the counter and sat down across from Tilda again.

"Wyatt," Tilda said, "I need to ask you a favor."

"Favors aren't easy for you to ask," I said. "That much I still know about you."

"I'd like you to show this obituary to my father."

"Why on earth?"

"Because the U-boats, the radio and everything else have got him halfway off his rocker, that's why," she said. "You're in the house, Wyatt. Don't act like you don't know exactly what I mean. And if Hans Mohring—*if.* If Hans should become my husband, then Dad's got to try and see him whole-cloth. I think the obituary might help Dad see Hans as someone who's not had an easy time of it. And that he loves me and I love him. Maybe we're both a bit head-over-heels. But so what? Maybe it's laughable, us all smitten. But it's not laughable to us. Anyway, my

hope is, this obituary, in his daughter's hand-
writing, might help convince my dad that Hans is
not just a German anybody. Understand, Wyatt?"

"You look like you're going to cry, Tilda," I
said. "It's too early in the morning to get so
worked up."

"Well, I started getting worked up about eight
o'clock last night," she said. "I've been getting
steadily more worked up ever since. Just please
give this obituary to my father, will you?"

Marlais, I did deliver those pages to my uncle
out in his shed, and he did read them, and then he
tacked them to the wall along with the newspaper
articles. He placed the obituary next in line after
the last reported U-boat sinking. Then he went
back to applying linseed to a sled. He didn't offer
a single comment about Hans Mohring's life.
What my uncle did say was "This is one inspiring
document Tilda's written up, don't you think?"
Later, I sneaked into the shed on my own and
retrieved the obituary.

Those pages, in Tilda's own hand, I've kept all
these years.

Always Leave a Little Room
for a New Purchase

NEXT MORNING, OCTOBER 6, I didn't bother
to go to work. Instead, at seven A.M. I went
to the bakery, and there sat Tilda again. She
looked all haywire, exhausted as I'd ever seen
her, I'd say more ravished, just this once, than
ravishing. She wore a gray fisherman's sweater,
dark loose trousers and galoshes. It was steadily
raining, with harder rain in the offing. The
moment I joined her at the window-side table she
said, "Hans has made an addition to his obituary."

Cornelia was behind the counter. On its shelf,
the radio was affected by the storm. There was
mostly static, with barely audible passages of
music now and then. Yet Cornelia made no effort
to find another station. I hoped that I was wrong,
but it was almost as if she was resigned to the
static itself being the featured program, human
expression the interruption. Tilda and I watched
her a few moments.

"Being a touch stingy with candy sprinkles on
those cupcakes, aren't you, Cornelia?" Tilda said.
Cornelia ignored this. Every day after school,
children stopped in for cupcakes. One to eat in
the bakery, sometimes up to half a dozen to take

home. Cornelia couldn't afford to slack off on them. The woodstove had only just begun to provide heat. Tilda and I were drinking coffee and eating toast and jam. "Want to know what he added?" Tilda said.

"I'm all ears."

"That he is survived by his wife, Tilda Hillyer, of Middle Economy, Nova Scotia."

We sat without talking for a few minutes. "Wyatt, I'll need you to give me away at my wedding," Tilda said then. "Considering recent events. Considering everything. I can't ask my father, now, can I? He'd refuse me."

"Tilda, have you just told me you've set a wedding date?"

"October tenth," she said.

"That's just four days from now."

"Coming up quick, I know. Reverend Plumly over in Advocate Harbor agreed to perform the rites. I thought five or so villages down the road wasn't too close or too far. When I told him Hans is a German citizen, all Reverend Plumly said was 'I won't charge additional money for that.'"

"Reverend Witt turn you down?"

"I try not to go where I know I'm going to get my feelings hurt," Tilda said. "No, I didn't approach him."

"I take it you've told Aunt Constance."

"Hans made the announcement in private to Mother, on her last visit, which was two mornings back. He asked her for my hand in marriage. Mother hugged us both, but then, she would, wouldn't she? No matter what she thought."

"I wonder if she's told Uncle Donald."

"Probably she's got to decide, would the news be worse for Dad now or later?"

"Promise me you'll never tell me how Hans proposed marriage," I said.

"He said he felt like he'd known me his whole life already, so why not continue that."

"Funny, since you've never been to Germany."

"You know how he meant it, Wyatt."

"Did Hans get that letter off to his professor?"

"Went out in yesterday's post."

Tilda looked out the window at the Minas Basin. Fairly close to shore, the usual cormorants barely preceded their wing-flapping shadows, low to the water. "I wish cormorants never got on Noah's Ark," she said. "I've always despised that ugly bird." No matter what the subject, no matter how glum the circumstances, Tilda never failed to make me laugh. "But they've got God's equal rights to the sea, I suppose."

"I suppose."

"Mom, when she's puzzled why something in nature's downright ugly, she makes holy excuses. Says on that day of Creation, God had a headache. Then I usually say, well, why didn't he correct his mistake once he invented headache powder?"

"Were you awake all night again?" I asked.

"I look a wreck, don't I? Plus, I'm just going on about nothing, aren't I?"

"No, you're going on, true, but it's got substance. I wish I could listen through another coffee, but I've got a sled to work on. It's my wages. Besides, Hans comes downstairs, sees us, I don't want him to get jealous."

"Would it do any good to say he likes you, Wyatt?"

"Tilda, get some sleep."

"Look in the mirror, eh?" she said. "The pot's just called the kettle black."

I finished my coffee and left the bakery. At home, I started for the shed, but when I got near and heard Donald yelling at the radio, I decided to go into the house instead. "Aunt Constance?" I said.

I found her standing in the dining room, her new wardrobe trunk open on the table, clothes stacked on three chairs nearby. "I leave tomorrow morning, you know," she said.

"I'd forgotten it was so soon," I said.

"My, my, my, look at these three pull-out drawers," she said. "There's so much room. Still, I want to be careful in my choices. Proper preparation helps make for proper travel—"

" '—and proper travel makes for peace of mind at one's destination,' " I said, quoting what she'd said many times before.

I kissed my aunt on the forehead and sat down in a chair opposite her clothes. "You know, whenever I pack a trunk," she said, "I think of Meticulous Spelling, who used to live in Upper Economy. Maiden name, Meticulous Bartlett. Married George Spelling. Anyway, she certainly contained opposites, Meticulous Spelling did, in that her housekeeping was sloppy as a drunk sparrow making a nest, and she couldn't spell worth a tiddly damn, and I know personally, because she used to drop by and ask how you'd spell this or that word, because she was writing a letter to her aunt Nadelle in Vancouver. Some people can't spell, some can, I suppose, but Meticulous Spelling was one who couldn't. And on the subject of not being meticulous, I witnessed that woman, in her own home, pack a trunk once. She was setting out to see the sights in Quebec City. I don't know why she bothered to iron her clothes in advance. The inside of that wardrobe trunk looked ransacked."

I smiled and said, "Oh, Aunt Constance, you're the cat's pajamas."

"Even those I'd fold nicely."

"I bet you would."

"Everything neat and clean and in its place."

My aunt concentrated on which dresses to pack, which blouses, which socks, which shoes, which everything. She'd neatly fill one drawer, remove the contents, replace them with a different combination. At one point, not looking up from the sweater she was folding, she said, "Donald's moved to the shed. Outwardly, I'm trying to be poised about it."

"How do you mean, moved to the shed?"

"I mean he's built a cot and has bedclothes out there. He's got the woodstove for heat."

"At least now you'll be able to turn off the radio when you want, Aunt Constance."

"I don't find that response in the least appropriate."

"I'm sorry."

"Apology only half accepted," she said. "You two may be on the outs, but don't forget he took you in and gave you a paying job, Wyatt."

"You yourself said he's not himself lately."

"Donald asked Leonard Marquette and a few other lobstermen, could he use their trawlers to try and ram a U-boat."

"Where would this take place?"

"Right, well, Leonard told Donald there's no U-boats in the Bay of Fundy. And apparently Donald said, 'Where you don't see any U-boats, that may be exactly where they're the thickest.'"

"In the shed two days ago, he accused me, right to my face, of being a coward because I hadn't signed up for the RCN. I didn't say I'd been thinking about doing just that. He wasn't in the mood to hear it."

"So you *have* been thinking of it, then," she said.

"Yes."

"Wyatt, don't sign up to prove you're not a coward. Sign up because of the deepest conviction of what you're fighting against. War's old as the Old Testament. However, there's an unusual amount of madness at work in this war. Though, as far as I know, you've never befriended a Jew, have you? Maybe you had a Jewish friend growing up in Halifax and you never mentioned it. Anyway, like Reverend Witt says, if there's even near the equivalent of a Christian hell on earth, the Hebrew race over in Europe is in it. They could use some help, eh? Zoe Fielding wrote in a letter that she'd seen a newsreel, made her sick. What the Nazis are doing to the Hebrew race. And she meant sick, right there in her seat. There's reasons to sign up. Those U-boats have gone to such great effort, haven't they? Come all the way across the Atlantic Ocean to bring war to Canada. Let alone marauding around inside Donald's head of late, eh? Who's to make those U-boats regret their efforts if not our Navy?"

"Maybe our government's about to conscript me anyway," I said. "That'd make my mind up."

"It's best to make up your own mind." She set the sweater in the wardrobe trunk.

I never made it out to the shed. The morning meandered to afternoon. I pretty much just sat with Constance, watching her pack, talking about this and that. She added a *National Geographic* and a *Reader's Digest* to the trunk. For some reason, I remember how she absent-mindedly ran her fingers over the ruffled silk pocket that spanned the side of the trunk that held the hangers and dowels. A silk pocket "thoughtfully secluded in back for underthings," as she put it. It struck me that my aunt was a little giddy about that pocket.

Close to eleven o'clock, Constance said, "Probably there's no perfect time to mention this, Wyatt, dear, but as I'm leaving tomorrow, let me get something off my chest. Tilda and Hans Mohring have set a wedding date."

"October tenth."

"Goodness."

"I met Tilda this morning at the bakery," I said. "She told me."

"My own mother used to say, anything other than in the local church or in your family house is eloping."

"You gave them your blessing, Tilda said."

"But I begged her, change the date. Because I can't postpone my visit to Zoe Fielding. It's her granddaughter's christening. It can't be helped. But it breaks my heart, really. I'll miss my own daughter's wedding. I'd already paid for my ferry tickets. You have to reserve rooms, since they get filled up with military and civilians alike. These days it's nearly impossible to book passage."

"It was a sudden announcement, Aunt Constance. Not your fault."

"Fine, but couldn't Tilda and Hans please, please put off the date? I asked, but no. Everything feels so urgent lately. And where will they live, I wonder. If Hans Mohring even hints at taking Tilda away from Nova Scotia, I'll speak up. Mark my words, I'll speak up."

"I'd like to take the bus to Halifax with you," I said.

"Thank you just the same," my aunt said. "Besides, knowing my wardrobe's packed so well, I'll probably sleep like a baby."

"No, I mean for my own reasons," I said. "I've made the decision to speak with the RCN recruiting office."

"Don't tell me my little speech already's had an effect."

"Like I said, I've been seriously considering it for some time now. I'm in good health. Of military age. When it comes down to it, what's my excuse not to sign up?"

"On the bus, once I've dozed off, you can find an empty seat and think things over," she said. "A bus ride's good for thinking, I've always found."

"There's always a vacancy at the Baptist Spa, so I'm not worried where to spend the night. I'll be back in plenty of time for the wedding. I'll represent the family. Tilda asked me to give her away."

"Did she?" My aunt looked momentarily flushed and stricken. "Did she, now?"

"In so many words."

"Donald won't, probably, be capable of attending. I understand that," she said. "This evening I'll stop by above the bakery and tell her I understand it."

"I'm sure she'll appreciate it, Aunt Constance."

"Of course, I wouldn't not stop by anyway. To say goodbye."

She placed an umbrella on top of her folded raincoat.

"There," she said, "it's done."

"It's a work of art, your packing," I said.

"I've left a little extra room," she said. "One should always leave a little room for a new purchase. I don't count on making a new purchase, but just in case."

My aunt closed the trunk, locked it, fastened the key to a piece of string she'd previously cut to length, then slid this bracelet onto her left wrist. "Do you mind, Wyatt, dear, setting this trunk near the front door?"

Yet before I even laid hands on the trunk, my uncle, standing outside the house, lifted a dining room window and said, "I've officially docked you a full day's wages." He hadn't shaved in at least a week. He looked exhausted, sallow, thinner in the face.

"I'll work this afternoon and tonight," I said.

"Don't bother," he said, and shut the window.

"Well, now," my aunt said, "not much effort at conversation, was there?"

"Not much, no," I said.

"Well, lately he talks with himself. Mainly."

"You know, Aunt Constance," I said, "given his seesaw moods of late, there's a chance that Uncle Donald might disrupt the wedding ceremony."

"Don't worry. He won't attend," my aunt said. "He might want to, but he won't. Donald won't go where he's not invited."

"I'd better get out my own suitcase," I said.

"It's two dollars fifty cents for the bus."

I lifted the trunk and placed it near the front door. My aunt went into the kitchen and put the kettle on. "I'd better bring Donald out some tea," she said. "Some tea for my husband of thirty-seven years, now sleeping in a shed."

Picnic on the Bus

CONSTANCE AND I BOARDED the Acadian Line at 10:05 on the morning of October 7. We took seats together, third row back, driver's side. She wore dark brown slacks, a white blouse, a sweater, a jacket. Comfortable shoes rounded out her travel attire. She had a scarf folded neatly in her handbag. Between Great Village and Truro we were the only passengers. Then, in Truro, two women boarded and sat together midway back of the bus, and immediately each took out a book to read. We had a thirty-five-minute layover in Truro. My aunt and I remained seated. She took out the thermos of tea she'd packed. Soon a vendor, a rough-hewn boy of fifteen or sixteen, walked down the aisle. He offered fried halibut sandwiches or ham-and-cheese. We both got the halibut.

The vendor went back into the depot. "Picnic on the bus," Constance said. "Life could be worse."

"You didn't have to pay for my sandwich," I said. "I have my own travel funds. Except for this past week, Uncle Donald's never been late with my wages."

" 'Except' means an exception, and there shouldn't have been one."

"I won't press him on it."

"Pack your suitcase carefully?"

"You'll never know."

"When we get to Halifax, may I carry out a quick inspection?"

"No, you may not, Aunt Constance."

As the bus idled, the driver, Mr. Harrison (he and Mr. Standhope worked this route), went out to lean against the bus and smoke a cigarette. My aunt saved half of her sandwich, wrapping it back up and placing it in her handbag. In about twenty minutes the driver returned, followed by two young men, Canadian soldiers in uniform, who sat in the back row, smoked cigarettes, talked and laughed. The driver steered us out of Truro, southbound on the two-lane. Passenger stops included, this leg was scheduled at three hours fifteen minutes, which would deliver us to Halifax at five-fifteen.

"You might want to take your nap now," I said.

"Not yet."

"Then I'd like to ask you something. Do you mind?"

"I didn't say yes to you as a travel companion if I wasn't going to be companionable," my aunt said.

"Here's what, then. Rack my brains as I might, I can't figure out why Uncle Donald—I mean, considering his *feelings* about the U-boats—why—"

"Why in God's name would he allow me to travel on the ferry in the first place. Take the *Caribou* up to Sydney, then across to St. John's. Treacherous waters, what with the U-boats and all. Is that your question?"

"Yes."

Constance opened her handbag, reconsidered the remaining half of the sandwich. Finally, she ate it as if she were famished. In fact, for the first time in my experience, a completely unheard-of phenomenon, she spoke with food in her mouth: "—slept in the shed."

"I didn't quite get that," I said.

I waited while she finished the sandwich. "I slept in the shed last night," she said. "I wouldn't be seeing Donald till after the christening, so I went out to be with him. In marriage you have to adapt, eh? I adapted out to the shed. And we talked, husband and wife. Though I admit it's not comfortable out there. Those newspaper head-lines on the wall are unpleasant. Anyway, to his credit Donald did desperately try to talk me out of leaving home. But I said it's a christening. It's Zoe's grandchild—my oldest friend's grandchild. Friendship is provisional, Wyatt—you have to keep earning it. Back and forth, give the gift that's only each other's to give, as the hymn says. How long have I been friends with Zoe Fielding? Since we were five years old! I reminded Donald of all that. We had tea in the shed. I turned the radio off. I said, 'I simply won't miss the christening.' And that's when Donald used strong language. God's name—in vain. Language I don't approve of, but it was heartfelt."

"Then what happened?"

"My husband and I called a truce and neither slept."

"You didn't sleep at all last night?"

"Though Donald had offered me the cot. But, yes, soon I'll need that nap."

"Everyone I love most can't sleep well lately."

"Somewhere in Tilda's book, it says, 'Plead, cajole and foist your opinion as you must, yet it does not necessarily change another's mind.' Donald tried and failed with me. The christening won out, and that's all there is to it. I've said to Tilda more than once: those platitudes aren't much good for predicting life, but they often manage to sum up what's just happened pretty well."

"I've never cracked the cover of that book. It's by Tilda's bed."

"Formerly her bed, eh?"

We were silent a few moments, then Constance said, "My husband asked why didn't I think ahead to go the first stretch by automobile. That'd limit it to only one, much shorter ferry ride, just across to St. John's. But drive all the way up to Sydney Mines in Cape Breton to catch that ferry? Those roads? At my age, with these old creaky bones?"

"By going out to the shed, you're saying what? That it's not just friendship that's provisional."

"Marriage is, too. Correct."

"Thirty-seven years, it's still—"

"More painfully than ever, *provisional.* Haven't you noticed?"

My aunt shut her eyes then. But she didn't sleep. Apparently she just wanted to talk with her eyes closed. "Reach into my handbag, there, Wyatt. I'm giving you permission. There's a folded-up sheet."

I found the piece of paper and read what was on it, a poem neatly printed in ink:

> *CASABIANCA*
> *Love's the boy stood on the burning deck*
> *trying to recite "The boy stood on*
> *the burning deck." Love's the son*
> *stood stammering elocution*
> *while the poor ship in flames went down.*
>
> *Love's the obstinate boy, the ship,*
> *even the swimming sailors, who*
> *would like a schoolroom platform, too,*
> *or an excuse to stay*
> *on deck. And love's the burning boy.*

In a few minutes, my aunt opened her eyes and said, "Mrs. Oleander, the librarian, brought this poem to Tilda's attention. Tilda then copied it out for me. What Mrs. Oleander found thrilling, and so do I, is that it was composed by a woman who had some of her upbringing in Great Village. Practically a neighbor! This very poem was actually published. The magazine's called *New Democracy*. Granted, it was published in 1936, but the poet, Miss Elizabeth Bishop, has published many others. According to Mrs. Oleander, Miss Elizabeth Bishop's something of a world traveler. But she visits our province now and again. And do you know what? Where you and I got on the bus this morning, the house across from the Esso station, is the very house in which the poet spent several years. She went to the Great Village school. Her mother—and this is actual fact, not merely gossip—the mother's in Nova Scotia Hospital. Across Halifax Harbor to Dartmouth. Some sort of nervous collapse or other. Nobody's business, really, but the family's. Poor thing, eh? Elizabeth was only a little girl when they sent her mother there."

I returned the poem to my aunt's handbag. "It'd take ten philologists to help me understand it as well as it's meant to be understood," I said.

"Don't sell yourself short," she said. "The way I see it? A poem reaches out exactly halfway, then you reach out halfway, then see what happens."

"Provisional, eh?"

"I only mean if you're thinking's willful and

generous toward a poem, the poem'll be equally those things back. As for meaning, it'll mean something different to each person. That's all you have to know."

" 'Poor ship in flames went down'—that's got a ring to it," I said. "And 'stammering elocution'—I know what that's like."

"See, already you've got a good start on coming to terms with it."

"Nope, that's enough homework for me, Aunt Constance. But I'm glad you like the poem so much."

"When I get back home, I'm pressing it into my daybook. Mrs. Oleander says there's every reason to have confidence that Miss Elizabeth Bishop will establish a permanent reputation."

"Already did, in Great Village, don't you think?"

"Of course," my aunt said. "But just imagine, letting dozens, maybe hundreds of total strangers in on your private-most thoughts. Poets suffer from this. Yet their suffering's to our benefit. Writing poetry, not just for the church bulletin, I mean, risks being too openly sophisticated. Sophisticated in ways the average person can scarcely comprehend. And right there I speak of myself as average."

My aunt looked out the window for a while, then did finally doze off. She woke up only when the bus wheezed to a stop at Halifax terminal. My uncle had rigged a kind of gurney to haul my aunt's trunk, basically a dolly made of planks sawed and hinged, about two feet wide and three feet long, with wheels taken from four children's scooters fitted to the underside. Mr. Harrison and I loaded the trunk onto it. Wobbled a bit but did the job nicely, and even drew some notice from pedestrians, all the four city blocks to the wharf, where a deckhand pulled it up the gangway onto the ferry *St. Michael's*. The *St. Michael's* would connect with the *Caribou* in Sydney Mines, Cape Breton, then cross the Cabot Strait to Newfoundland.

"Enjoy yourself here in the city," my aunt said. "Take in a movie. Eat in a restaurant. A seat by the window makes you feel less alone, I'm told. But try to postpone moping about things at home, at least till you get back home. I'll send a post-card, eh?"

"Have a wonderful time," I said.

"Wyatt, it's good for the soul, isn't it, to visit Joe and Katherine."

"I could go out to the cemetery straight from the wharf."

"You take care, darling," my aunt said. "And especially good luck at the recruiting office. Those young men in uniform on the bus—your age, about. I pray God lets them measure up, wherever they're sent. I love you very much. I think you'll decide things well for yourself."

We hugged, and I watched my aunt until she reached the top of the gangway. On deck she waved, then disappeared. I bet they serve tea and biscuits, and that's where she's gone, I thought. I opened my suitcase to take out a sweater and found a small tin of lemon cookies. Purchased from the bakery, I knew; my aunt never made lemon cookies. I opened the tin. Then I realized that while I was helping to get my aunt's wardrobe trunk on the dolly she must've inspected my suitcase, because she'd placed a note inside the tin: *Adequate job.*

Walking through the city, I stopped in at the Baptist Spa on Morris Street. The proprietor, a Mrs. Campion, was cordial. I paid for a room, number 4, left my suitcase on the bed and set right out for the cemetery. My parents' graves were near the entrance, to the right of the iron gate. Very easy to locate.

Which reminds me, Marlais. In Nova Scotia, your mother's favorite of all the cemeteries she'd come to know was the one in Great Village. And believe me, Tilda was tough in her judgments. Again I jump ahead here, but one time—after the war—Tilda came home from being a mourner in McCallum Settlement. "The cemetery there's a disgrace," she said. "No one's weeded there for ages. Hoodlums have scrawled up a number of stones and the road in is badly rutted. Still, I did a good job and was paid on the spot. Yet it was everything I could do not to criticize the care-taker. The deceased was named Darwin Timbertea, age ninety-one, succumbed to pneu-monia. Other than clergy, the only one there was a nephew. After the service, the nephew drove me to the bus. In the car, I couldn't hold back and harshly criticized the caretaker, and the nephew said, 'My uncle Darwin *was* the caretaker.' "

At four P.M. I went to the recruiting station, corner of Duke Street and Argyle. The desk atten-dant, in Navy uniform, was direct. "You're here to kill Germans, I hope, and to do Canada proud, I hope. What's your name?"

"Wyatt Hillyer, from Middle Economy."

He said, "Did they teach you to write in Middle Economy?"

"I already knew how by the time I got there."

"Fill out these forms, then."

"I'm not decided yet," I said.

He leaned forward over the table filled with recruiting pamphlets, his face an inch from mine. "See that poster?" he said. He grabbed my shoul-ders and spun me toward the wall and I saw a recruiting poster. It showed a Navy warship drop-ping depth charges down at a German U-boat with Hitler's face on its hull.

"I'm not here to help you not piss your pants, Hillyer. You want to be on that ship, doing what that ship's doing, sign up. Me, I'm from Nells Harbor—men from there get their sea legs in the womb, eh? How about boys from Middle Economy?" I signed the papers. He said, "Spend Christmas at home and come back January fifteen. Right here. My desk." He saluted and I saluted back.

It remained for me to pass a physical examination, but for all intents and purposes, I was in the Royal Canadian Navy.

I ate supper in a restaurant on Lower Water Street, lingering long past dark, looking at the harbor, thinking I'd write Tilda a letter that would begin, "Well, I'm going off to war." But to what purpose? The letter, I mean.

Directly from the restaurant, I went to a pub on Bedford Row. Among the customers were some students from Dalhousie University, men and women, talking about philosophy and music. I heard "Beethoven." I thought Hans Mohring might know them. I felt envious. I had philosophies of my own. But I didn't invite myself to join them. After an hour or so, in walked the Navy recruiter, accompanied by three other men in uniform. Ashamed to say, at the bar I spent far too much money, throwing back shot after shot. In the wide mirror back of the bar I noticed that the fellow who'd recruited me kept looking over, shaking his head, all mockery and disgust, I thought. Who knows, really, but you get my frame of mind.

There was an excellently built sled hanging on

a wall, with a dart board at its center, darts stuck along the slats. At one point, a pretty woman, with dark red hair and wearing an overcoat and leather boots up to her knees, sat next to me and said, "I haven't seen you at Dalhousie. Are you a student?" I said no, I wasn't, and she said, "I'm Mary Conklin, from Dublin. I'm studying art history. Do you play darts? I have five brothers, I was raised on darts, so your pride be warned."

I introduced myself, then we pulled the darts from the sled, stepped back, and she said, "You go first." So I threw a dart toward the board. I didn't have my sea legs, to say the least, not after all that whiskey, so I didn't see my Navy recruiter step into range on his way to the jukebox. My dart struck him high on the arm, almost his shoulder. From his grimace, I expected the worst. "Oh, Lord, that's not the bull's-eye ya had in mind, I bet," Mary Conklin said. However, my recruiter just grinned, yanked the dart out, blood specking up, and said, "See you January fifteen, Hillyer." His mates roared with laughter. He continued on to the jukebox and stood there studying the choices. Mary Conklin said, "That was the shortest game of darts I've ever had," then left with her friends.

Around eleven o'clock—maybe it was later—I paid up and made my way out into the city. Stumbling along, I stopped at the first hotel I came across, the Essex House, on Bishop and

Lower Water, where I paid the night clerk and somehow managed the stairs up to my room, 403.

Early the next morning, the kittiwakes and gulls were keening so loud and close, I thought they should've pitched in on the room rate. It was cold and rainy, and I'd left the window open. The bureau doily was soaked through, and on the doily, rain had gathered in a glass ashtray. I could hear the loading cranes at Smith Wharves.

Standing at the sink, splashing water on my face, I suddenly remembered I'd signed up for the RCN, and felt neither good nor bad about it. Not righteous or patriotic or thrilled to the task— what sort of Canadian did that make me? And yet I could hear my aunt's admonition ring in my ears: "Indifference is a sin." If at that moment I'd sat down and written a questionnaire on hotel stationery, it would've included: *Did I join up because I wanted to kill Germans, do my bit? Did I join up because only a coward wouldn't?* Question after question after question. Despite all the accounts of battle I'd heard on the radio, I had no goddamn idea what combat was like. Why wouldn't a U-boat find my ship? Why wouldn't I be listed among the missing in a newspaper article whose blaring headline was tacked to my uncle's shed wall? I'd like to think that I was of as sane and similar a frame of mind as the next fellow—hundreds of us in Nova Scotia alone— awaiting orders. Both wanting to get on with it—

should be getting on with it, no doubt—and scared out of our wits.

To top off the morning, vicious hangover included, it wasn't until I'd walked all the way to a café on Granville Street to get some coffee that I remembered I'd taken a room at the Baptist Spa, paid for in full. Where my suitcase would still be on the bed.

That afternoon, on the bus to Great Village, I was so agitated I changed seats twice. I kept thinking: I should've said to Constance most of the French I knew, *Bon voyage.* I should've waited longer at the dock. I should've watched her ferry gain the harbor. What had been my hurry? The cemetery could have waited. You can't be *late* to visit parents in a cemetery, can you? All of this filled me with regret. Aunt Constance always said, when it was too late to help something, "Oh well, water under the bridge," but that was a phrase I no longer much liked.

All that. And Tilda's wedding in two days. (The love of my life's wedding.) And my church suit to get pressed and cleaned. That couldn't be done in Middle Economy. That would have to be in Truro.

1,789 Gramophone Records Splintered

FIRST THING, once I got back to Middle Economy, I drove my church suit to Truro. I hadn't attempted to seek out my uncle, though I knew he was working in the shed; I could hear the radio out there. Anyway, Winterson's Cleaning Establishment was in downtown Truro, on Phillips Street. The owner, a woman named, according to the plaque on the counter, Bettina Winterson, said my suit would take two days. "A prediction's not a promise," I said, being impolite for no good reason. I didn't realize at the time that I'd quoted *The Highland Book of Platitudes*.

"Okay, then, here's a promise. You'll have your suit tomorrow, by four," she said, "or I'll owe you a free cleaning. Trousers, shirts, anything you please. One-time offer, of course. How's that for a promise?"

Leaving Truro, I felt confident that, clothes-wise at least, I'd be presentable at Tilda's wedding. Driving along Route 2, I put stubborn will to work and tried not to think about much at all. Jettison all worries and concerns and vicissitudes and whatnot—and this seemed to take effect, because soon the inside of my head was the same as the general view of the boat-empty expanse of the Minas Basin, the day's last gull disappearing below the horizon.

I met Tilda at the bakery the next morning. I realized I'd begun to look forward to these meetings, rely on them, all the while realizing they couldn't go on for much longer. Still, there she was, bundled up in double sweaters, a thick scarf, a pair of Hans's trousers rolled up to reveal winter leggings. She looked a touch disheveled, and I said, "Night on the town, eh?" She yawned as if it was painful to her face. She struck me as a flibbertigibbet—all nerves—and at first could not meet my eye. But then she did what she always did when she wanted my full attention, which was to place her hands firmly over mine, press a fingernail into my knuckle and talk.

"We've pushed our wedding date up," she said.

"To when?"

"Actually, Wyatt, we got married at five P.M. yesterday."

"I don't get it. You asked me to give you away."

"I gave myself away."

"In Nova Scotia you need a legal witness, I thought."

"Cornelia volunteered. She was between baking scones and baking cupcakes and was available. In fact, she reminded us we needed wedding bands. I said we didn't have any, so she cut lengths of twine and we used those. I'm hoping Mother will advise on real bands when she gets back. She and I could make a day of it in Halifax. Anyway, as for using twine, Reverend Plumly didn't so much as blink."

"Maybe he suspected it was a German wedding practice."

"Wyatt, you're starting to sound like my father."

"No. Donald's dangerously tilted. Me, I'm just all envy, in case you didn't notice."

"I've noticed a lot of things."

"I still don't understand exactly why you changed your wedding date."

"Here's why. Reverend Plumly had to officiate at a funeral in Advocate on the day we were supposed to get married, and the family—the Dewis family—wants me to mourn at it. It's one of the uncles who died. Everett Dewis. He was on the outs with the whole bunch. The rest of the Dewis family are going to Montreal. So graveside it'll be just me and Reverend Plumly. Hans and I can really use the fee."

"Why didn't you wait till Constance got home?"

"Because Reverend Plumly was leaving to visit his sister in Quebec City right after the funeral. We asked everyone else who came to mind to marry us. No takers. Two justices of the peace— no. Reverend Mann in Glenholme—he's had three men from his congregation killed in the

122

war. He said no directly to Hans. Don't be so thick, Wyatt. Can't you see we felt lucky Reverend Plumly obliged us?"

"So you took who wanted you when. Well, things have a way of working out, don't they?"

"Mom was going to miss the wedding anyway," she said. "Strange, I was thinking of a platitude: When a wedding and a funeral meet on the road, the funeral should always step aside. Except I've just stepped aside my wedding for a funeral, haven't I?"

"Look at it any way you want, Tilda."

"Wyatt, I *did* leave a message for you at the Baptist Spa. It was the first long-distance telephone call I'd ever made. I knew you couldn't get back home in time. At least I wanted you to have notice."

"I never got the message."

"Did you ask after any messages?"

"I spent all night with prostitutes. Please don't tell Aunt Constance."

"Oh, well. You'll have to describe that experience some time, Wyatt. If it's still the truth by the time you're ready to describe it."

"I'll relate it to Hans, man to man."

"I'm sure my husband will learn something new."

"Does your father know you already got married?"

"To that end, we paid Reverend Plumly an extra amount. He drove over and told Dad."

"But you haven't seen Donald."

"No. And no surprise, he hasn't visited the newlyweds."

"Are you planning a honeymoon, then?"

"In two years, we hope. Given our present finances."

"So probably you'll move to Halifax."

"Hans has to finish his degree. And Dalhousie's in Halifax, isn't it? A man and wife live together, don't they?"

Hans stepped into the bakery, looking a little the worse for wear himself but with an expression of surprise and great relief, as if he hadn't seen Tilda in ages and was dumbstruck by the very sight of her. "Good morning again, my angel," he said, and kissed Tilda's hands. Hans was wearing a winter coat, and he'd brought a shawl and set it around her shoulders. "Hello, Wyatt," he said. "Tilda's my wife now. But you can meet her for breakfast like this any morning. If she approves. You are fortunate cousins, I think. It would be nice to have my own cousins living as close by."

"Where are your cousins, anyway?" I said.

"Denmark and Germany," Hans said.

"No, I guess Denmark and Germany aren't *close by* Nova Scotia, are they?"

"I wrote down a phrase the other day," Hans said. " 'An ocean separates us.' "

"You're filling up those notebooks left and

right. Keep up the good work, Hans," I said. "Tilda, where's Cornelia?"

"Gone to get more flour," Tilda said.

"Wyatt," Hans said, "I have an idea and I want to speak with you about helping me with it. Let's all have breakfast together, then—Wyatt, do you have to go immediately to work with toboggans, or might you have time to speak with me?"

"Lately, Hans, my employment situation's up in the air."

"I hope it comes down," he said.

"What is it you want to talk about that you can't say in front of your wife? Not, if you ask me, an honest way to start married life, eh?"

Hans sat down at the table. Tilda brought over a pot of coffee and cups for all three of us on a tray. She set the pot on an oven mitt on the table. She slid open the glass display case and took out a plate full of day-old scones and set it on the table, too. Hans said, "All right, good. Thank you for the lesson in marriage. But Tilda already knows my idea."

"We talked about it for hours," she said.

"I probably will fail," Hans said. "But I'm wanting. Very much wanting. To—how did you put it, Tilda?"

"Make amends," Tilda said.

"Make amends with Donald Hillyer. He's my father-in-law now. I'd like to make amends with my father-in-law."

I said, "You've got a better chance of having afternoon tea with Jesus."

Tilda laughed, because she remembered the title of one of Reverend Witt's sermons: "Is Afternoon Tea with Jesus Possible?" Hans looked puzzled. With that title, Witt had intended to make people curious about simple day-to-day faith—if Jesus dropped by one day for tea and a chat, off the cuff, what might you most want to discuss with him? Tilda kissed Hans and said, "Not laughing at your expense, darling. Go ahead. Go on. Tell Wyatt what you have in mind."

"Like an archaeologist, I glued pieces of Mr. Hillyer's phonograph records together," Hans said. "They're too damaged to play, of course. But I was able to write down the names of the composers and the compositions, you see. And my idea is, you accompany me to Halifax, because I frequent a classical music store. The proprietor's name is Randall Webb. Randall and I are friends from almost the first day I arrived to Halifax three years ago. In exchange for German language lessons, Randall allows me to borrow music."

"Hans, darling, no need to start every story with Genesis," Tilda said. "Just tell Wyatt what's the plan."

"All right, yes," Hans said. "I hope to purchase new copies of my father-in-law's phonographs, the ones he left broken on our bed."

"I get the picture," I said. "You need my car, so

here's what. I will drive you down to Halifax. But only because Aunt Constance would be pleased to have those records back playing in the house."

"That's reason enough, Wyatt," Tilda said.

"How are you going to pay for this big scheme of yours?" I asked.

"I'm pitching in my soon-to-be-earned mourner's fee," Tilda said. "And Hans has scholarship money left. Not much, but some."

"You can figure out your family finances on your own. My part of the bargain, though, is that I don't want to wait. I want to drive down to Halifax today. I'll even loan you some money if you need it. What do I spend it on, anyway?"

"Halifax prostitutes, I thought," Tilda said.

Hans practically spit out his coffee. "Where, Wyatt, that building on Lower Water Street? Or that small hotel near Citadel Park?"

"How'd you come by such information?" Tilda asked.

Caught up short, Hans took Tilda's hands in his and said, "Some seniors from Dalhousie frequent these places. At least that's my understanding."

"By the bye, I'm tagging along," Tilda said.

"My car's right outside."

"I'll need a few things," Tilda said. "Be back in a jiffy."

"Sit in the car with me, Hans," I said. "I'll explain 'jiffy' to you. I could tell you liked that word. See how I'm getting to know you?"

When she returned, Tilda sat between Hans and me and we drove out of Middle Economy. "I have to make a stop in Truro," I said. When we got to Truro, I parked in front of Winterson's Cleaning Establishment. Hans and Tilda waited in the car while I went inside. Since I was no longer going to give Tilda away in marriage, I'd intended to take my suit back unlaundered and save the money. But Bettina Winterson said, "Your suit's ready." I paid her and carried the suit on its hanger to the car, opened the door and laid it across the back seat.

"What's that?" Tilda asked.

"Wedding suit," I said.

"How much did it cost to clean?" she asked. "I'll pay you back so I won't feel bad."

"It had to be cleaned eventually," I said. "Let's leave it at that."

We hardly spoke the rest of the way to Halifax. Once in the city, Hans directed us to Ballade & Fugue, his friend's store, on Trollope Street. I locked my suit in the car. The store consisted of one large room with narrow aisles of bins packed with gramophone records. It smelled musty and the front windows needed washing. Music was playing on a gramophone behind the counter; I didn't know the composition. A blackboard announced NEW ARRIVALS, a list underneath. A big contraption of a cash register sat on the counter. Hans and Randall Webb greeted each other in German and said two or three additional German sentences, laughing a bit at the end. I noticed that the one other customer, a man of about thirty and wearing an RCN uniform, stiffened his shoulders, worked hurriedly through a bin for a minute, said to Randall, "Sorry, fella, nothing here for me," then left the store.

Randall shrugged. "He'd come in asking for— how to say it? More popular types of music. Oh, well."

Randall was well over six feet tall, lanky, with a generally bedraggled look and ill-fitting clothes. But he had a lively, alert face beneath his long black hair, parted straight down the middle, revealing a white furrow. He wore wire-rimmed spectacles. I could see into the storage room. There was a sink, a toothbrush in a water glass, pajamas hanging on the back of a chair. There must've been a mattress or cot back there, too. I thought Randall Webb must live in his store, or at least stayed there on occasion. Hans introduced Tilda and me.

"Tea?" Randall said.

All of us declined. Hans said, "Here's a list, Randall. I was hoping you might have these."

"Hans, my friend, let me read it." Randall studied the list, looked up and said, "Mostly you're in luck. Nix on the Schumann Piano Quartet in E-flat and the Piano Quintet in E-flat, though. By the way, that's got Schumann's three string quartets, all on the same recording. I haven't had one in stock for about a year. But there's a store in Montreal I do business with. I can try them. You pay for the long-distance call, I'll make inquiries."

"Let's just start with what you have in stock," Hans said.

Consulting the list, Randall moved through the aisles. A few students meandered in, browsed, chatted in French, but didn't make a purchase.

"How long have you had this shop?" I asked Randall, and he said, "Going on eight years."

Watching Randall scour the bins, I recalled Constance's "always leave a little room for a new purchase," and thought to send a postcard, even splurge on a telephone call or wire to Newfoundland, in which I'd recommend, if she still had room in her trunk, that she stop by Ballade & Fugue. She might find a gift for my uncle—and herself, of course.

The inventory of gramophone recordings was overwhelming. The bins held composition after composition I'd never heard, let alone knew existed—the shop seemed to be a crowded exhibit of my lack of musical knowledge. In fact, I pretty much knew only the works Donald had played every evening, and a few others from *Classical Hour.* Tilda shot me a disappointed, even embarrassed, look when I said, "Randall, can you tell me the name of the greatest composer born and raised in Nova Scotia and point out the right bin?"

Hans said, "That might take more research than Randall has time for just now, Wyatt."

That didn't help my confidence in the least. So it was a great kindness when Randall said, "Anything to do with classical music, I'm willing to find out. I admit I don't know such a composer, Wyatt. Professors in the music department come in here often, and one or two mention they've got talented students in composition, though they're mostly from Europe. I attend a student concert now and then, too. But to my knowledge, no Dalhousie student has gone on to make a reputation in the big wide world yet."

I was so grateful for his indulgence, I said, "Randall, would you pick out something for my aunt? She's already been up to her ears in Beethoven and Bach and Chopin. Maybe you can recommend something that will surprise her. Just make your best guess."

Randall seemed more than pleased. He walked to a bin against the far wall, took up an album and handed it to me. "This might work," he said.

Hans was curious and came right over and looked. "Selections from *La Bohème*, by Puccini," he said. "Tilda, does your mother enjoy opera?"

"For the life of me I don't know," Tilda said.

"Add this to my list, please, Randall," Hans said.

"No," I said. "Keep it separate. This is my gift to my aunt."

"Can you play it for us, Randall?" Tilda said.

Randall took the record from its sheath, carefully lifted the needle from the gramophone, then replaced one recording with the other. He set the needle down again, and as the overture began, he displayed the CLOSED sign on the front door, slid in the lock, lowered the door's shade and said, "It's a crime if *La Bohème* gets interrupted."

Randall brought out a chair from the storeroom. I sat on the chair, and Tilda and Hans sat on the frayed sofa, holding hands. "Did Puccini ever visit Canada?" I asked, nearly whispering to Randall as he walked past.

"I know for a fact he didn't," Randall said.

Ten minutes into it, I knew this music—and it didn't matter that I couldn't understand the words—wasn't going to allow small emotions. Tilda slid close to Hans and closed her eyes, a peaceful expression on her face. Randall lay down in an aisle, head resting on the stack of records he'd gathered from the list.

Hans changed records and sat back on the sofa with Tilda. Again they held hands. I looked over to the front window and saw three men, all in RCN uniforms, peering inside. I recognized one as the customer who'd been in Ballade & Fugue when Hans and Randall had greeted each other in German. Each Navy man had his eyes cupped and shaded by his hands, adjusting to the interior light of the store, probably wondering why the CLOSED sign was up. I'm certain they could hear *La Bohème.* One face disappeared, and I noticed the front door handle being tried. Randall, Hans and Tilda were lost to the opera. And right then and there I got a sick feeling, a bad feeling, but I made no logical connections, not like in a game of Criss Cross. I thought it had to do with the uniforms, the realization that I was officially in the RCN, that I might soon be out among German U-boats and every other horror. It could have been a thousand things. Then the three Navy men disappeared.

"Randall," I said, "that CLOSED sign turned away a few customers, I'm afraid."

"Look at it this way," Randall said. "What if they wanted to buy *La Bohème* right when we were listening to it? I only have the one set."

When the arias ended, Randall finished filling whatever of the list he had in stock. The money Hans had in his wallet fell a little short. I was going to offer some, but Randall said, "The rest we can work out in German lessons." He gift-wrapped the records individually and wrote out a receipt.

"We should be getting back home," I said.

"What on earth for?" Tilda said, and I had no good answer.

"Want to listen to more opera?" Randall said.

"Once I put the sign up, I don't take it down till morning. My hours are my own." (I saw Hans jot down that phrase in a notebook.)

But we left Halifax shortly. The recordings were on the back seat. Once in Middle Economy, we went directly to the bakery, famished. It was already closed, so Tilda used the key Cornelia had given her. When we stepped inside, we found a note: *A bit under the weather—there's half a cake on the counter.* That cake with vanilla frosting was our dinner. I left the bakery at about nine P.M.

The next morning I was violently shaken awake. I squinted up at Uncle Donald, his unshaven face gaunt and derelict, breath like he'd been chewing sawdust. He was holding up the *Halifax Mail.* "See this, Wyatt!" he said loudly. "Right here on page two. Some Navy boys took direct action in Halifax last night." He tossed the newspaper onto my face and I heard him leave the room.

I went into the kitchen, ran cold water from the spigot and splashed some on my face, then sat with the *Mail* at the kitchen table. A headline on page two read: POLICE INVESTIGATE BREAK-IN; THREE RCN QUESTIONED. Underneath that: "Owner of Record Store in Serious Condition in Hospital."

Really, Marlais, I could scarcely believe my eyes. The article, which ran to two columns, informed readers that late the previous night thugs had broken into Ballade & Fugue, torn the place apart and "systematically splintered 1,789 gramophone recordings of classical music, according to owner Randall Webb's inventory." I knew it had to be those men who'd peered in through the window, the ringleader maybe the man who'd heard Hans and Randall speak German to each other. The rest of the article described how they'd attacked Randall in the storeroom, "rained blasphemies and indecencies on him, and had, in the course of a beating, broken his nose, cheekbone, and four ribs, punctured his spleen and left him with a severe concussion." It wasn't until four A.M. that Randall had managed to telephone the police, who immediately dispatched an ambulance. To my amazement, it was Officer Dhomnaill—I recognized his face in the photograph; he was standing in Randall's store—the newspaper quoted: "We jimmied open the door and found Mr. Webb unconscious and bleeding on the debris here in his shop."

I drove to the bakery to deliver this news to Hans and Tilda. It was already nine A.M. but they'd just sat down for breakfast. I'd heard rumors that newlyweds sometimes slept in like that.

Murder

IN THE END, the Dewis family decided not to put out the money, and Tilda lost that mourner's fee. "No good deed goes unpunished" was Cornelia's response, after she'd informed Tilda that Reverend Plumly had called to cancel her services, with apologies. "And here you'd gone and changed the date of your wedding on their behalf." Yet the same day Tilda got another offer to mourn, in the village of Lorneville.

"It's arranged through Reverend Greene at Lorneville Methodist," she said.

"Didn't he refuse to perform your wedding service?" Cornelia asked.

"One of many who did," Tilda said. "I don't have to be his best friend, I just have to work with him half an hour."

"Practical of you," Cornelia said.

Over the next few days—October 11, 12 and 13—I lived like a hermit. I pretty much kept to the house, scarcely laying eyes on my uncle, though I'd hear his truck come and go. And what I'm going to tell you about now, Marlais, which occurred on the night of October 13–14, I didn't see as a premonition at first. Yet it must've been a premonition that led me to wander into Donald and Constance's bedroom and sit on my aunt's side of the bed. I use the word "premonition" because, a few days later, an article in the *Mail* substantiated that the ferry *Caribou* had been torpedoed and sunk at about the same time of night.

I hadn't been able to sleep. My uncle was out in his shed. Sitting on the bed, I waited for my eyes to adjust to the room, then toured the ancestral portraits in frames on the walls. I looked at my aunt's hairbrush on the bureau, her hand-held mirror, the vase of dried flowers, her blue cotton bathrobe on its hook on the door. I looked out the window. The moonlit view was down the scrub pine slope, a number of ponds, a stream that eventually widened out into the Minas Basin.

There were several lights on in Betty and Abel Wickersham's house; possibly they were already up and about. I recalled how a week earlier at the post office Abel spoke to me about the change in Donald's character. "This war—all of us are coming apart at the seams," he said. "That young man from Advocate Harbor and that other from Diligent River shipped home in coffins. Fellow from Portapique, what family was he from, the Cogmanaguns, wasn't it? Reverend Witt says people need to use all the old prayers more often, but come up with some new ones, too, to fit this war in Europe. So much sadness and not always knowing what to do about it."

"I sure don't know what to do with mine," I said.

"It's nothing new to our part of Nova Scotia," Abel said. "Being from Halifax you may not know, but during the Great War not one man of conscription age from Great Village ever came back. Not a goddamn single one survived. That whole generation of men, absent like if you woke up and discovered your middle finger had disappeared. After that, if you were a young woman from Great Village wanted to marry, you looked elsewhere."

"The world's gone haywire again, Abel, hasn't it."

"Who doesn't feel that? So tell me, what gives Donald the right to poke his finger into our chests, hectoring about U-boats as he's been doing?"

"You got me there."

"Look, I've known Donald Hillyer my entire life, and I'd be the last to contend he's mild-mannered by nature. But he never used to hector like that. Understand, I'm less filing a complaint than mystified."

Moonlight flooded the wide field behind Patrick and Marcelline Bastow's house, down the road to the west of the Wickershams'. The Bastows had only their porch light on. Their son, William, served with the ambulance corps in France. Tracing their road farther west, I came to Reverend Witt's house. Witt lived alone and raised about a hundred sheep, which brought the behind-his-back comment that a Christian flock wasn't enough for him. Not more than ten days before, Reverend Witt had dropped by the house and told my aunt that Donald had asked to deliver a sermon in church.

"Donald getting up in front of all those people?" Constance said. "He couldn't have been serious."

"Here's the list he gave me of his ideas," Witt said. "See for yourself."

My aunt and I both read it. My uncle's every topic was U-boats, no surprise there. My aunt could only shake her head, incredulous, and say, "My Donald's got smoke blowing out of his ears. Tea, Reverend Witt?"

The three of us sat down for tea. Witt said, "Just so you know, I told Donald that I had sermons composed for the next long while. I could see this didn't sit well with him. He said, 'If that's the best answer you've got, I might approach churches elsewhere.' "

Now, I realize, Marlais, that human memory is an unreliable stenographer of such conversations, but you get the gist of them. The one with Abel Wickersham, the one with Reverend Witt. In fact, many of the people who'd had run-ins with Donald had come to a similar conclusion: my uncle in effect had (to paraphrase Scripture) become what he beheld—U-boat atrocities, radio war reports. He'd become those and was almost a broken man for it.

The night of October 13–14, I tried to sleep on top of the quilt on my aunt and uncle's bed, but couldn't. At first light I went to the shed to attempt to make amends, but my uncle was nowhere to be found. I killed some time—doing what, I can't remember. Around noon I drove to the bakery, and Cornelia said that early that morning Donald had dropped by for coffee. "He was on his way to get toboggan runners from the blacksmith in Truro," she said. The blacksmith's name was Steven Parish. He'd fashioned runners for my uncle for two decades, had only once raised his price, in 1934, but not before or since.

"Tilda around?" I asked.

"She and Hans went to visit Randall Webb in hospital," Cornelia said.

I got in my car and drove to Truro. My uncle's truck was at the blacksmith's shop. The shop was across the road from a restaurant that featured a view of the Tidal Bore, the berserk tide that filled the long cove in just minutes. The cove was not fifty meters from the restaurant, though locals regarded the Tidal Bore as a world-class phenomenon of nature. In fact, the restaurant, McKay's Diner, bragged-up the Tidal Bore at the top of its menu—a drawing of a couple, daredevil in a rowboat riding a tall wave, eating a big stack of pancakes. The printed motto was "Our blueberry pancakes fill you up fast." For my aunt's sixty-first birthday, January 5, 1942, we'd gone to this restaurant for breakfast, Donald and Constance, Tilda and me, and the pancakes were excellent. When Donald had started in on a story from his childhood about his competing in an ice-skating race despite a sprained ankle, my aunt said, "Husband, don't be a tidal bore." I laughed loudly, so did Tilda, and so did our waitress, who'd been refilling our coffee cups. But then the waitress asked my uncle, "Well, did you win or not?"

The sign on the door of Steven Parish's shop read BLACKSMITH AT WORK, and when you stepped inside, that's exactly what you found. Parish was born and raised in Truro. He was about fifty years old, handsome, with curly black hair usually tied back from his forehead with a bandanna, taut of build. He wielded the tools of his trade with precision and grace, especially considering his "youthful arthritis," as Constance called it. Anyway, when I opened the door into the heat-blast of the forge, Parish, wearing a smudged leather apron, goggles and thick asbestos gloves, saw me and walked over. He pressed the working end of a hammer against my chest and said, "Wyatt, whatever's on your mind, I wouldn't speak a single word of it to your uncle. He's in my office listening to a nightmare bulletin on the radio. So I'd get right back in your car and drive home, is my suggestion."

"How do you mean 'nightmare'?"

"German U-boat sank the *Caribou*, and Constance might've been on it, on her way home from St. John's."

Parish stepped over to a dozen or so runners leaning against the wall, tapped one with his hammer and called out, "Take these with you." He went into his office. Before he shut the door behind him, I caught a glimpse of my uncle pounding his fist on the table. His face was contorted in a way that twisted up my own stomach. I loaded the runners into the back seat of my car, then drove straight to Middle Economy.

I carried the runners into the shed and went inside the house. As it happened, Tilda had also learned from Cornelia that Donald had gone to Truro, and what with his being absent like that, she took the opportunity to gather up a few personal items from her old room. I found her there paging through *The Highland Book of Platitudes*. When she looked over and saw me in her doorway, she said, "Randall's in bad shape, every breath painful, but he says he's going to build his record shop back up from scratch, and Hans and I said we'd help."

I didn't respond.

"What's the matter, Wyatt? Don't tell me nothing, because your face is all mayday! mayday!"

I sat on the bed next to her and took her hands in mine. "Tilda," I said, "one of the ferries Aunt Constance was taking. It's called the *Caribou*."

"Jesus wept!" She pushed me away, stood and walked to the window and stared out. "Is it sunk for certain?"

"All I know is, I went to the blacksmith's shop to try and find Donald, and when I got there, Steven Parish said a radio bulletin had come in. And he said—"

Without turning from the window, Tilda said, "What? Steven Parish said what?"

"He said the *Caribou* was lost."

"But is it for *certain* Mother was on that particular run? Those ferries, every week or twice a week or whatnot, go Newfoundland–Nova Scotia and vice versa, correct? Plus, she said she was going to be a tourist along the way, remember? Gone a month like that. Ferry after ferry."

"I didn't know her exact schedule, Tilda. I only know Aunt Constance was ticketed twice on the *Caribou.*"

Tilda took five deep breaths, counting each one out loud. "Now, here's what I'm going to do," she said. "First off, I'm going to walk to the bakery. You won't drive me, because it's a good specific distance, to allow crying. Crying about what's not yet known for certain. Because, sad as any ferry sinking is, I realize my mother might not have been on that particular *Caribou* run, right? And as we speak, she may be fully alive, laughing and smiling at the christening—but I can't for the life of me remember the date of the

143

christening. I know she was making a stop or two along the way. Or was that on the way back?"

"Today is October 14, is all I know," I said.

Tilda sat on her bed and immediately stood again. "Then once I get to the bakery, I'll go upstairs," she said. "Because Hans is organizing papers. Organizing papers toward his thesis in philology. We'll turn on the radio, and I'll say to my husband—"

She bit her lip and the rest of her thought never arrived, at least not out loud. Clutching *The Highland Book of Platitudes* to her chest, Tilda then hurried from the bedroom and the house, striking out for the road to the bakery.

For many of the next daylight hours, I slept the sleep of the dead on my aunt and uncle's bed. No dreams. After eating a dinner of leftover stew with bread and a glass of water, I heard my uncle's truck pull up. This was around seven P.M., already dark. He didn't come into the house, though. He went directly to the shed.

I left a floor lamp on in the living room, and the porch light, and drove to the bakery. I went right upstairs and knocked loudly, and Tilda let me in. Hans was sitting at their kitchen table, which was stacked with papers and books, some in German, some in English. Without a word, Hans went to the cupboard and brought out a quarter-full bottle of vodka, hesitated, then brought out a second bottle, that one new. He made room for the bottles on the table. Tilda set glasses down and Hans poured.

We raised our glasses, stymied for a moment as to what to offer as a toast. Tilda finally broke down and sobbed. Then she managed to say, "My mother didn't know how to swim. When I was a little girl, all those times she took me to the beach over at Parrsboro, and a few times to Advocate Harbor, where all the driftwood washes up. Muggiest summer day, she didn't so much as stick a toe in. Whereas me, I'd just fly into the water."

It seemed a stalwart obligation for Hans to try and distract Tilda away from thoughts of her mother, so he put Schubert's Impromptu in A-flat on their gramophone. I wondered, however, was it possible that Schubert's piano composition could incite Tilda to think all the more intensely about Constance? It had that effect on me. Because not a minute into it, I had the image of my aunt flailing in the ocean, not being able to reach a lifeboat. An image I might have got from one of those newspaper accounts on the shed wall.

"Where'd you get a gramophone?" I asked.

"Pawnshop," Tilda said. "The few phonograph records we've got here, Hans bought at a pawn-shop, too. When we went to visit Randall."

I threw back my entire glass of vodka. It burned going down my throat, and I half choked out, "I admit I've never drunk this stuff before."

"Hans says to drink it cold as possible," Tilda said.

We sat in candlelight, drinking and listening. When Hans turned over the record, set the needle and sat down again, he said, "Wyatt, I understand what has happened."

"We don't know what's happened yet, Hans," I said.

"I think we do know, yes," he said. "I think a submarine from the country of my birth has killed my mother-in-law, Constance Bates-Hillyer."

"Constance might not have been on that particular run," I said.

Hans said, "Fine and admirable, Wyatt, to hope against hope. Yes, but I have studied the shipping news, as it's called. I went to the library and studied it in the newspaper. Also, I used Mrs. Tell's telephone. I paid her for five telephone calls to Halifax, to the ferry port. To the newspaper, Wyatt, I asked my questions. I've studied the ferry schedules, and I am deeply worried."

And that was pretty much all any of us said the remainder of the night. Sip by sip by sip we finished off both bottles of vodka as Hans played every one of the gramophone records they owned, twice over. We probably kept Cornelia awake, certainly troubled her sleep, but there was no knock on the door, no complaint. What's more, when it became light out, she slid a note under the door: *I heard the news—may I have breakfast with you?* Tilda, Hans and I were numb and exhausted from the vodka, our fear-of-the-worst. When would we know for certain?

Hans said, "I better wait awhile before I give Donald his gramophone records, don't you think?" He had only slightly slurred his words.

"Hans, I married a student in philology," Tilda said. "I did not marry a member of the crew from whichever U-boat sank the *Caribou.* I'll make everyone see that."

"Hans is right," I said. "He should wait on those gramophone records."

Hans went to the bedroom and returned with a framed photograph of his parents. They were standing in front of a restaurant. "This was taken in Copenhagen," he said, handing me the photograph. "I only wish I could speak with them. But that is impossible, isn't it? Quite impossible."

"Coffee might be what the doctor ordered, eh?" Tilda said, standing up from her chair. She sat right back down. "Still a little woozy. Maybe I'll leave coffee up to Cornelia."

"The bakery's open by now. I'll go downstairs to find her," I said. I went into their washroom, and while there I overheard Hans say, "Tilda, I want to add something to my obituary."

"Now, Hans?" Tilda said. "I don't know if I can spell correctly. My head's stuffed with cotton."

"Yes, I'm afraid so, Tilda, *now,* please. And

Tilda, it doesn't matter, your spelling," Hans said. "Please add, 'He loved the Schubert impromptus best.' "

Tilda took the obituary out of the roll-top desk drawer, then sat at the desk and began to write. I went down to the bakery. Cornelia was behind the counter; the radio was giving the weather forecast.

"Oh, Wyatt, there you are," she said. "I heard your vigil all night, you three. Young people gathering together against terrible news. Now that's resourceful. My worry is, if my own mind, just here in the bakery, has gone to hellish places, I don't want to imagine where Donald's has gone to."

"Cornelia," I said, "you are my aunt's closest friend. You yourself must be out of your mind with worry."

She brought a pot of coffee and a cup to a table and I sat down there. Tilda walked in and said, "I completely forgot, it's today I've got my funeral up to Lorneville. Completely forgot, completely forgot."

"Tilda, speaking on your behalf here," Cornelia said, "I'm not sure going to a cemetery's the best idea in the world. But I suppose work is work."

"Whatever the truth about Mother is, it's going to be the truth in three or four hours, or whenever I get back. Besides which, I promised the Drake family up there. Mom always said, a true gentleman or a true gentlewoman always keeps their promise, no matter what the rest of the world's like."

"I take it you want me to drive you to Lorneville," I said.

"It's a Mrs. Winslow Ledoyt Drake who passed," Tilda said. "Age ninety-four and outlived everybody who might've otherwise attended. Mrs. Drake's two daughters have been informed in England, but the war's got them stuck there, so it's just going to be me and Reverend Greene and the weather. Anyway, Hans isn't coming along. I said he shouldn't be alone. We didn't spat, but he didn't budge on this, so, yes, I'm turning to you and asking you. You don't have to get out of the car. During the service you could drive around if you wanted to."

This cannot reflect well on me, Marlais, but I was glad for the opportunity to be alone with Tilda, not to mention get away from my nerve-racked uncle and the empty house. So I accepted. Tilda had two cups of coffee in a row, and I had a second. "I'm going upstairs now," she said, "to change into my black dress." In fifteen or so minutes, we set out due east along the two-lane through Bass River, Portapique and finally to Glenholme, where we turned onto a well-kept dirt road. We traveled north, slowly curving westward, past Londonderry Station, then slowed down considerably in order to find the narrower dirt road leading into Lorneville. The only thing

Tilda said the entire time was "Actually, this dress is quite comfortable."

The cemetery was within sight of the village of Lorneville. It had at least twice as much property as the one in Great Village. The service was scheduled for ten A.M., and we were right on time. Reverend Greene must have walked to the cemetery, or was dropped off, as there was no other car in sight. Smoothing down her dress, then fixing a bobby pin to her hair, Tilda said, "Well, here goes. The way I'm feeling, it's as if since yesterday I've stored up grief like rain in a rain barrel. I'm afraid this old Mrs. Drake's about to get drenched with tears. Then again, she might get short shrift if I decide to save everything for the news about Mom. We'll just see."

She attempted a smile but fell short, and when she got out of the car, I got out, too. I kept about three gravestones back, by the fence. Reverend Greene wore a heavy overcoat and fedora, as it was chilly and windy out and felt like it might snow, but Tilda went coatless. As it turned out, the grave had already been filled with dirt, properly tamped. And what did it matter, really? The moment Tilda stepped up to him, Reverend Greene said to her, "Shall we begin?" When he'd read about ten words from the Bible, the wind blew the hat off his head. It tumbled along the ground, smack into a gravestone. He didn't bother to retrieve it.

He spoke briefly about Mrs. Winslow Drake's lifelong devotion to Christ our Savior, to family and friends, and to the painting of miniature schooners built by her husband, Abial Drake, which graced fireplace mantels in many of her neighbors' homes. He kept looking over at me, maybe because having three was more respectful—less stark—than having just two people participate in the service. Especially since he and Tilda had both been hired.

Between the gusts of wind I was able to make out most of his words, right on through the Lord's Prayer. After the "amen," Reverend Greene added, "And Lord, please accept a separate prayer on behalf of Mrs. Winslow Drake's surviving daughters, Sadie and Vivian, who along with their husbands and children are under terrible siege and bombardment in London, England, on this very day. Please protect and keep them, so that someday they may visit their mother's grave and perhaps return to live in Nova Scotia."

He nodded to Tilda, stepped aside, and Tilda took over. I wondered if Reverend Greene had ever seen a professional mourner at work. As my aunt liked to point out, Tilda seldom did anything halfway, and as I soon observed, mourning was no exception. What's more, she was trying to build a reputation, so this would be a chance to impress Reverend Greene. In turn, he might recommend her around the province, if that's how it worked. But given how heavily thoughts of her mother must've weighed on her, I doubt she cared about ambition as she fell into a strange marionette's flailing of arms, wailing and moaning. To my eyes, at least, it was an authentic letting go.

In that windswept cemetery, as Tilda mourned a complete stranger, I recalled how stiffly I'd stood at my own parents' graves, how life felt tilted off-true, how I'd mainly wanted to sleep, how out-sized my funeral suit had felt, even though it fit me perfectly. I realize all such comparisons are nonsense, but there in Lorneville, I thought: My dear aunt Constance may well have been drowned last night, whereas my mother and father . . . And then a snippet of a skip-rope song girls used to sing at my elementary school came to mind: "When the sea cried 'Repent! Repent!' only the sea obliged." Sometimes the girls would repeat "repent" ten times or more in a row. Like a lot of those skip-rope songs, it sounded happy-go-lucky, but actually it came from a dirge about a schooner lost in a storm, leaving widows, and children half orphaned, and empty graves in the village cemetery. And though I was remembering back a dozen or so years, it seemed I could really hear those girls singing, hear the slap and whir of the skip-rope, bells jangling on the wooden grips, their feet hitting the playground tar, their voices meshing into one voice. When I snapped out of this memory, I looked toward Reverend Greene and saw him leaning over Tilda, who had fainted and lay sprawled on Mrs. Winslow Drake's grave.

I ran to them and Reverend Greene said, "I don't imagine you have smelling salts."

I didn't know what I was doing, really, but I slapped Tilda's face back and forth, and she opened her eyes and said, "All right, Wyatt, that stung, and I'm cold."

Reverend Greene said, "Should I try and find a doctor?"

"I'll get her home now," I said.

Reverend Greene appeared too awkward to speak; he just couldn't wait to get out of there. He stuffed a small envelope into my coat pocket. It contained Tilda's fee. He walked over and picked up his hat, then set out toward Lorneville. When Tilda was able to stand, I fitted my coat over her shoulders and got her to the car. In the back seat she fell right to sleep.

Back home in Middle Economy, Tilda took immediately to her bed. Hans came down to the bakery and said, "She's asleep now, Wyatt. Thank you for getting her home."

"That's fine. You're welcome."

"What happened out there, do you think?"

"Hard to say. She really got worked up."

"Worked up?"

"Maybe too much wind got in her ears. Maybe she should've been wearing a hat pulled down over her ears, Hans, I don't know. She went all out, I can tell you that much. Tilda really earned her keep."

"Wyatt, do you know what time the first bus leaves tomorrow morning?"

"I think eight-forty."

"All right. Now I'm returning upstairs."

"Why ask the bus schedule?"

"It might be a good time to leave for a while."

"To where?"

"I was thinking Prince Edward Island. I studied its location on the map."

"Hans, a U-boat recently attacked a civilian ferry in the Northumberland Strait, along Prince Edward Island. The memory of that has to still be fresh up there, is my guess. I'd study your map again if I were you."

"Yes. I see. Now I'm going upstairs."

I drove toward my house with no small amount of dread, but almost right away I discovered, in my coat pocket, the envelope containing Tilda's fee. I turned the car around, drove back to the bakery and left the envelope with Cornelia, asking her to give it to Tilda at her nearest convenience. Then I drove even more slowly back home. When I got there, two trucks and one car were parked out front. Just inside the front door, I heard the radio: "—and what heroic measures are needed in the

154

face of such atrocities—" Loud static for a moment. "*—the escort ship* Grandmère *searched the area for survivors. Those fortunate ones told of the screams and cries for help they heard all night in the darkness . . .*" Static and more static.

Scowling and cursing, my uncle adjusted the dial, but the static prevailed. He turned to the other men at the table, offered a downward smile and said, "You probably didn't know, but my Constance couldn't swim."

Then he saw me and right away turned down the volume on the radio. He looked to have a week or more stubble of beard. He was wearing the same clothes he'd worn to Steven Parish's shop the day before. There was a bottle of whiskey on the table. "We're bivouacked here with the radio," he said. "Where's your manners, Wyatt? Shake hands with our guests."

Simon Perkins, whose lobster boat was named *Sprightly*, stood up and we shook hands. I shook hands with Warren Heddon, who was the proprietor and cook at the Glooskap Restaurant in Parrsboro, and as my uncle once put it, "Me and Warren have shared thirty-some years of Sunday breakfast, and not once late to pick up our wives and children at church and spend the rest of Sunday with them." I shook hands with Miller Shiers, a house painter, who had famously painted Reverend Witt's church in three days' time, including two nights without sleep, using lanterns hung on his ladder to work by. There had been no particular rush or reason for him to paint the church like that, except, as Shiers said, he'd simply decided to. I shook hands with Gus Breel, who was the constable serving eleven neighboring villages. He'd been born in Upper Economy, and had, in his fifty-six years, lived only in Upper Economy, Middle Economy and Lower Economy, and had been married and divorced in each place. Cornelia had said, "You know, they should name a new village after Gus Breel. There'd be Upper Economy, Middle Economy, Lower Economy—and then for Gus's sake they could add Just Plain Broke."

Looking at these men at our kitchen table, I said, "I don't ever remember this many people in the house since Tilda's eighteenth birthday."

"So much for pleasant conversation," Donald said. "Because as the situation now stands, our concern's not who's *here* as much as who *isn't*."

The room fell silent. Then Warren stood and said, "Well, Donald, we just wanted to sit here with you." The others nodded in agreement. Warren, Miller, Simon and Gus filed out of the kitchen. I heard their car and trucks start up in quick succession.

"Our last night together, Constance slept in the shed with me," my uncle said. "If that isn't something, nothing is."

And it was at that precise moment the telephone rang. My uncle stood and answered it on the third ring. He did not say hello. I could hear a voice at the other end inquire, "Is this the residence of a Mrs. Constance Bates-Hillyer, please?" Stretching the cord to its full length, my uncle stood at the counter and faced the cupboard. I sat down at the table.

"Yes, this is her husband, Donald Hillyer," he said into the receiver.

Marlais, I can tell you that my mind was a whirligig. The room was spinning. I didn't want to hear, I didn't want to hear, and then I heard: "Well, now, Secretary Macdonald, just because my Constance's wardrobe trunk was recovered, doesn't necessarily mean—" My uncle listened a moment, then moaned from deep in his gut and more or less reeled backward against the kitchen table, finally crumpling to the floor. He looked up at me. "Nephew, Secretary of the Navy Macdonald has personally called just now, and he's informed me that Constance Bates-Hillyer is officially numbered among the missing."

Quickly, then, my uncle was alerted to a different voice on the telephone, and he pressed his ear close to the receiver. "Not the slightest room for doubt," he said. "I understand." He stood up, leaned against the table for balance and handed me the telephone, which I hung up.

My uncle sat at the table. "We never went to a walk-in cinema together," he said. "And last time we were in Halifax—when was that?—1939, I believe. March 1939, two nights at the Hotel Dumont, breakfast included free of charge and no limit to how long a patron could sit in the lobby. Constance snuck out during my nap and took a dance lesson from the in-house instructor—the *foxtrot* at her age! Now, I know that might not sound like something your aunt Constance would sneak out to do. But she knew I wouldn't have taken any dance lesson. Besides, I had my nap to take. I asked her how much of the foxtrot you can really learn in one lesson. 'As it turns out, quite a bit,' she said. Showed some temper, too. We ate supper at the hotel, and we were finished with time to spare. The cinema was just three blocks from the hotel. I really don't know why we didn't walk over and take in a picture."

My sense was, all this sadness and regret provided a calm interlude. I knew it couldn't last long.

"Uncle Donald, might they return Aunt Constance's wardrobe trunk?" Honestly, this question served no good purpose, but it was all I could think to ask.

"Now, right there, Wyatt, is a true blessing," he said. "That is a true spot of grace in all this. Because Navy Secretary Macdonald's assistant said the wardrobe trunk will arrive here by bus. They promised."

"A keepsake," I said. "For Tilda."

"What's best for me now, Nephew, is to go out to my shed. I can do some sanding. I can sand for an hour or two and think. Plus, I have my own radio out there, as you know."

"I'd like to work out there with you, Uncle Donald."

"You know what I think? It's possible my Constance isn't going to be found in all of eternity," he said. "We should cobble together a family this evening, is what I think. Will you invite Tilda and her husband for me?"

"Listen," I said, "do you know what Hans Mohring did? Out of his own pocket, he bought new copies of just about every one of the gramophone records you smashed to pieces, Uncle Donald. He bought them at Ballade and Fugue."

"German-owned record shop?"

"No, sir, the owner's name—you go back and read the newspaper article, Uncle Donald. The shop owner who those RCN beat up—Randall Webb is not German."

"Consorted with them, though."

"You like Beethoven, Randall likes Beethoven," I said. "Uncle Donald, please listen to what I'm saying. The important thing: Hans glued the pieces together and figured out which they were. Maybe it was as much to please Aunt Constance as anything. But he specifically said he did it to make amends with you."

"Where are these gramophone records?"

"His and Tilda's rooms."

"Well, I'm seeing things in a different light now. All right, how about this? To make amends, Hans should bring those gramophone records to the house. And Tilda should be here, too. Her mother's gone, Wyatt."

"Tilda doesn't know that yet. She's been waiting for news just like you. She doesn't know Secretary Macdonald telephoned."

"You know the best thing I can do for Tilda, so recently in wedlock? I should try and knock some sense into my son-in-law's head. Maybe he and Tilda should go to Montreal. Or to *someplace.* Sit out the war, and he could tell people his accent's Swedish or from Denmark. See, *considering what heroic measures should be taken,* like the radio said. I think it's my father-in-law responsibility to point out it's dangerous times for a German in Nova Scotia. See, that'll be the give-and-take, right there. He'll give me the gramophone records—'Thanks, thanks'—and I'll give him solid advice."

I drove to the bakery and went directly upstairs, where I found Hans and Tilda each packing a suitcase.

"Navy Secretary Macdonald just now telephoned Uncle Donald," I said. "Aunt Constance isn't coming home."

"I knew it was true," Tilda said. "In my heart of hearts, I knew." She and Hans embraced, but

160

Tilda got a bit frantic and suddenly held him at arm's length. "I have to go see my father."

"Yes, he's a widow now," Hans said.

"I know he wants to see you, Tilda," I said. "In fact, he wants us all, you, me and Hans, over tonight. He said Hans should bring the gramophone records."

"You told him about that?" Hans said.

"I was speaking on your behalf, Hans."

"We're taking the morning bus out," Tilda said. "It's for the best."

"How's that?" I asked. "How for the best?"

"The people in Middle Economy, they're good, gentle people for the most part. But they don't know Hans."

"There's not been enough time to know him."

"It all adds up to the same thing, Wyatt," she said. "Nobody's fault. They just don't know him. They don't yet know us as a married couple. And now look what's happened. The U-boat that killed my mother will be in Reverend Witt's sermon on Sunday, mark my words."

"I don't wish to make anyone here uncomfortable," Hans said.

"Have you listened to the radio, Hans? The whole goddamn world's uncomfortable!" I said. "What's *uncomfortable* got to do with anything?"

"Shut up, Wyatt. Just shut up," Tilda said. "Listen, Hans has a university friend in

Vancouver, graduated last year. Hans telephoned him, and he'll take us in."

"Vancouver—all the way to the west coast of Canada," I said.

"Yes, Wyatt, that's where Vancouver's located," she said.

"All right, all right, all right, I can see your thinking. Still—"

"We counted our pennies," Tilda said, "and it's just enough, or almost."

"All right. I'll drive you to the bus personally," I said. "But you have to promise to come to the house tonight. Jesus Christ on the cross, just now I don't know any of what's what anymore."

"The world's a shithole," Tilda said. "That's what."

"About leaving tomorrow—your mind's completely made up?"

Tilda sighed deeply and said, "It's two weeks and five days by bus to Vancouver. There's a number of transfers. Off one bus, onto another. I won't promise you a postcard along the way, but I promise one once we've arrived, Wyatt." She went into their bedroom, and I could see her scrutinize each item of clothing in the bureau, rejecting, accepting. Either way, everything got neatly folded and put back in a drawer or into her suitcase. And I thought, Like mother, like daughter.

I went downstairs first and told Cornelia that

Constance was gone. We all shared a supper of sandwiches and tea, the talk smaller than small, all life-and-death subjects avoided. Cornelia cleared the dishes. Then Hans said, "Tilda, I'd like to have a short time with your father alone, please."

"You sit with me awhile, then, Tilda," Cornelia said. "We'll talk things over."

"One hour at the most, Hans," Tilda said. "I mean that as much as I've ever meant anything. In one hour I'll be at my house."

"Why not let's walk there together, Hans," I said. "I'll leave my car for Tilda."

"Good," Hans said. "Good, good, good. Let me get the gramophone records and we'll go."

I took a flashlight from the glove compartment of my car. When Hans returned carrying the records, wrapped in a couple of shirts, we set out along the road. The weather was typical for October, cold rain. Hans tucked the records inside his overcoat. Our hair was immediately soaked, and I said, "Oh, well, it's not that far." The flashlight beam made almost a solid tunnel out ahead, and rain could be seen etching across it slantwise. We bent into the wind and walked at as steady a pace as we could. Finally, still out on the road but directly across from the house, Hans threw his arm over my shoulder and said something, but I couldn't make it out. "What?" I shouted.

Hans cupped his hands over my ear and said, "This is the same kind of night our child was conceived. Tilda is quite certain of which night it is on the calendar. We were out on the road and we saw the library. Tilda had a key, so we escaped inside. We didn't leave till morning."

Hans then crossed the road, so there was no chance for me to reply, let alone take in his news. I hurried to catch up. There were a number of lights on. Thick gray smoke was torn to rags as it rose from the chimney, gone into the darkness. Hans waited on the porch, and when I joined him I opened the front door, heard the radio, stepped in and said, "Uncle Donald?"

From behind me I heard, "You're not sleepwalking, are you, Hans?"

"No, sir, I'm not," Hans said, laughing a little. "Why would you think so?"

I turned to see my uncle. He'd arrived unnoticed around the side of the house. Hans hadn't seen him yet; he half smiled and began to unbutton his overcoat, no doubt reaching for the gramophone records. That was when my uncle brought a toboggan runner down on Hans's head. The sound was sickening. I can't compare it to anything.

It took that one blow, is all. Hans collapsed on the porch. The gash was deep, and blood matted with the rain in his hair, and as my uncle stood there, almost transfixed by his deed, I punched him in the forehead, then punched him again near his left eye, and this caused him to drop the runner. I picked it up and struck my uncle with it across his knees, and he buckled but didn't fall. He stumbled back a few steps. Barely able to keep his balance, he said, "Blindsiding the man wasn't what I'd intended."

"You wanted to look him in the face, is that it, Uncle Donald? What'd Hans Mohring ever do to harm you?"

I went unsteadily down the porch steps. Then I vomited, violently, and dropped the runner. Neither my uncle nor I picked it up again. I leaned against the house and retched my guts up, and the only thought I had was, Tilda might've seen this.

I stepped back up to the porch. Hans lay on his back, his face ghostly in the porch light. He loosed a kind of gurgling moan, blood frothed on his tongue and dribbled down his chin, his right arm twitched, his mouth opened and closed with a popping smack of his lips, twice, three times, like he was attempting to catch raindrops. My uncle reached into his back trouser pocket, removed his World War I revolver, pressed it against Hans's chest, said "Mercy on his soul," and pulled the trigger. The shot was muffled by Hans's overcoat and the gramophone records inside. Hans jolted, arching his back, then fell flat to the porch again. Even I, who'd never seen a dead person close up, outside a coffin, knew that Hans Mohring was dead.

My uncle tossed aside the revolver. He slapped my face hard and said, "Pull yourself together, Nephew!"

Things then seemed to happen in a dream—I mean, in the way a dream can tamper with all common sense, make you feel you're both participating in something and watching at some remove.

"Get a tarp from the shed, Nephew, and let's get him rolled up properly in it."

So I was fully volunteering in the aftermath, because I followed my uncle's instructions flat-out: hurried to the shed, lifted a tightly rolled tarpaulin from the corner, carried it across my shoulder back to the porch. My uncle took it from me, went inside, unrolled it in the dining room and said, "Now let's situate the body right in the middle."

He reached under Hans's shoulders and I clasped both his ankles and, half lurching, we lifted and carried him into the dining room and set him on the tarpaulin. I reached under the overcoat and took out the gramophone records, placed the bundle on a chair. We then fitted the tarpaulin tightly around Hans. My uncle removed the flowered tablecloth and twisted it into a kind of rope, which he used to secure the tarp at the top. He slid off his belt and fastened it around the tarp at the bottom. I could see the soles of Hans's shoes.

"I'll pull the truck around," my uncle said. I didn't know what he had in mind, exactly. "This rain'll wash the porch clean, but you'd better take a mop to the blood in the house."

I found the mop and bucket in the pantry, ran water into the bucket, adding some liquid floor soap. I then mopped what blood I could detect in the dim light. Things were moving almost faster than I could keep up with. I emptied the bucket in the kitchen sink and washed and squeezed out the mop and put them back in the pantry. I heard my uncle's truck. He'd driven it right up to the house.

My uncle got out of the truck and went to the shed. He returned carrying a toboggan. Runners hadn't been attached to it yet. He set the toboggan on the porch and said, "Let's get him on this." We carried Hans Mohring over and set him on the toboggan. My uncle took a length of rope from his truck and we tied the body to the toboggan, then lifted it onto the bed of the truck. I climbed into the cab and my uncle got in and we drove, not a word between us, to the dock at Parrsboro.

"We'll use Leonard Marquette's boat," Donald said when we reached the dock. "He won't mind one bit. Not one bit."

Now I understood: it was my uncle's intention to take Hans Mohring out to sea. I figured we'd set the toboggan on the deck, and once we got far enough offshore, we'd slide it into the water. But that isn't what we did. My uncle insisted that we lower the toboggan down the ladder fixed to the dock and set it afloat. Then he used a jackknife to sever a lifesaver from its white rope, tossed the float on the deck and used the rope to fasten the toboggan to the boat. I stepped on board and stood at the stern. The toboggan kept its balance, rolling gently in the swell, knocking against the barnacled pylons. My uncle went to the wheelhouse, started the engine, switched on the running lights and slowly navigated through the fog and pitch black, out into the Minas Basin.

My best guess, it was half an hour before I went to the wheelhouse. "We're almost to Cape Split," my uncle said. "Just about five minutes more, I'll cut the engine but not anchor. Then we'll do what's necessary."

"What do you think, Uncle Donald," I said, "that Tilda will believe Hans went for a dangerous *swim?*"

"No, I'll own up to it. I'll take my medicine. But first I feel obligated to send this German fellow to the bottom."

"German fellow Tilda's *husband* you just murdered. Obligated to whom?"

"Now suddenly Hans Mohring's your best friend, huh? Retch off the rail, Wyatt, if you feel so disgusted."

The lighthouse at Cape Split swept its beam, which didn't quite reach our boat, but I glimpsed a flotilla of sleeping ducks about fifty or so feet away. The lighthouse's foghorn was in good working order. In any other circumstance a person might've felt peaceful and sequestered at sea like this. Catch a few hours' sleep before setting lobster traps, say, or fishing nets, and always the surprising color of the dawn light as it tinged the horizon, a normal day in this part of the world, ship-to-shore chat with the local dispatcher, or your wife if your own house was equipped with a two-way, as many in Parrsboro and neighboring outports were. No war bulletins coming in over the airwaves, the static innocent, only interrupting things like "Try to make it back by supper if you can, because Emmeline Bellinger's first birthday party's this evening."

"Let's take him back," I said. "Let's not do this, Uncle Donald. What are we? Let's take him back home."

"We don't have enough petrol to get across to Germany, Nephew." His little joke. "Besides, all those U-boats out and about? No, sir, I'm afraid it's a more local watery grave for Herr Mohring here"—he looked back at what we were towing—"and then I'll go to prison for the rest of my life."

Well out in the Bay of Fundy, he cut the engine. I could see fog swirling at the running lights, but otherwise, nothing. "Fetch a flashlight from the rack there," my uncle said. I found the flashlight and followed him from the wheelhouse to the stern. "Point it so I can find the rope." He opened his jackknife and cut the tie rope and we watched as the toboggan drifted away. "This far out, the winds and tide should favor a long ride, take him straight out the bay. Or any minute he might sink away—that's possible, too. Anyway, I checked the gauge. We've got just enough petrol to get us home."

"Let's get a gaffing hook and pull him back," I said. "Uncle Donald—what are we?"

"I can't tolerate the idea of my daughter weeping and carrying on over his grave."

My uncle returned to the wheelhouse. I stood at the stern the whole return trip to the wharf at Parrsboro.

Tilda had parked my car in front of the house. Not a single light was on. When my uncle and I walked into the dining room, Tilda was sitting at the table. A candle was lit in a brass holder. Tilda wore her black dress. A string quartet by Beethoven was playing. Suddenly there was a horrible screech as the needle failed to leap the bullet hole. The needle caught again, repeating a passage, repeating, repeating, repeating. Tilda had folded the two shirts Hans had wrapped the gramophone records in and set them on the table next to the toboggan runner, which lay crosswise.

My uncle and I stood in the doorway, staring at the objects of incrimination, laid out right where we'd had so many family meals.

"Pop, you never once—not *once*—mopped a floor in this house," Tilda said, her voice strained, as if speaking at all caused excruciating pain. "In fact, Mother's the only one ever mopped a floor in this house. Yet it's been freshly mopped, hasn't it?"

Her hands had been under the table, but now she lifted them, and the revolver was pointed at her father. Then at me. Then she put the barrel to the side of her head. "Where is my husband?"

Left to Right Like a Book

OKAY NOW. OKAY NOW," my uncle said. He slowly approached Tilda, then tried to pry open her fingers and take the revolver. She didn't put up a great struggle, but didn't let go, either. Grasping her wrist, he levered her hand toward the candle, and when the flame touched her skin, she said, "Oh!" and lost her grip. My uncle placed the revolver next to the gramophone. He lifted the gramophone's arm and set it on its cradle.

Tilda was glaring at me. "Wyatt," she said, just above a whisper, "where is Hans?" My uncle violently pushed me along out the front door, and with Tilda now screaming, "Where is my husband? Where is my husband?" he and I got back in the truck. A short way down the road, I turned and saw Tilda in front of the house. She'd dropped to her knees.

A folded copy of the *Mail* fell open from the dashboard onto my lap. On the front page was a photograph in which dozens of suitcases and trunks had washed up in Sydney. In the photograph you could see the rain. Two men were hauling in a trunk with gaffing hooks. AT SYDNEY, NS, SEA DELIVERS PERSONAL BELONGINGS OF *CARIBOU* VICTIMS.

"Today I lost both my wife and my daughter," my uncle said.

I had to reach across and switch on the windshield wipers.

We drove straight to the police station in Truro. There my uncle put things directly to the desk sergeant. "In all my days!" the sergeant said. "This is some novelty. Two men show up out of nowhere. Murder and accessory to murder's my educated guess. Best to leave all that up to a magistrate. Is there a vehicle?"

"My truck's right out front," my uncle said.

"Keys?"

"On the seat," my uncle said.

"I'll take you to lockup. Got anyone to telephone?"

"No, sir," I said.

So, Marlais, on October 23, 1942, a magistrate's hearing was held in the library in Middle Economy. It was an irony, locally noted, that Magistrate Dean Junkins, who'd been sent out from Halifax on October 18, was put up in the rooms above the bakery. Cornelia had tidied things up nicely. Tilda had packed up her and Hans's belongings and moved back to the house. Donald and I were delivered by an RCMP officer named Bernard Remmick by car to the library. In the newspaper it was called a paddy wagon, but it wasn't any such thing; it was an automobile like any other. The *Mail* also referred to the hearing as "a preliminary inquiry into the murder of the German student Hans Mohring," but as it turned out, it wasn't preliminary to anything but itself, because the hearing was completed by the end of the day on October 23. My uncle served as the only witness, and since he flat-out testified against himself, that was the end of that. I imagine Magistrate Junkins was home in time for a late supper.

The morning of the twenty-third there was a hard rain. At least 150 people had packed into the library. They'd come in from all the Economys, Great Village, Bass River, Five Islands, Glenholme. Cornelia had brought my uncle's and my suits to Truro, and we wore them to the hearing.

The proceedings began promptly at nine A.M. Despite the gravity of the situation, my uncle looked so uncomfortable it had a comic effect. He was among the people he'd known all his life, yet he couldn't meet anyone's eye. He constantly fidgeted, smoothing down his black tie at least a dozen times, before the magistrate, sitting at a table next to the witness chair (a chair from Cornelia's bakery), said, "Mr. Hillyer, I authorize that this hearing has commenced. You may have your say now."

The library hushed right down. My uncle took a sip of water, cleared his throat, looked at Tilda, who sat nearby but not in the front row, then stood up to read his handwritten statement. I'd seen him working on it in his cell.

"You aren't obligated to stand," Magistrate Junkins said.

"I'd prefer not to," my uncle said.

"Sit down, then," the magistrate said.

My uncle sat down and read: "We do not wish to see our hand in what happens, so we call certain things terrible accidents. We call them terrible accidents, but that's not true of what I did. Not true at all. It was no accident, and to my mind, for that reason redemption is far less possible."

Magistrate Junkins, right off sighing with impatience, said, "No religion or personal philosophy is necessary here, sir."

But my uncle seemed to ignore this and said, "Likewise, if a person is dedicated to the truth of his actions, then much can be stated directly. Hans Mohring was age twenty-one only. He wanted to be a philologist. May I consult the dictionary over there on the shelf?"

"You may."

Buttoning the three buttons of his suit coat as if he was about to encounter a sudden chill, my uncle stepped over to a nearby shelf, took up the well-thumbed *Webster's* dictionary, carried it back to the witness chair. He removed the leather bookmark and set it on the small table in front of him. "And 'philology' is defined thusly," he said.

And do you know, Marlais, I had never heard my uncle utter the word "thusly" before. " 'Philology: The science of language, especially in its historical and comparative aspects.' And there's another thing philology means: 'the love of learning and literature.' That German student, philology was his interest. My daughter told me they'd talked about philology on the bus ride out from Halifax, when they'd first met.

"Now, stated as plainly as a person can state anything: I, Donald Hillyer, admit to murdering the German student Hans Mohring. Furthermore, I admit, earlier in the evening, to requesting my nephew Wyatt Hillyer, who's sitting right here up front—requesting that he invite Hans Mohring to my house. Wyatt had no earthly knowledge of my intentions. Hans Mohring and my daughter had got married, and Hans wanted to declare himself to me somehow—and by the way, the marriage was performed legally by Reverend Plumly in Advocate. Anyway, once Hans Mohring stepped onto my porch, I struck him with a toboggan runner and then I put a bullet from my revolver into his chest. If it can be put any plainer, I don't know how."

My uncle folded his statement in two, then stood up, probably confused, thinking he'd been standing up and needed to sit down. A current of laughter went through the room, at which

Magistrate Junkins said, "I don't see anything humorous in Mr. Hillyer's account or his present demeanor." The room quieted and my uncle sat down again.

"Is there anything else in your initial statement?" Magistrate Junkins asked.

"No," my uncle said.

"Then it's time for my questions."

Magistrate Junkins consulted his notes, and I'm fairly certain that many of the people in the library that day had never seen a magistrate consult notes, and every gesture he made was scrutinized and would, I felt, make for conversation later on.

"Donald Hillyer," Junkins said, "I've had two full days to review the information gathered. Now, I understand that you admit to the murder of Hans Mohring. Be that as it may, back up in time and recount, if you would, for my further understanding, what, in your view, drew you to that heinous act."

But before my uncle could reply, Tilda stood up, and with all eyes on her, she picked up the *Webster's* and returned it to its place on the shelf. She then left the library.

My uncle said, "That day—the day it happened—there were two things that tore me up. First was the radio static. And then came the call from Secretary of the Navy Macdonald, who telephoned my house in person. Those two things."

"For the record, Mr. Hillyer," Magistrate Junkins said, "we must note why the Navy Secretary of Canada would make such a call. For the record, please."

"Well, sir, all right. The facts are these. The Newfoundland car ferry *Caribou* sailed from the terminal at North Sydney, Nova Scotia, destination light-to-light was her home port at Port aux Basques, Newfoundland. They sailed at about midnight."

"This was October 13–14, then?"

"October 13–14, yes, sir."

"Proceed."

"It happened at about—according to newspaper accounts, which I see you have on your desk there. It happened about three-forty-five A.M., blackout enforced on all ships, when a torpedo slammed into the *Caribou*. My wife, Constance Bates-Hillyer, had traveled to visit her friend Zoe Fielding. There was the christening of her grandchild, and Constance had promised to attend. She was taking a vacation, is how she put it. That was the circumstances. And my wife was a victim of that attack. Constance Bates-Hillyer, possibly killed outright, but finally put in the sea, Lord have mercy on her soul."

"Take your time, Mr. Hillyer."

"It wasn't so much the telephone call in general. Specifically, it was mention of my wife's wardrobe trunk."

"I don't understand."

"Navy Secretary Macdonald said her personal wardrobe trunk had been identified. Naturally, my wife'd sewn her name and address on the lining— who wouldn't have? Anyway, Secretary Macdonald said, 'Her body's not yet recovered, but the trunk has been,' and those were his exact words."

In my chair in the front row, I closed my eyes and pictured my aunt's black 2 x 2 x 3 Hartmann cushion-top wardrobe trunk, which had small brass studs along the seams, two wide black hinges in back, brass cornices and a brass lock. She'd purchased the trunk in Truro, and when it arrived by bus, Donald brought it home and set it on the dining room table. Donald, Tilda and I stood there when she first opened it, and she said, *"Wallah!"* like a magician, and she showed off its three inside drawers, its wooden dowels and five wooden hangers. "I looked at any number of wardrobe trunks," she said, "but this one all but said, 'Take me to Newfoundland!'"

"But as for radio static?" Magistrate Junkins said. "As to the relevance of radio static. By the way, Miss Teachout, are you keeping pace?"

I forgot to mention that Lenore Teachout was the stenographer and sat to the front and right of Magistrate Junkins.

"Yes. I had all of January and February at court in Halifax, you might remember," she said. "I'm well trained."

"Continue, then, Mr. Hillyer."

"We had the Grundig-Majestic on the kitchen table," my uncle said. "Bad weather, and I was trying to get a clear human voice. We'd get snippets. We'd get parts of updates and bulletins: 'the sinking of the ferry *Caribou*'—static static static—and then 'Axis U-boats plying their grim trade, no common humanity'—then more static. It can be like that with a radio, but that day it seemed outright cruelty. You see, whenever I'd put 'Angels of the Highest Order' pieces by Mr. Beethoven on the gramophone—Mr. Beethoven's a German. I'm not without appreciation for that particular German mind. Anyone who knows me can attest to that fact."

"Mr. Hillyer—"

"No, no, no, listen. I say all of that because my gramophone is old, and the recordings I had were scratchy. That's not an entirely unpleasant sound, not to my ear at least. The scratchiness, I mean. It makes you feel like the music has wended its way forward from another century. But *radio* static, now that's a different thing. Radio static's democratic, that I admit. It intervenes on good and bad news alike, eh? Terrifying war news or trivial information on what to purchase and in which shops. I understand all of that."

"And the point of this disquisition—?"

"The *point,* sir, is that when you're trying to get vital news about a loved one—"

"Sir—"

"—static intervenes. And that afternoon, before Secretary Macdonald telephoned, there was just too much goddamned static, sir."

Yet during the couple of days after the *Caribou* had been sunk, plenty of information had gotten through loud and clear. Personal testimonies of survivors were even quoted on the radio. To this day, I recall what one survivor, a Mr. Leonard Salter, said: "—right over the trough of a heavy swell, I was near a lifeboat and for an instant the light from floating parts of the burning ferry was such—and I've always had grand eyesight anyway—but I could see on the deck of the *Laughing Cow* its sailors bustling fast into the hatch. The submarine dropped out of sight then and I got pulled up into a lifeboat. Cries, wails, pleadings from the water all around. Prayers—"

The captain of the *Laughing Cow*—the U-boat that torpedoed the *Caribou*—was Ulrich Graf. His cowardice was reported in yet another broadcast. Once the *Caribou* had gone under, Graf took his sub down and directly beneath the survivors, who were in lifeboats, scattered on rafts, holding on to planks, holding on to anything at all for dear life. Graf had figured that the escort ship *Grandmère* wouldn't drop depth charges there. And in that, Graf was correct.

"Are you capable of continuing, Mr. Hillyer?" the magistrate asked.

Just before he clasped his head in his hands and rocked forward and back, forward and back, nearly falling off the witness chair, my uncle said, "Everything I love most used to happen every day: wake up, see my wife's face, maybe an improvement on a sled or toboggan already in mind. Eat breakfast. Look at the sea. Go on out to the shed. Come in for lunch. But not that day. The day Hans Mohring came to make amends, that day was hell on earth. Two, three, four months earlier? I couldn't've found a day like that on the map. And now that hellish day's my permanent address."

Tilda returned to the library around eleven A.M. and sat in a back corner. Magistrate Junkins shifted his attention from his notes to my uncle, removed his reading glasses and said, "Now, Mr. Hillyer, if I understand correctly, you're something of an expert in Navy battles and have more than a general interest in the fates of seagoing vessels off Nova Scotia and Newfoundland."

"Naturally, expertise in the subject has caused torment."

"So you'd say that your mind was steeped in, or at least preoccupied with, said subject. I quote a neighbor of yours—"

"Which neighbor is that?"

"—who remains anonymous," Magistrate Junkins said in a reprimanding tone. "I quote"— he put on his spectacles again and read from a notebook—" 'Donald Hillyer became a walking

182

history lesson, often of the browbeating sort. And this lesson was unfolding on a day-by-day basis. He was fairly steaming about the U-boat sinkings. Steaming like a—' "

"My wife Constance's lungs are filled with seawater."

Magistrate Junkins closed his eyes, sighed deeply and followed that with shorter sighs. He continued reading: " 'Steaming like a—' "

"Feelings of gloom and spitefulness, that's what took over," my uncle said. "How difficult is that to understand, sir?"

" 'Steaming like a teapot on the boil.' Mr. Hillyer, is it true that the walls of your work shed are covered with newspaper articles about recent tragedies at sea?"

"They are German-caused murders of great proportions, whatever else you might call them." My uncle sipped some water.

There in the library I pictured the walls of the shed, all but completely covered with newspaper headlines and articles and photographs. You read the incidents left to right like a book, in the chronological order in which they happened. All the U-boat attacks off Atlantic Canada were represented—the ferries lost, the number of casualties, the number of dead and missing and presumed lost, photographs of people waiting at docks and wharfs, of church gatherings and wakes.

For instance, on the wall on the immediate left as you walked in, headlines about the Battle of the St. Lawrence, as it was popularly known, which occurred on the night of May 11, 1942, when *U-553* torpedoed and sunk the British freighter *Nicoya* off the Gaspé and the Dutch ship *Leto* in the lower reaches of the St. Lawrence River. Both ships were bound for England. That attack roiled my uncle in the extreme.

Now, Marlais, I won't inventory the seventeen merchant ships sunk by U-boats, plus an American merchant ship and two Canadian warships that were sunk near the St. Lawrence over sixteen months, starting around May of 1942— and the *Caribou* right in the center of all of it. But before the *Caribou* went down at sea, each time any sort of vessel was attacked, up went an article on the shed wall. And since I was working in that shed long hours every day, I couldn't help but practically memorize them. Against my will, almost, I was becoming a student of these incidents. The shed walls became my harrowing reading life, you might say. "The walls ran the gamut," as my aunt put it, "from you-wouldn't-think-it-could-get-sadder to sadder-yet. 'Lost at sea' has its own strange quality. Out to the cemetery, you put on the stone 'Sacred to the Memory,' of course. But since the body's not in the ground, it's somehow a more hollow feeling. Read the newspapers. Listen to the radio. Talk to your neighbors. Even sermons in church. These past few years it's as if the whole of Atlantic Canada feels hollow."

And then came the incident that really sent my uncle into a tailspin. On Sunday, October 11—my aunt was already on her travels—*U-106* sunk the British freighter *Waterton*, which had been traveling from Corner Brook, Newfoundland, to Sydney, Nova Scotia, carrying a cargo of paper. The *Waterton* went down in seven minutes, but as one article said, "The crew was rescued and nobody got a foot wet."

"Broad daylight in the Cabot Strait," my uncle had said. "That's in our back yard! Constance is traveling those waters! I wish she'd wire us."

"I'm sure she's fine, Uncle Donald," I had said, weakly.

"You know what I dreamed? Good Lord. I dreamed about stacks of paper on board the *Waterton*. In my dream, I saw it as ten thousand Bibles not printed, ten thousand personal letters never sent. Don't say I had this dream to anyone in Middle Economy, all right? Kindly don't mention it."

But back to the hearing. The library was quiet again. My uncle took another sip of water.

"Yes," he said, now looking at Magistrate Junkins. "I was steaming. Yes, sir, indeed yes. I was steaming. As any good Canadian should have been."

"Every good Canadian did not murder this German student," Magistrate Junkins said. "I'm obligated to put that fine a point on it. Let me remind you that the reason we are here. Today. In this library. Are your *actions,* Mr. Hillyer. And how the province of Nova Scotia determines the consequences of those actions. And recommendations to such—a profound responsibility—begin and end with me."

He shuffled some papers and stared out the nearest window, lost for a moment to the rain, it seemed. Then he said, "I'm afraid no one's thought to provide me with a glass of water yet."

Cornelia went into the library's small pantry and returned with a glass of water, which she set in front of Magistrate Junkins.

"Thank you."

To which Cornelia replied, "You only needed to ask."

"Now, then, Mr. Hillyer," Magistrate Junkins said, "in establishing your state of mind on the last day of Hans Mohring's life, can you recall when you decided which—*method,* let us say. That is, how you would press an attack on Hans Mohring?"

"Are you asking was it 'thought out'?" my uncle asked.

"I refer to your use of a toboggan runner," Magistrate Junkins said, "as a weapon of choice."

"I chose it because it was leaning against the

shed wall closest to the door when I decided to go see if Hans Mohring had come to my house yet."

"Simple as that."

"My hand on the Bible," my uncle said.

At this point Tilda more or less cried out, then gained enough composure to walk to the shelves, take down the *Webster's*, carry it over and set it in front of her father on the table. "Swear to me, Pop"—she forced his right hand onto the dictionary and pressed her own hand down on his— "swear to me on his favorite book that you didn't mean to kill my husband. Swear to me you couldn't help yourself, because of Mom dying. Because of Mother being killed. Father, swear to me it was all a conspiracy of the brain."

"We will take a recess—*now!*" Magistrate Junkins said.

He stood, went through the pantry and out the back door of the library, but it took a long time for anyone else to leave, and it wasn't just the pouring rain. Though finally, Tilda and her father were alone together.

Marlais, your mother never told me what they said to each other. If anything was said.

Before the afternoon session began, Magistrate Junkins announced, "If you have sandwiches or any other such thing, kindly keep to the back." He sat down. And it was true, quite a number of people had packed lunches or had slipped out and gone to the bakery and returned with a sandwich or slices of honey bread or even halibut cakes. I noticed that Cornelia had left the library earlier, right after she'd brought Magistrate Junkins a glass of water. She figured that during a recess people would want to get something to eat at her bakery.

"Now, to begin with," Magistrate Junkins said, "Mr. Hillyer has informed me he has an announcement to make, and I'm going to allow that." He nodded to my uncle.

My uncle said, "I'm officially leaving my sled and toboggan concern to my nephew Wyatt. He and I haven't had the time to discuss this, but those are my intentions."

Now, two things about that statement, Marlais. First, it might seem a separate thing altogether from the grievous matter at hand, yet everyone was interested—you could tell from their faces. They knew Donald would soon be off to prison. No doubt about that. They didn't know exactly when, or to which prison, but they knew my uncle would not be building sleds and toboggans for some time, possibly never. Second, considering the fact that in his written statement my uncle had mentioned that I'd fetched Hans Mohring to the house on the evening he was killed, there was no doubt a high probability in everyone's mind that I had witnessed the murder. The question then was, did I do anything to help or hinder, and would I confess, and would I be going to prison, too? If I did confess, what would become of the sled and toboggan business—all of local concern and curiosity.

"I don't much care," Magistrate Junkins said.

My uncle turned toward his neighbors. "Wyatt's better at toboggans than sleds," he said, "but he'll manage all right."

"Mr. Hillyer!"

Magistrate Junkins checked his notes and said, "Now, then, you had asked your nephew to— what again?—invite Hans Mohring for supper?"

"No, no, because who was going to *cook* supper?"

With this, Magistrate Junkins had no possible recourse but to allow people to laugh until they stopped laughing, because those who knew our household knew that my aunt Constance would let Tilda (who was a bang-up cook herself) cook only on Saturdays, and they knew that Donald could scarcely manage to scorch a butter biscuit with a bonfire, as they say. In turn, Magistrate Junkins allowed himself a slight smile. I think he realized that people weren't mocking justice, just letting a breath of fresh air into the proceedings, since the proceedings were mostly about a life being taken.

"Magistrate Junkins," my uncle said, "I don't know where you were born and raised, nor how people there think. But I believe if you sully the sea, it comes back at you tenfold. Now, I've written out a list here. Let me read you the times I know for certain when I've sullied the sea." He reached into his suit jacket pocket and produced a piece of paper, then read from it. "First time was when I was ten years old. I was out in a dinghy with Paul Amundson, same age as me. His family was of Norwegian ancestry. We went fishing. Of course, we'd been fishing a lot, but this day he'd caught all the fish and me none. He had a bucketful. When we rowed back and tied up and got out of the boat, I pretended to stumble, and spilled his bucket into the sea. Doesn't sound more than a jealous prank, eh? But Paul knew I'd done it on purpose, even though not a word was said of it. I'd done it on purpose. Spilled betrayal and deception out of the bucket, and therefore sullied the sea."

"Enough!" Junkins said. "You may submit your list to Miss Teachout here."

Lenore Teachout got up from the stenographer's table, took the list from my uncle, sat down and immediately began copying it into her transcript. But my uncle didn't wait for her to finish: "Skipping to number *ten,* I sullied the sea by dumping Hans Mohring's body into it."

And I believe he didn't mean to say what he said next, but he did say it: "Out in the Bay of Fundy, my nephew assisted. On my instruction."

The weather had by now mostly cleared, but you could still see, through the library windows, a departing curtain of rain and dark clouds over the Minas Basin. I turned around in my chair, and it appeared that more people had crammed into the library for the afternoon session than were at the morning session. I looked over at Tilda. I noticed that, during the time the hearing had been recessed, she'd gone home and changed clothes. She now wore one of my aunt's dresses. It was pale white, slightly frayed at the hem, with outsized white buttons and a black scallop stitch along two wide pockets, and it fit Tilda loosely. I think wearing it must've been a comfort to her.

My uncle continued on his own volition: "That evening, the German student got to the house. Like I said, Wyatt had fetched him as requested. Then, I recall the heft of the runner. Oh, yes, also the rain, I remember the rain, and I brought the runner down. I don't know what he might've felt, but it wasn't the hand of God caressing the lamb, like Constance Bates-Hillyer used to call it when a breeze ruffled a child's hair at a church social, say."

"I'd imagine it wasn't like that at all," Magistrate Junkins said flatly.

"No, it wasn't. No, it wasn't."

"And once Mr. Mohring was deceased, you took him out to sea."

"We wrapped him in a tarp. We tied him to a toboggan. We put him in the flatbed. We drove to the Parrsboro dock. We took my old friend Leonard Marquette's boat—"

"For any other reason under the sun, you could have borrowed my boat without asking, Donald," Leonard Marquette said from three rows back. "But now I can't ever wash down that deck well enough, can I? I might as well sell the damn thing."

"Leonard, I can't take back what I did," my uncle said.

"This testimony is over," Magistrate Junkins said. "It's finished. I have your complete statement written out by hand here in front of me. Everyone rest assured I will study it at great length."

"—out on your boat, Leonard, the strangest thing," my uncle said. And Magistrate Junkins could see it was necessary to the crowd and even proper in some way to let my uncle finish. "I had a terrible vision, out in the dark like we were, my nephew and me. This German U-boat rises to the surface and somehow it catches the toboggan right on its deck, and the hatch opens, and out climb a bunch of German sailors. To catch a breath of good Canadian air. So they come up and 'Lo and behold, will you look at that!' Of course that couldn't happen. Of course it couldn't. But it goes to show, I was in the throes of a desperate imagination—God strike me dead, eh?—desperate as my imagination was that night."

Ghost Child

SOME OF THE OLDEST people living in Middle Economy may still use the phrase, Marlais, but it was once quite common, that a child lost before birth was referred to as a ghost child. Said child being gone but still present. For instance, when a friend of Constance's, a woman named Lillian Swinaver, miscarried, my aunt said, "Poor little ghost child." Then there was a woman named Anna How, who lived in Glenholme and had miscarried four times. Story goes that one summer afternoon at a church social, she sat with her husband at a table set with plates, forks, knives and napkins for six. "We're simply a quiet family," she'd said.

Then there was Tilda Hillyer, who lost a child on January 2, 1943. Cornelia had informed me of this in her one letter to me at Rockhead Prison, which was on a bluff behind Africville, in the northern part of Halifax. The letter, dated January 5, took, through channels, ten days to reach me.

Wyatt,
Our Tilda lost her child and I am looking after her for a while since no nurse's

training, just good common sense, is necessary according to Dr. Bryce Stady of Montrose, who did the examination and kept Tilda overnight in his guest room. Mrs. Stady has a steady hand in such matters and she was fully present as well. I have enclosed a flowery Get Well card and postage stamp as I imagine you don't presently have such homey items available for purchase. You should send it.

From Reverend Witt's pulpit Sunday prayers are offered, less on Hans Mohring's behalf, I must say, than for forgiveness for Donald, and that doesn't sit well with some of my customers, whereas with others it seems just fine. I'd say it's cut opinions in our village pretty much in half. At any rate, Tilda has sent a long letter to Hans's parents in Denmark. She obtained their address from the president of Dalhousie University himself, so I was told. Tilda of course has a way with words but I could scarcely imagine that task. She hopes that the war allows her letter to arrive. Well then, Wyatt, see you—I'm afraid later than sooner. That's presuming your decision is to return home, though maybe you no longer see Middle Economy in that light. Which to my mind would be understandable but a mistake.

Cornelia Tell

Immediately after the hearing, Donald had been escorted by two RCMP officers back to the lockup in Truro and, after sentencing, to Dorchester Prison, where he'd spend the remainder of his life. Then, on December 10, Cornelia drove me to Halifax. Since I was officially in the RNC, I was assigned to the military prison near the Citadel, in the middle of Halifax, but within a week I received my Navy discharge papers.

Therefore, Marlais, your father had served Canada in the war for exactly not one single day.

Since there were a lot of cases backed up on the docket, I didn't have my own magistrate's hearing in Halifax until December 15, 1942. A Magistrate Quill presided, and Lenore Teachout was the stenographer. It was nice to see a familiar face. My hearing took less than an hour. I didn't have to go through the murder again myself. More, I agreed with a detailed indictment read by Magistrate Quill, who got it right. The truth is the truth, and in the end it can't be lost to excuses, cowardice or lies. There wasn't any doubt that I'd conspired in the whole sordid incident. "You aren't to be exonerated" is the one sentence I perfectly recall from my hearing. Despite everything—separate from everything—I loved Tilda to the point where her grief, sadness and anger became my conscience, so how could I not own up? Convicted of "aiding and abetting a homicide," I was remanded the next day to Rockhead Prison. My release was to be in early June 1945.

Hans had been murdered. I thought it was a fair sentence. Especially as Cornelia had told me to expect worse.

In prison, the days and nights were empty but for the radio. The prison library saved me. I read all of Charles Dickens in there. All of Victor Hugo. Three works by another Frenchman, named Stendhal, my favorite being *The Red and the Black.* As for my spirits, well, on any given day—and especially at night—standard-vintage melancholy would've been a reprieve. For my whole sentence, I was assigned to the wood shop, where I made bird feeders that were sold all over Canada, the proceeds going to the War Orphans' Fund in Ottawa.

The library had a fairly large window overlooking Halifax. In fact, close enough so that I saw the fire that ripped through Barrington and Sackville streets, which caused $130,000 worth of damage. Saw the *Queen Mary* tie up at Pier 20, and the thousands of people who awaited the arrival of Winston Churchill. "This is not the first time I've visited Halifax," I heard him say on the radio, "but it is the first time I have been accorded such a welcome." The *Mail* had a front-page photograph of Churchill holding up a London *Times* whose headline read: ALLIES HAMMERING AWAY TOWARD SIEGFRIED LINE. I hadn't had any contact, none at all, with Uncle Donald, except for an envelope he sent me from Dorchester Prison that contained only newspaper articles about how, on December 24, 1944, a U-boat had sunk the minesweeper HMCS *Clayoquot* five miles off the Sambro lighthouse at the entrance to Halifax Harbor. I imagined the walls of his cell were covered with headlines.

And, Marlais, though I kept up with all the now-it-can-be-told stories in the *Mail*, the fact was, I sat out much of V-E Day itself—Tuesday, May 8, 1945—bedridden with a hacking cough and grippe. But that night, and for a few nights after, through the library window, I saw and heard some V-E Day celebrations run amok, police flares above buildings, sirens and rioting and what the *Mail* called "sailor-led lootings."

I forgot to mention that, late in my sentence, a new policy was instated, and we prisoners were allowed a movie. On April 30, 1945, eleven of us—accompanied by three RCMP officers—went to see *Mr. Winkle Goes to War*, with Edward G. Robinson in the starring role.

There were some bureaucratic glitches, so to speak, but I was finally released on June 15, 1945. I took a room at the Baptist Spa—since I had last stayed there, the room rate had gone up fifteen cents per night—and right off posted a letter to Cornelia Tell, saying which bus I'd be taking home. She must've told Tilda, and so it was the world's biggest surprise that it was Tilda who met me at the Esso station in Great Village, at about seven P.M. on June 19. Why she would decide, against all logic, to do that, I hadn't the slightest idea.

What with dusk tinged rose and magenta on the horizon, it was a lovely evening, clear all the way across the Minas Basin. Tilda was driving her father's pickup. "You look a bit of a scarecrow," she said, referring to the fact that I'd lost so much weight in prison.

"I'm happy to see you."

"What other family do I have left?"

Tilda herself showed some changes. For one thing, her hair was cut quite short, or let's just say its thick wildness took up less room. Also, she wore horn-rimmed glasses, and I noticed, when she pushed them back on her nose, that her fingernails were chewed to the quick. Tilda noticed me notice the eyeglasses and said, "I'd been getting headaches. Dr. Stady up in Montrose thought I should make an appointment to have my eyes checked, so I went to Halifax for that. Turns out, I'm a touch farsighted. I use these specs mainly to read books."

"Have you been reading many books?"

"Almost nightly. In the library."

Then the bus driver, Mr. Standhope, walked up and said, "You'll want to take the wardrobe trunk home. Let me help you with it."

He turned the luggage bin's latch handle, opened the door, set the hinge, slid the trunk to the edge. I held one leather handle and he held the opposite one and we loaded the trunk onto the bed of the truck. When Tilda climbed up next to the trunk and ran her hand along the seam, her eyes teared up. "I didn't know it was on the bus," I said. "Really, I had no idea."

Mr. Standhope got back on the bus and drove off. For some reason, Tilda wanted to look inside the trunk then and there. Lifting the cover, she inspected each drawer. A dress, a pair of slacks and two blouses on their wooden hangers. All the clothes seemed present and accounted for. I wondered if Constance ever got the chance to read her *National Geographic*, her *Reader's Digest*.

"It took them long enough to return this trunk," I said. "They must've had hundreds."

"I'm pleased to see it again," Tilda said. "I never expected to."

Tilda discovered an envelope tucked inside the collar of the topmost folded sweater. She tore open the envelope, took out a piece of paper and read aloud: *"Clothes laundered and returned with condolences from the Christian Ladies' Auxiliary of Sydney, Nova Scotia."*

"All neat and clean, isn't it?" she said. "They've made it seem like Mom hasn't left for Newfoundland yet. Those Christian Auxiliary ladies sure know a thing or two about wishful thinking in hindsight, don't they?" She slid the note back into its envelope, set it on the sweater and closed the trunk. She hopped down and got in behind the wheel. I put my suitcase next to the trunk and then sat on the passenger side.

"I'm grateful you met my bus," I said. "I didn't expect it."

"Well, I'm hardly grateful to see you, Wyatt, but nonetheless I've put supper on the stove. Only because Mom would have." She could have said much, much worse.

She turned the ignition and started off for Middle Economy. I wanted to remark, "Beautiful evening," but refrained. And we hadn't traveled more than a hundred feet when she stopped at the side of the road. Staring straight ahead, Tilda said, "You *do not* mention Hans's and my ghost child. You do not ever refer to that. Not once, not ever." Then she drove on, and when the road curved close to the water, we saw two cormorants flying, and Tilda said, "Since you've been away, my thoughts have coarsened even more toward that bird."

As soon as we got to the house, we carried the trunk in and set it on Constance and Donald's bed. I retrieved my suitcase, and when I got back inside the house Tilda said, "Try and make yourself at home." First off, I put my suitcase in my old room. I took off my shoes, just to better feel the creaky wide-planked floor again, with all the knotholes sanded to level. "Your old overstuffed chair's in the town library," Tilda said from the hallway. "They needed a comfortable chair for people to read in, by the fireplace."

I made a little tour. The rest of the house felt at once familiar and unfamiliar. She'd rearranged all the furniture, had different wallpaper put on the parlor walls and had replaced the white kitchen paint with yellow. I noticed some gramophone records in a three-tiered iron shelf. "Steven Parish designed that for me," she said. "The albums are from Randall's shop. He moved to the bottom of Morris Street, cheaper rent. Those RCN were allowed to ship out, no punishment at all for practically killing Randall. The newspaper said they were just hotheaded. But do you know, Randall lost the hearing in one ear from what they did to him. But he told me when he thinks of how Beethoven was deaf a good deal of his life, he can't feel too sorry for himself, Randall can't. I've been to his new store five or six times."

"How are you living, Tilda? How are you paying for things?"

"Mourning professionally all over the province."

"I imagine that scarcely makes ends meet, though."

"Mom and Dad had some savings. Some little savings. But you know how frugal I am anyway.

I cut the apple in half and save three-quarters for later."

"What's on the stove smells good. I'm starved. Do you mind?"

"Help yourself, Wyatt. I won't sit down with you, but it's Mom's French stew recipe. And by the bye, along with the other changes in décor, you'll notice there's no radios. They both went off to church charity."

"But the gramophone's still here. That's nice."

"Play it all you want. You have my permission."

"Maybe I'll just sit here for a while. In the kitchen here. It's bigger than my cell at Rockhead."

"Good idea. By tomorrow, you can graduate to the great outdoors. Why not drive over to Advocate Harbor, take a long walk, get reacquainted with the driftwood beach and breathe the sea air, eh? You always keep things close to the vest, Wyatt, so I don't imagine you'll much want to talk about what Rockhead was like for you. Anyway, painful to tell's painful to hear. That's a Highland platitude."

"I'm glad it's over—that's all anyone needs to know," I said.

"I'm in the rooms over the bakery again. I didn't want to be in the same house with someone I still have such hatred toward, you know?"

When Tilda left the house, I sat down for supper. I ate at a hurried prison pace, which habit I felt, given time, would probably change.

There's a saying, "A murder doesn't keep hours." I heard it a few times from a Reverend Oostdijk, a second-generation Dutchman in Halifax who used to counsel prisoners at Rockhead. He meant that if you'd participated in such a crime, don't be surprised if it comes back to haunt you at unpredictable moments. That's your punishment and salvation, as he put it. (I understood the *punishment* part.) Day or night it might happen. Morning or afternoon. Or, in my case, while eating the stew Tilda had prepared. I looked up from my plate and saw—or thought I did—myself and Uncle Donald standing in the doorway, clothes soaked through, wild-eyed, the truck's headlights swirled in fog behind us. The thing was, I was viewing us from the exact chair and place at the table Tilda had that October night, 1942, Hans Mohring already in the Bay of Fundy, rain like it was riveting Braille into the puddles on the road out front of the house.

It's one thing to hear "A murder doesn't keep hours," quite another to experience its content, like I just had. I fairly reeled from the table to the sink, turned on the spigot and threw cold water on my face. If this happens again, I thought, I can't stay here. I wondered if it happened to Tilda. And if so, how often. Every night?

By nine P.M. I was worn to a frazzle and fell asleep in my clothes, in my old bed. In the morning I was amazed to hear birds. I found my car keys above the driver's side visor. I turned the ignition and the old buggy started right up, which meant Tilda or someone else had kept it ship-shape in my absence.

I drove to the bakery. This was about seven-thirty, and Cornelia was washing her front window. She had swirled thick white cleaning liquid in overlapping eddies on the glass so that you couldn't see into the bakery, except a little where the liquid had caked to lace patterns. Cornelia was a kind of shadow figure on a stepladder, opening up a new clean area with every tight sweep of a sponge. I stood there as she stretched overhead to arm's length, then worked her way down, finally clearing a space that offered a view of the street, and she saw me. She half smiled, lifted the sponge to her mouth, obviously an invitation for me to come in and have a cup of coffee or tea. I went inside and sat down at a corner table and watched her complete the window. She stepped back, appraised her work and said, "Now I can see this fine June day like I'm right out in it, eh, Wyatt, my long-lost friend."

"You did a good job there, Cornelia," I said.

"The only problem with so clean a window is, now and then a sparrow or blackbird collides with it, just flying along la-de-da, the end of its days. Did you have a window at Rockhead?"

"The prison library had two."

"Well, you can come sit and look out this one at your convenience. During bakery hours, of course."

"That's welcoming to hear, believe me."

"Just who else in Middle Economy have you talked to so far? Tilda, I imagine."

"You and Tilda, that's it."

Cornelia slipped off her rubber gloves, tossed them in the sink, then brought me a cup of coffee and sat down at my table. "Got any plans?" she asked. "Past finishing your coffee, I mean."

"I'm going to go out to the shed and see what shape the sled-and-toboggan concern might be in. That first and foremost, I guess. The accounts have to be delinquent, all of them. Honestly, I don't know what's left. Maybe nothing."

"Oh, I forgot to ask. How about a scone? I'm out of practice with you."

"Cranberry?"

"Three of those left. Do you want all three?"

"Yes, please."

"Breakfast's on the house, but don't tell anyone."

"I won't even tell you."

"You're thin as a rail. I'm going to slather some extra butter on those scones."

The scones were delicious. Coming out of all

those months of drab prison food, I practically wanted to bite into the pat of butter, dappled as it was with scone crumbs from the butter knife. But having such a clean, clear window was best of all. And just sitting with Cornelia was nice, too. But then she looked at her watch and said, "Wyatt, I need to give you some advance warning. In October last year, Leonard Marquette fell and broke a hip and was laid up for weeks. He quit commercial fishing—doctor's orders— and now he's sitting on a forklift half of each day in a warehouse in Truro. According to him, he's pretty much his own boss and gets to give his hip a rest any time he wants. The reason I'm telling you this is because Leonard comes in for coffee and a blueberry muffin eight o'clock on the dot, sits for fifteen minutes, tops, so he's on the road and on time for his shift. His warehouse gets a late start but stays open later than most at the other end of the day."

"So Leonard will be here any minute—so what?"

"So, from Leonard you might experience some harshness, is what. You might experience it right to your face. There's no predicting Leonard's moods ever since his nephew was killed in France."

"Philip Marquette?"

"Yes, Philip, who was a student where Hans Mohring was a student. Dalhousie. The first Marquette to go to university, and that's a big family. Born and raised in Pembroke, where Leonard's sister and brother-in-law still live. But growing up, Philip was often to my bakery. My, my, my, that young man artistically carved wood like he was born to it."

"I think my uncle once tried to employ him."

"That's right. But Philip went to university."

"What was he studying?"

"Marine science, I believe it was called. In Pembroke he must've looked at the ocean every day for seventeen years, then took classes to find out the nature of what he'd been looking at. There's a nice continuity to that, eh?"

"I remember he carved bowling pins," I said.

"Here's something. When he was ten, he carved the smaller pins, called duckpins, for an alley up near Shediac Bridge, and what was unusual was, in that particular bowling establishment the lanes actually crossed into New Brunswick. Of course, there's no dotted line between provinces, is there, and besides, who cares, anyway? Nobody was smuggling bowling balls across the border. Back then, duckpin alleys had fallen in popularity, but not near Shediac Bridge, apparently, because Philip Marquette was paid handsomely to carve fifty duckpins. His parents put the money away. Come to think of it, he might've used it at Dalhousie to purchase textbooks. Who knows?"

"Are you saying don't mention Philip, it'd be too painful?"

"No, it's not that, Wyatt. It's that Leonard's lately been brooding all over again—he might never have stopped brooding, come to think of it. About Donald and you using his boat that night."

"But I didn't know we were going to use Leonard's boat until we got to the wharf."

"Most people understood that."

Indeed, at eight o'clock, give or take a minute, Leonard parked his dilapidated dark green truck with side gates in front of the bakery. He couldn't *not* have made me out through the newly washed window.

Once inside, Leonard stood at the counter. Cornelia set a blueberry muffin and a cup of coffee on the table closest to the counter. But Leonard kept standing, and he reached over, picked up the coffee and took a sip. "Wyatt, your time in Rockhead must've seemed an eternity to you," he said. "But it went far too fast for my liking. Personally speaking."

"I was sorry to hear about Philip," I said.

Leonard looked at Cornelia. "Knowing you, Cornelia, you probably gave Wyatt Hillyer those scones gratis. Welcome-home present, knowing you."

"None of your business, Leonard," she said.

Leonard gobbled the muffin in a few bites and then, holding his cup of coffee, sat down at a table. "Wyatt, did you notice I walk on a slant?" he said. "Permanent limp, all because I slipped on the deck of my boat and broke my hip and now I take a pill for the pain. In fact, I'm going to swallow one right in front of you and Cornelia." He reached into his jacket pocket, took out a vial, twisted off the cap, emptied a pill onto the table, set the pill on his tongue and stupidly displayed it there for five or so seconds. Finally, with an exaggerated gulp and a loud slurp of coffee, the pill disappeared. "It takes me a full minute to get out of bed in the morning, let alone limber up, just so I can get into my truck."

"Boo-hoo, Leonard," Cornelia said. "It takes me *three* minutes to get out of bed, and neither of my hips has ever been broken."

Leonard frowned and said, "It's not just that I slipped on the deck of my boat. It's that I slipped on invisible blood. Far-fetched as you might think that is, Wyatt, you didn't slip on it, so how in hell would you know?"

"Leonard, pay up and get on out of my bakery now, please," Cornelia said.

"I was out on my boat," Leonard said. "It was a clear day. No waves to speak of. The Bay of Fundy was between storms. Deck was dry as paper. And I slipped. Now, even a mesmerist at twenty-five dollars an appointment could not persuade me out of believing the deck of my own boat hadn't become ghoulish. No, sir, that German boy's blood was there—I just couldn't see it. And down I went. Thank the Lord that Tom

Ekhert was working nets with me that day, or I'd've had my very first and last swim lesson, seeing as I'd started to roll right into the soup when he caught me."

"I hope the forklift breaks your other hip, Leonard," Cornelia said.

"Always a pleasure to see you, Cornelia. And the muffin was good as always," Leonard said. He set some money on the counter. "I'm a paying customer."

After Leonard drove off, Cornelia and I sat drinking coffee, not talking, admiring the new day out her window for a few minutes.

"Whew, what'd you think of your homecoming parade just now?" she asked.

"Not so harsh that I lost my appetite and can't finish these scones," I said, which made her laugh. "Have you seen Tilda this morning, by the way?"

"She has a rendezvous about this time every morning," Cornelia said.

"Where—with whom?"

"At the Parrsboro Wharf with her late husband," Cornelia said. "And I mean *every* morning. Mourns her husband. And she doesn't care who's watching—school kids to fishing crews, she doesn't care. You do something on that regular a basis, people not only get used to it, some eventually come to rely on it as a fixture. From what I've been told, she's very dignified about it."

"Every morning makes sense to me, since Hans was the love of her life."

"Hard to know what to think, really. She talks out loud and tells Hans about how things went for her yesterday. Things like that."

"When did these rendezvous begin?"

"Next day after Donald was escorted off to Halifax," Cornelia said. "Tilda out there on the wharf like that? Sometimes I think of it as admirable, but one thing's for sure—it's mysterious far beyond normal wifely obligation, no matter how devoted."

"Has she gone mad, Cornelia? Is it madness?"

"Often in a marriage, there's a husband you just don't know if he's hearing you or not, but the wife keeps trying." Cornelia smiled. "All kidding aside. No, if Tilda's mad at all, she's mad with guilt. If she didn't go to the wharf every morning, it might swallow her up, that guilt."

"Guilty of what?" I said.

"Like Tilda herself told me, she shouldn't have ever let Hans go to the house with you that night. Had she been along, Donald—she thinks—couldn't have committed that murder. I'm not sure I agree with her, but my opinion's hardly the point, is it?"

When I got back home, I went out to the shed. Inside, it was all stale air, and as far as the sleds and toboggans were concerned, there was much disarray. Tilda had peeled the U-boat news, all those headlines and articles, off the walls. I opened the windows and let the breeze in. Spider webs were in every corner. I swept those away with a broom. It had to have been Tilda who'd also organized, in separate stacks held by rubber bands, invoices, letters of request and other correspondence on the workbench. I sat opening and reading these for an hour or so and concluded, Well, you need to have some employment, let's see what you can do.

Skipping lunch, working well into the afternoon, I wrote to each of the twenty-three customers to whom a sled or toboggan was due—some for nearly two years!—beginning each letter with, *My uncle Donald Hillyer is no longer employed in this line of work. I'm Wyatt Hillyer, his nephew, and I was apprenticed to him for a good while. I will be carrying on with the business. I think you will be satisfied with the results.*

The thing was, Marlais, I had no idea whether I could manage the paperwork, let alone construct the sleds and toboggans on my own—and how many of these customers would still want their sled or toboggan? Yet what was my choice? Close to age twenty-three now, I had no other skills to peddle. Honestly, the thought of asking for work on a fishing or lobster boat crew was daunting, even laughable. Who would hire me? What was I in this village anymore?

Pariah, I worried. The rancor I'd felt fairly steaming off Leonard was the first step in confirming the fear that I'd brought shame to my neighbors. And come to think of it, on which side did my own private sympathies fall? Should Reverend Witt be praying for Hans Mohring's passage to heaven, or for my uncle's redemption? Why shouldn't Witt pray for both in the same breath? Minute by minute my thoughts would start out in a straight line toward a hopeful conclusion, then would suddenly detour and get lost. Naturally, I considered leaving Middle Economy for good. Just getting out. I even imagined that Randall Webb might hire me to work in his music shop. My childhood house on Robie Street was rented out, to a childless couple, last name of Pullman. I could give them notice. I could move back there.

Detour, detour, detour into late evening; finally, I was just grateful I'd left enough stew for supper a second night. Especially that French stew, because the flavors settled in more deeply. Have you ever noticed how that works with leftovers?

After supper, fully dark out, it started to rain and I switched on the front porch light. Washing the dishes, I looked out the window and saw rain spill over the iron birdbath Tilda had given Constance in the summer of 1940. Steven Parish had worked on it like a sculptor, adding a special feature, a circumference of dancing angels at the solid, heavy base. There was quite a downpour now. I put on a phonograph record from an album containing a set of Beethoven's sonatas for cello and piano—Sonata in A Major, Sonata in C Major and Sonata in D Major—then settled onto the sofa. I had wanted the Beethoven to transport me out of the world, but in a short time the music turned out to be only an accompaniment, not an antidote, to my restlessness. I lifted the needle, set it on its holder, turned off the gramophone, took a kerosene lantern from a shelf, set a lit match to the wick and carried the lantern out to the shed.

Once inside, I lit a second lantern and placed the two at opposite ends of the worktable, and this made for adequate light. I started in on the toboggan long promised to a Mr. and Mrs. Kormiker, originally from Iceland but now living in Copenhagen. Mr. Kormiker was in banking. On a visit to Halifax they'd seen my uncle's brochure, probably in one of the hotels. It was very professionally done, that brochure, not inexpensively produced, either. Steven Parish had provided drawings of sleds and toboggans, as he had done for his own brochure of iron works—fireplace tongs, candelabra, stovepipes and such—that he forged on commission.

Now, Marlais, you might ask, why start up again with this particular toboggan?

Because while going through all the correspondence, I'd read the letters that Mrs. Kormiker had sent to Donald and Constance. Eleven letters in all, each cordial and filling no more than three-quarters of a single page of personal stationery. Her written English was excellent. In one letter she wrote, "Our granddaughter is now two years of age. Is it possible to have a toboggan made by your hand delivered for her sixth birthday?" This letter was dated April 11, 1941—the war had allowed it to cross the Atlantic. What most struck me was the faith that a simple transaction in life, with patience—because think how far in advance they were planning—could eventually take place between people an ocean apart. A bargain had been struck, and I'd inherited an obligation. I felt desperate to do some small dignified thing. What's more, I figured that if the granddaughter was two in 1941, that meant if I worked hard on the toboggan, I might not be all that late.

Mr. and Mrs. Kormiker wanted a 12-by-3-foot three-board called a dog toboggan, with an upright backboard. I had to hire Steven Parish to forge the triangular hitch with handle. I'd been concerned he wouldn't want to do the work for me. But as it turned out, he was noticeably only a little less friendly than he'd always been, which wasn't too friendly at all. He looked at my rough sketch of the toboggan and said, "Sure, I'll make the hitch. But I'll make it because Donald said you were a proper nephew to him, for the most part. But you have to pay me before I start."

Parish made the hitch with handle in two days. When I went to pick it up, he said, "Bring me any work you need done, Wyatt, and I'll do it. By the way, I've been up to Dorchester five or six times. Bleak place, eh? I made Donald a candle holder for Christmas last year. I never thought to ask if they allow him candles. Anyway, Donald's getting by."

Though the Kormikers' toboggan could be pulled by hand, it was really designed to be tied to a haul rope or reins. And they also wanted an attachable cargo box, so their granddaughter could fit snugly inside. There'd be plenty of room for quilts or blankets or overcoats in there, too, I learned from one of Mrs. Kormiker's letters: she and Mr. Kormiker had made their choice on the basis of sketches of five different types of toboggans my uncle had sent them.

And that's what I spent three full days and nights doing. Little sleep, no radio. My uncle had already fashioned the bow to three feet of curl. What was left for me to do was sand and attach the crosspieces, hinge the backboard behind the next-to-last crosspiece, and build the slush board my uncle had promised as an "extra." In addition, I had to build the cargo box from scratch, including gunwales, eyebolts and hinges. I had to fix the runners. Finally, I had to shellac the entire thing, curl to stern.

On my third morning of work, I completed the toboggan at about six A.M., but I hadn't been able to feel the tips of my fingers as I applied the shellac, because they were raw and numb from hours of sanding. My uncle had jars of salve for immediate relief after such long bouts. The salve was from Norway. I worked some into each of my fingertips but didn't feel that, either.

The toboggan weighed about thirty pounds. I set it across two sawhorses to allow the architecture to settle and plugged in an electric fan to help dry the shellac. It looked just fine. I recalled how when we finished a sled or toboggan, or the occasional horse-drawn sleigh, Donald would pour us each a shot of whiskey and we'd clink glasses and he'd say, "One down, and if we're blessed, ten thousand to go." I cleaned the tools, hung them in place, tidied up the shed and went in to wash up at the kitchen sink. Then I drove into town.

But instead of stopping, I drove past the bakery and on to Parrsboro and, as I thought I might, saw Tilda out on the end of the dock. If anything, it was raining harder than during the night, and it had rained all night. Now rain blew fiercely in from the Minas Basin. Half a dozen trawlers pulled at their tie ropes and knocked against the pylons. It was quite the storm, and yet there was Tilda, dressed in a rain slicker, dungarees, galoshes and a fisherman's hat tied under her chin, right out in it. To me the remarkable thing was that three men—I recognized Todd Branch and his neighbors Ralph and Alvin Drakemore, all from Upper Economy—just went about their business. They weren't going to head out in this weather and were battening things down on the deck of their trawler, shouting words I couldn't make out. They completely ignored Tilda, or so it seemed at first. But then Todd Branch went below, emerging with, of all things, a steaming cup of molasses tea, or coffee or cocoa or whatnot, and brought it to Tilda, and cupped Tilda's hands in his as she lifted the drink to her lips, as if he was helping a person to recover her strength after a deathly illness. The other two men didn't even look up. Tilda took another sip, nodded to Todd Branch and turned away from him. She went back to tasting the rain in her cup and talking to Hans Mohring. Todd stepped onto the deck of his boat. It seemed to me he carried out all of this like it was matter-of-fact, no more than a recently added chore. How many mornings had he brought a hot drink to Tilda?

The moment I stepped into the bakery, Cornelia set a cup of coffee and a cranberry scone in front of me, without my having asked for either. She sat down opposite me at the table closest to the window. "Look at that, will you?" she said. "Wind blew mud all the way in and my perfectly clean window's not perfectly clean anymore." She took a bite of toast.

"I saw Tilda at the Parrsboro Wharf just now," I said.

"You know, I thought that was your car going by."

"There she was. Just like you said."

"I saw her out there three mornings ago, and guess what?" Cornelia said. "Some schoolboys were taking potshots at whichever birds—cormorants mostly. And all at once, Tilda reached over and grabbed that rifle and took a few potshots of her own. Of course she missed everything except the water, but the sight made me laugh so hard. I was on my way back from picking up cranberry preserves from Mrs. Gerard's in Parrsboro when I saw that."

"I think she might've seen me," I said. "I hope she didn't think I was spying on her or something."

"You just gave in to curiosity, Wyatt. That's pretty human of you, and besides, Constance Hillyer confided in me."

"Confided in you what?"

"Confided in me about your feelings for Tilda," Cornelia said. "Look, Tilda's been a widow for merely a couple years. And I suppose life's as bewildering to her as it would be for any war widow, of which there's recent thousands, eh? Do you know, she spends half the night in the library, due to Mrs. Oleander's tolerance and hospitality. That's her narrowed horizons. House, wharf, library. Know what else? I think Tilda forgot how to sleep. I hear her playing the gramophone upstairs."

"Anyway, my *feelings* for Tilda, as you call them?" I said. "They aren't in the least well met by her. How could they be? I put her husband out to sea, may he rest in peace, and I mean that. So my *feelings* are hardly the thing that'll solace her, if that's what you're saying."

"I'm saying what I just said, that's all."

"She must've been even more in love with Hans than I thought."

"No denying, Hans was allowed all her beloved places, village she grew up in to pillow talk, all so soon after they met, too. It fairly took your breath away."

"I thought about that night and day. In prison, I mean. Thought hard about that. And about other things, of course."

I tried lifting the cup of coffee Cornelia had brought to the table, but I dropped it and it smashed on the floor, coffee splattering.

"My goodness," she said, "you're a clumsy oaf this morning."

"Sorry. I worked on a toboggan all night. All that sanding numbed my fingers."

"Want another cup?"

"No thanks."

I picked up the pieces of the cup and put them in the wastebasket. Cornelia handed me a sandwich wrapped in a napkin. "It's halibut, onion, tomato and mustard," she said. "You put that in the larder, eh? I doubt anyone's making you lunch these days."

"Thank you. I'm a bit short of money just now, though."

"Do I look like a debt collector to you, Wyatt?"

"No, you don't, Cornelia. Thank you for the sandwich."

"Tilda should be back any minute."

"She'll come see me if and when she wants. I think that's best."

"I hope you try and make a go of your uncle's business, Wyatt."

"I got that toboggan finished, didn't I?"

Much of the rest of the day, not counting the time it took to eat the sandwich, wash some clothes in the sink, rinse and hang them to dry on a length of twine I'd rigged taut in the pantry, with three buckets side by side underneath to catch any drip, I drew up a rough design for a box in which to send the toboggan to the Kormikers in Denmark. Under a tarpaulin in back of the shed there was more than enough plywood to build it to adequate dimensions. The construction itself took about two hours. When I inspected the results, I thought, If I'm honest about it, this thing looks like a long coffin. A rueful, though not all that original, observation. And then your mind sometimes doesn't stop to charitable purpose: I thought, I'm sending this coffin to Denmark, a toboggan inside, whereas Hans didn't get even this much.

There was rain and more rain, and it was dark all afternoon, more a deepening of the morning's darkness, really. It felt like the Minas Basin had gotten an early start on summer storms, impatient for the turbulence. I put a pot of tea on to boil and listened to many gramophone records in a row. In prison, this was something I daydreamed of doing, and one time asked a guard, Mr. DeForge, "Who do you like more, Beethoven, Chopin or Vivaldi?"

"I'll personally drag you out of that cell and stuff you up your own asshole," he said, "you ever ask me that kind of question again."

I'd just put on Beethoven's Sonata in F Major when the telephone rang in the kitchen. I looked at the clock: 1:20 A.M. I picked up the receiver and said hello, and Tilda said, "Wyatt, there's two crows somehow got into the library. They're in the library right now. Listen—"

She apparently held the telephone receiver in midair, because I heard a definite *cawwwr-rrruuup* loud and clear. "Hear that?" she said. "I can't read with this going on. I can't concentrate. I'm going crazy. A drawer in the card catalogue was left open a crack, and a crow plucked a whole bunch of cards right out. The other crow watched from Mrs. Oleander's desk."

"Tilda, are you asking me to drive over?"

"I've told you about these crows—do what you want."

I got to the library in maybe ten minutes. Lightning over the Minas Basin. Opening the library's front door, I heard a crow's weird voice. I left the door open. By the light of a floor lamp next to the overstuffed chair, plus shadow-flickering light cast from the fireplace, I saw Tilda in stocking feet in the corner, dressed in dungarees, a pale blue shirt and a black button-down sweater. And she was wielding a mop.

"That one crow there just shat on Mrs. Oleander's desk," she said.

"How'd they get in, do you think?"

"I'm pretty sure the wind knocked out a window upstairs. This library's got an attic, you know."

"No, I didn't know that."

I saw the file cards all over the floor. One crow was still on Mrs. Oleander's desk, silent. The other was on the long reading table, producing coughs and clicks, tearing out the page of a book, holding the cover open with its claw. I took off my shoes and threw one at this crow, who dodged the shoe and fluttered up, page in its beak, landing on Mrs. Oleander's desk. Both crows hopped about. I threw my other shoe, this time striking one crow, and both flew right at Tilda, who waved her mop, redirecting them out the front door.

Tilda slammed shut the door, then slid to the floor, laughing as hard as I'd ever known her to laugh. I threw myself onto the overstuffed chair and said, "Some life you've got now, Tilda. I see you've given up on people altogether. It's just you and books at night and crows, huh?"

"I telephoned you, didn't I? Damsel in distress and all that."

"That's never been you and never will be."

"Think what you want."

We looked at each other a moment, then Tilda said, "Before those birds flew in, you know what I was reading, maybe for the tenth time?"

"I've never read anything for the tenth time. Which book?"

"*In a German Pension*, by Katherine Mansfield."

"How far along were you?"

"Page four. Then all hell broke loose."

"I should leave you to your reading, then."

"Want to hear it, Wyatt?"

"Want to hear what?"

"*In a German Pension*."

"The whole thing?"

"I'm ready and willing."

Tilda sat in the overstuffed chair on the right side of the fireplace. I added a few logs to the fire and brought Mrs. Oleander's chair close to the left side of the fireplace. Both chairs now faced the fire at an inward slant. When the flames steadied, we could hear rain hissing in the grate.

Tilda opened the book and said, "The first story's called 'Germans at Meat.' Once I start reading, don't interrupt me, Wyatt. I never interrupt myself when I'm reading alone, and I prefer it that way."

"I always wanted to be read to."

"Then this is your big moment."

She moved the floor lamp closer, settled back into the chair and began to read: "Bread soup was placed upon the table. 'Ah,' said the Herr Rat, leaning upon the table as he peered into the tureen, 'that is what I need.'"

Why do I still remember those sentences, Marlais? For the next three hours—at least that long—Tilda read story after story. Besides "Germans at Meat," I remember the titles of two others, "The Child-who-was-tired" and "The Sister of the Baroness," but I think there were thirteen in all.

She read each one with the same dedication.

"Well, that's that, then," Tilda said when she'd finished. "I see you're still awake, Wyatt." She set the book down on the hassock. A silence fell between us, not just defined by being in a night-time library, or noticeable because rain drumming on the roof drowned out most other sound. No, it was something else altogether. It was as if a fleeting chance was presented us by mute angels—to reference a hymn—who couldn't later report us to God even if they'd wanted to. Tilda and I seemed to have been, for a brief time, offered a secret life, sequestered, outside the scrutiny of our neighbors in Middle Economy, a safe haven from all recent ghosts. True, no dictionary definition of love might apply to what happened between us that night, but my choice is not to consult a dictionary. Whatever else, we didn't worry to near madness what was to be done with our bottled-up emotions. There we were, in a room without any history between us, a room we'd never been in together before. It took place only that once, ending with daylight, pale in the rain-streaked windows. Clothes scattered. Fingertips less numb. The desk lamp still lit.

Marlais, father-daughter decorum insists that I not describe any more. Besides, I'd be too embarrassed, even in a letter. However, I'll risk mentioning that when you were six months old, the three of us were in the kitchen, and Tilda looked across the table and said, "In the library that night, when we sat in the overstuffed chair, tucked together like we were, I knew the moment our daughter was conceived."

You were born six pounds eight ounces at Truro General Hospital, 11:58 P.M. on March 27, 1946. Cornelia Tell and I were called in from the waiting room to see you, all of half an hour old, held in your mother's arms. You were named Marlais Constance-Hillyer. Marlais, after Marlais

Winterhew, the author of *The Highland Book of Platitudes*. Tilda chose the name.

Your mother was the love of my life. I was not the love of hers. You became the love of both of ours.

The Rooms above the Bakery

MARLAIS, AT MY KITCHEN table here at 58 Robie, I'm looking at the Monday church bulletin from Middle Economy dated October 25, 1948, and the heading reads: DANISH CITIZENS VISIT MIDDLE ECONOMY.

Marcus and Uli Mohring, now officially Danish citizens, arrived to Middle Economy by bus on Friday, October 15. Since you were about two and a half years old at the time, you probably don't—do you?—remember meeting them at the bus in Great Village. It made all the sense in the world when Tilda requested, during the few days Mr. and Mrs. Mohring set up in the house, that I keep to the shed during the day and stay in the rooms above the bakery at night. As a result, I never so much as caught a glimpse of them. Best for everyone. Naturally, their presence caused a lot of local curiosity and astonishment. It resurrected much sadness, too.

Until the magistrate's hearing took place in the library back in 1942, Donald, Constance, Tilda, Cornelia and I were the only ones who knew much about Hans. Since then, two newspaper hacks had attempted to write about the murder in Middle Economy "during the war," but nobody

in the village gave them enough time, information or opinions to support a feature story. One
reporter, Abigail Montrose, said in a brief article
in the *Mail*, "The citizens of that outport generally met my inquiries with cold politeness." Now
and then somebody stopped into the bakery and
asked Cornelia where "the house where the
murder took place" could be found. Or words to
that effect.

"Yep, once was too often for my taste,"
Cornelia said. "My attitude is, serve them something to eat, let them pay for it, and don't tell
them a goddamn thing. If that goes smoothly,
fine. But if they don't want anything to eat, I say
the townspeople aren't here to provide a dog-
and-pony show." One morning I was in the
bakery, this was in August 1946, I think. A
middle-aged couple—Cornelia said they were
from Halifax—were just leaving. They had
unfriendly expressions on their faces, no doubt
because they'd dealt with unfriendly Cornelia.
When I sat down at a table, Cornelia said, "I'd
bet that in Halifax a tour of houses people got
murdered in would take longer than the five minutes it'd take in our little village, don't you
think?"

"I'd bet whatever you'd bet, Cornelia, and add
ten dollars," I said.

"Besides which, that man and wife who just left
didn't order as much as a scone to share between

them. You know what I offered them gratis, though?"

"No, what?"

"Offered to show them the door."

You may wonder, Marlais, about the history behind Marcus and Uli Mohring's coming to visit. Well, in May of 1947 Tilda had received a letter from Uli Mohring, in which she wrote, "My husband and I would like to see Dalhousie University, where Hans was so happy, and the village of Middle Economy." Tilda wrote them back directly. When a second letter arrived stating their travel dates, Tilda told them to Reverend Witt, which, in terms of getting the news around, was like having their plans broadcast on the radio.

Mr. and Mrs. Mohring's visit fell on a weekend. They attended church. Reverend Witt acknowledged them from the pulpit but didn't refer to their son in his sermon. No need to, since Hans's murder was no doubt what all the parishioners had in their thoughts, no matter what the subject of the sermon was. "Certainly, seeing them in our church caused a once-in-a-lifetime bunch of emotions," Mrs. Oleander said to Cornelia the next morning in the bakery. "And I was shoulder to shoulder with Mrs. Uli Mohring, third pew from the front. That's not something I'm likely to forget."

In the kitchen above the bakery late that

Sunday afternoon, October 17, Tilda told me that Uli and Marcus Mohring had made an impression as nice people. "They're taking naps now," she said. "Mrs. Mohring is fifty-nine and Mr. Mohring's sixty-three. They have accents much thicker than Hans's was. Following the sermon and hymns, right there in the pews, they sat with twenty or so people, maybe more. They actually apologized—can you believe it?—if anyone was made ill at ease by them. Here's what else they said: 'It was very difficult traveling here. We had third-class steamer passage. But we only wanted to see where our son spent his last days. We wanted the opportunity to tell you what a good person he was. He was a good, serious student. We received a letter from Hans. It took a long time to reach us. It said he was married. That he married a Canadian young woman. We hoped to meet her.' And when they passed around photographs of Hans as a young boy, Mrs. Oleander got choked up. So did Reverend Witt. So did Charlotte Butler, from the sewing shop, and her husband, George, got choked up, too." Tilda stopped talking a moment in order to catch her breath. "And those aren't exactly sentimental types, the Butlers especially. Goodness, they were sobbing up to the rafters, the Butlers were."

"You don't have to tell me any of this, Tilda," I said.

"There *is* more to tell, but if it's all the same to

you, I'll keep it to myself. One other thing, Wyatt. I read Uli and Marcus my obituary, and they helped me write it better."

"Write it better how?"

"Details from Hans's childhood. Some other facts, too. They want to see that their son is well served. Reverend Witt's going to finally put it in the church bulletin. Sunday next, he promised. Better late than never, I suppose."

"Did they ask about—"

"They already knew who'd done what, from my original letter, back from when you were in Rockhead. No, they only wanted to speak about their son and meet me." She stared out the window. "Hans looked a lot like his parents, my goodness. He had the same way of walking as his father, same eyes and eyebrows, but his mother's mouth and smile. And Hans was taller than his dad."

"Difficult, I bet, for you to see Hans in them like that."

"No. You have no idea how happy it made me."

"How did they take to Marlais?"

Tilda didn't respond right away. Instead, she got up and steeped a pot of tea. I went into the bedroom and found you sitting on the bed, Marlais. You had sheets of paper spread out, and you were drawing funny faces of people, though some had cat whiskers. I put Chopin on the phonograph and went to the kitchen. Tilda set a cup of tea in front of me. She poured her own cup, carried it to the table and sat across from me.

"We four sat together in the kitchen of my house—me, Marlais, Mr. and Mrs. Mohring," she said. "And Mrs. Mohring held Marlais on her lap, and they were peas in a pod, let me tell you. I never heard Marlais so chatty. They drew with crayons on napkins, at first nothing but silly likenesses of each other. But then Uli asked Marlais to draw a picture of her family. And Wyatt, that picture turned out to include just me and Marlais."

"And I was nowhere in sight—on that napkin."

"Well, your car was there."

"Maybe that meant I was in the shed working."

"That's anyone's guess."

Tilda sipped her tea slowly and we listened to the music. You walked into the kitchen then, Marlais, and showed us a drawing you'd done of some boats and a big sun overhead, with long sun rays sticking out, but only at the top like porcupine quills. You were in stocking feet and had on a button-up shirt and overalls.

"That's wonderful," your mother said, and gave you a hundred kisses, you giggling the whole time. When you went back to the bedroom, Tilda said, "I wanted to talk with Uli Mohring alone, so Marcus took Marlais for a walk."

"So you and Mrs. Mohring had a nice talk, did you?" I said.

"Talked and talked, yes we did."

"Well, good."

"The thing is, Wyatt, at one point Uli Mohring smoothed out the napkin on the table—you know, the one with Marlais's family portrait on it. 'Tilda, dear,' she said. 'You have not once mentioned the father of this lovely child. Why not come live with us in Denmark?'"

"That was direct."

"Well, if something's to the point, a point's been made."

"And you said, on my behalf?"

"It's not what I *said,* Wyatt, it's what I *thought.* What I thought was, I'd be surprised if I couldn't fit everything Marlais and I would need in my mother's wardrobe trunk."

You know, Marlais, so much is difficult to tell you, but it's the truth.

I never believed in the phrase "it all comes back to me now," because not all of anything that happened in the past comes back whole cloth. But I do clearly remember that scarcely five minutes after we brought you home from hospital, you fell asleep in the crib I'd made. Tilda had done a splendid job of setting up her old room as your nursery. You'd wake, fall asleep again, wake. Your little lungs were like bagpipes. You cried loud and clear, wild forceful opinions without words. Tilda and I tried to resist holding you every time you cried, because Cornelia had warned us that if we did, from the start we'd come to see our child as a constant emergency. Still, not rushing to the nursery seemed against all natural instincts.

All that first night, your mother and I stayed up. We played gramophone records and talked—kept the bottles of baby formula warm, sterilized the rubber nipples in boiling water before feeding you—probably about as intimate as we'd ever be without touching. Mainly, we talked about how difficult it might be to raise you in Middle Economy. We imagined we'd have to weather the coarse opinions and snipes of our neighbors. You know, maybe you'd suffer from being a child born out of wedlock, and from the incident of murder that was part of your inheritance. However, setting aside all such big concerns, we loved you beyond words, Marlais. Please never doubt you were a beloved child. Adored.

Cornelia Tell became grandmother, nanny, advice giver, our one real friend in the village, a blessing, and she loved you. Because of her kindness, a few people played out their godly judgments by no longer frequenting her bakery. "I get the picture," Cornelia said. "Pretty simple, though. They chose against me, and I chose against them right back." And it got peculiar with Leonard Marquette. At one point he actually paid good money for an attorney to try and take me to court to recoup his medical bills. But during their

235

first meeting, when Leonard claimed he'd slipped on a pool of invisible blood, the lawyer, a Mr. Auchard—he'd thoroughly reviewed the stenographic report of the magistrate's hearing—quit the case on the spot.

In those days, there were no nearby bed-and-breakfasts, and the closest inn was in Truro, so shortly after you were born, I moved into the rooms above the bakery. That brought gossip, of course. It couldn't be helped. One morning, Cornelia lamented from behind the counter, "My failing is that I never kept a guest book. I mean, in just the past five years, look who I've had stay upstairs! Look who could've signed a guest book! Do you know what was most unexpected, though?"

"I can't imagine," I said.

"What was most unexpected was how complicated life got in the rooms above a simple bakery, that's what. I mean, I could write a book—if I could write a book."

In time, though, to Tilda's and my great surprise and relief, all sorts of neighbors came around to look at you, like they would any newborn. They brought stuffed animals and other gifts. Mrs. Oleander knitted you mittens and a tiny hat with ear flaps, which you wore every time we left the house in cold weather. You were a beautiful child. It was frequently commented on that you had many of your mother's features—already at age one, for instance, you showed a mop of unruly black hair just like Tilda's! You were practically being raised in the bakery, we sat with you there so often. We showed you off like any new parents would. I'd purchased a second gramophone from Randall Webb and set it up in the shed, and you'd fall asleep to music, snug in your bassinet, while I worked on a toboggan.

I arrived to the kitchen for breakfast every single morning without fail. But the truth was, we didn't add up to a family. We just could not have. It was, Cornelia said, more like a mother and father with their own addresses, unwed, permanently fixed in workable estrangement. Though we did share your beautiful life. Your beautiful life.

One could say that it was more than many people had.

Still, from the night Tilda and I had spent in the library, it was an uphill climb. One night, a little drunk and drowsy from two glasses of wine at supper, Tilda said, "To be honest—and I don't mean to be hurtful, Wyatt."

"That probably means you will be," I said. "I'm ready."

"Next morning, I was disgusted by what happened in the library. Add remorse. But as for our daughter, she's made me the happiest I could ever imagine being in my life. How's that for tricks?"

Tilda's and my life together was the steepest

uphill climb, is how it felt. During the very last conversation Tilda and I had, not more than three hours before you left Middle Economy for Denmark, we'd sat at the kitchen table, of course, above the bakery. Tilda said, "I don't ever want our daughter to think it was only because of her that you and I stayed together. Eventually, out of guilt or out of something, we'd probably have got married, just to sanction us being parents in the eyes of God. Like Reverend Witt already asked us to. Fate has it, our daughter has loving parents who don't love each other, not in the way they should, which she'd figure out sooner or later. I'll have to explain a lot while she's growing up. Where's her father? I know I'll need to tell her. But on the ship overseas Uli and Marcus will have time with Marlais. Then in Denmark they'll have us, and we'll have them. And let's just wait and see where life takes us, as Mom liked to say. Let's just wait and see."

"Won't it be as if Marlais is half orphaned, what with you living in Denmark and me living here?" I asked.

"I'd say come visit, but the thought of you stepping foot outside of Nova Scotia?" Tilda said. "If that actually happened I'd believe miracles never cease. On the other hand, Marlais is your daughter, too. Denmark is locatable, Wyatt. A train to Denmark arrives to Denmark. You wouldn't get lost.

"Uli and Marcus say it's a beautiful country. You bring your saws and chisels over and learn to live there, maybe some nearby town from us. Learn to live there. Just like Marlais and I now have to learn to live there. To my mind, it's no more impossible a prospect than Hans faced when he wanted to live here in Canada. But, Wyatt, I simply can no longer raise Marlais by this part of the ocean. I cannot stay in Middle Economy. It took Uli's invitation for me to come to my senses about this. But I came to them."

"Do they have professional mourners in Denmark, I wonder."

"I don't know. But if they do, I'd need to learn the Danish language for that, don't you think, to do it properly? No, probably I'll find a different line of work. I'm resourceful, eh? The good thing, no matter what, is that Marlais will have, not exactly grandparents, but close as you can get."

"So much conviction, Tilda, that your plans will work out for the best."

"Less that, Wyatt, than I'm basing my decision on what I know of our past. Yours and mine."

I parked my car just down from the Esso station, close enough to watch your mother and you, hand in hand, climb onto the bus to Halifax. Mr. and Mrs. Mohring had left on an earlier bus. They were to meet you at the Lord Nelson Hotel. Then you'd steam across to Europe. A few days later I received a postcard: *Bon voyage to us,* it read. It was signed *Your cousin Tilda Mohring.* The way she put her signature made for more distance between us than the Atlantic Ocean.

You and Tilda were gone. And one final thing that convinced me that Tilda was genuinely starting a new life: she left behind *The Highland Book of Platitudes*, in clear view on her bedside table. I'd moved back into the house.

The day the church bulletin printed Hans's obituary was the day I began to let the sled-and-toboggan concern fall apart. Early the next morning, a Monday, I tacked the obituary to the shed wall near the door. I didn't hit a nail, sand a crossboard, fix a runner to a frame or paint a stripe—didn't attempt to do any work at all. I put on a gramophone record, cannot recall which one. Yet when the needle bobbed in the last groove, when the static began, I could hardly lift myself from my uncle's cot. Instead, I threw a hammer, which struck the tone arm, making the needle screech off the record.

Soup for supper, and afterward, all evening, no gramophone music in the house, no child's voice. Sitting at the kitchen table, I got the picture, as Cornelia might say. Absolutely, absolutely, absolutely, I got the bleak picture: this is how my days and nights in the house would be. And though it took a full two months to dismantle the business my uncle had built up over thirty years, it was just four days after you'd gone that I sat at the long table in the library and consulted the Halifax telephone directory, jotting down the names, addresses and telephone numbers of hotels. I composed letters to twelve hotels, asking about availability and rates. I enclosed a return postcard and stamp in each envelope. In a sense, I was already gone from Middle Economy.

I did manage to take an inventory, but it was an inventory of sleds and toboggans I'd never make. Sleds owed and promised, toboggans owed and promised. The shed was full of half-mades, slush boards not yet shellacked, cargo boxes not yet fitted. I brainstormed about selling the business, but after posting notices in the church bulletin, the *Halifax Mail* and the Truro newspaper, there were no takers. Not a single telephone call or postcard of inquiry. But what should I have expected? As Cornelia put it, "You know, Wyatt, when you think about it, who'd be interested? Probably have to be somebody who already makes sleds and toboggans and wants to move to Middle Economy. The only persons I think actually ever could fit that bill are Donald Hillyer and you." Eventually I sold off the surplus wood to Todd Branch.

In the bakery, on the morning of November 27, 1948, I said, "Cornelia, I'm moving back to Halifax."

"To your childhood house?"

"No, I need the money from rent."

"How much is it to rent a house in the city? I always wondered."

"Generally, I can't say. But mine costs fifty per month."

"It'll cost you nearly that much in petrol, since now you'll have to drive so many hours to sit here with me and eat my scones. And since my scones are sold out by nine A.M., think how early in the morning you'll have to leave Halifax."

"Rumor has it there's scones served in Halifax."

"Not mine, though."

"No, not yours."

"And as for a roof over your head?"

"I have enough savings to live on for I'd guess three months."

"Rooming house or hotel or whatnot, right?"

"Just yesterday I secured a hotel room."

"Write down the address, okay?"

I copied it out on a napkin from the return postcard I'd received. Cornelia cut off a piece of masking tape from its roll and stuck the napkin on the first page of a ledger. "My goodness," she said, "will you look at that? I've started an address book!"

We sat drinking coffee and looking out the window. It was a dreary overcast day, and if I remember correctly, one car and one pickup truck went by, and Mrs. Oleander stopped in for a sandwich. She joined our conversation, then went back to the library.

"I've kept this private," Cornelia said, "but before the war I used to take a bus into Halifax. I'd get a hotel room and I'd go to the cinema. Sometimes I'd go three nights in a row. Sometimes I'd see the same picture twice. Lately I'm considering starting up again."

"Your money's hard-earned, Cornelia. Why shouldn't you enjoy it?"

"And since you'll be in Halifax, you could escort me. Of course, that'd be like escorting someone your mother's age—may your mother rest in peace. And I'd understand if that'd be an embarrassment."

"It so happens, I did escort my mother to the cinema, on more than one occasion, in fact. Sometimes my father tagged along, sometimes he didn't. But I'd be honored, Cornelia. You were the kindest to us. Me, Tilda and Marlais. Always and by far the kindest, never a thought about yourself. You let me know when you're next visiting Halifax, and I'll expect to go to the cinema with you."

She fluttered her hand against her heart. "I'm so relieved to get that conversation over with," she said. "I might close the bakery just to rest up."

"By the way, thanks for putting me in touch with Mr. and Mrs. Leaf."

"That worked out, then, did it?"

"As we speak, they're unpacking their clothes in my house."

"The deed is still in Tilda's name, right?"

"Yes, it's in the town clerk's files."

"Well, it's unlikely she'll be back soon, if at all. On the other hand, who's to predict anything? I always liked that proverb, I think it's Jewish: 'If you want to make God laugh, tell him your plans.' Reverend Witt used it in a sermon once, back when I was attending his sermons."

"My only plan, whether God laughs at it or not, is to move to Halifax and get a paying job."

"Do you know the exact date you're leaving?"

"The Leafs want to sleep in the house starting three nights from now. I've sold them my automobile. Tilda's truck stays out behind the shed, though. I've made that clear."

"Come for breakfast every morning till you leave, okay?"

"Thank you, Cornelia. I accept your invitation."

So, Marlais, over the next couple of days I organized everything belonging to you and Tilda, bed quilts to dolls to crayons to clothes, up in the attic. Except for *The Highland Book of Platitudes*, which I'd honestly intended to return to the library, but made it a personal keepsake instead. On the morning of December 1, I asked Mr. Leaf to help me load the toboggan in its box onto the truck, accompany me to the bus stop in Great Village, then drive the truck back and park it behind the shed. He graciously complied. The bus was right on time.

In Halifax, I paid full passage for the toboggan to be transported first on a ship, the TSS *Athenia*, bound for Greece, then for France, and then sent by train to Sweden and on to its final destination of Copenhagen. I was concerned that the Kormikers no longer lived at the same address that was on their envelopes, but that was a chance I took. Nonetheless, I was relieved when, two months later, I got a letter acknowledging the toboggan's arrival. The address I'd enclosed with the toboggan: Wyatt Hillyer—resident, c/o The Evangeline Hotel, 227 Brunswick Street, Halifax, Nova Scotia, Canada.

The Photograph in Rigolo's Pub

I'M MAKING A NOTE here, Marlais, to not forget to tell you about a photograph in Rigolo's Pub.

Living on the little savings I had from wages paid by my uncle, which Cornelia had kept in her combination-lock safe at the bakery, and rent from my Robie Street house, I'd looked for employment all winter of 1948–49. During that time I twice changed rooms in the Evangeline Hotel, each time downward in rent a few dollars a week. The Evangeline was quiet, and the manager, desk clerks and bellmen were friendly and pretty much left me alone. But the cleaning ladies, Mrs. Tompkins and Mrs. Delft, seemed to run the place. For instance, they kept no formal schedule, and my being blunt with them, that I didn't like sitting in the lobby at all hours, waiting for them to attend to my room, hardly put me better in their favor.

I applied for all sorts of work, and finally, in late June of 1949, I was hired on as a "detritus gaffer," as it was officially categorized on the payroll of Harbor Associates, which was the principal custodian of Halifax Harbor and subcontracted out specialty jobs such as detritus gaffing.

I was now part of a crew made up of two women, Evie Michaels and Hermione Rexroth, and three men other than me, Tom Blackwell, Sam Kitchen and Sebastian Firth. We cleaned up around Queen's Wharf and Smith Wharf, along all the beachfronts on both the Halifax and Dartmouth sides, the whole coastline all the way out to Pennant Point. Our main task was to maneuver around in lifeboat-sized outboards, or lean from tugboat railings, gaffing in flotsam and jetsam in order to keep the lanes clear for the Halifax–Dartmouth commuter ferries, fishing trawlers and behemoth freighters. And Marlais, you can hardly believe everything that finds its way into the harbor, and I mean everything, from picture frames to lampshades to shoes. One time a crate full of brooms, another time a shipment of exotic potted plants.

We were required to itemize everything we hauled in. But the time Evie Michaels and I gathered up a set of the *Encyclopaedia Brittanica*—individual volumes bobbing out there under the Angus L. Macdonald Bridge—Evie said, "Say, Wyatt, you know what? My family doesn't own a complete set like this. So if you don't mind, I'm not going to write these up. I'd like to dry them out and hope they're still readable. My kids could really use them for homework."

All manner of death and near death, too. For instance, we often found waterlogged gulls, and we had a sea duck choked on a plastic necklace, a goner. Then there was a pet dachshund in a wooden crate with breathing holes. When we approached, we heard the dog barking and whimpering, so we knew it was okay. Sorry to say, we've had one suicide, too, floating face-down near the mouth of the harbor. Fishing line had twisted his fishing pole around his leg like a splint. That sight was hard to take. Again that day Evie had partnered with me. We held the poor fellow against the hull of our boat with gaffing hooks, used the walkie-talkie, and waited there until the harbor police took over. We knew it was a suicide because next morning the article in the *Mail* said he—his name was Russell Leminster—had left a note to that effect. "Who knows," Evie said, "what goes through someone's mind, eh? Maybe he felt a sense of order was important, so he went fishing first. Then came the next thing."

We each were issued a one-piece dark blue uniform with an accordion waist. Also dark blue caps with *Harbor Assoc.* stitched in cursive across the front. We were given galoshes, a rain slicker, thick sweater, insulated vest, five pairs of woolen socks and two pairs of waterproof gloves, and if you lost an item of clothing, Harbor Associates replaced it but docked the price from your next paycheck, no exceptions. I admit that sometimes I wore one of the pairs of socks or galoshes or a sweater outside of work, as part of my day-to-day wardrobe.

I don't know why I just used the past-tense "wore" when I should've used "wear," because I'm about to enter my eighteenth year as a detritus gaffer. In fact, along with Hermione and Tom, I'm a senior gaffer and have received an increase in salary—beginning at $18 per week—every year, plus there's the Christmas bonus. Philosophically speaking, in 1949 when I first landed the gaffing job, I remember feeling that I'd come up in the world from being in Rockhead Prison, but I'd come down in the world from building sleds and toboggans.

Considering what I do for a living, I realize it's a pretty awful pun to say that motion pictures are the one thing that buoys up my spirits. Nonetheless it's true. I trust that your mother told you that for fifteen years now, I've put $20 a month into a Halifax bank account under your name. But aside from that, motion pictures are my one sizable expense. With rare exceptions, I take supper at home, and I'm provided breakfast and lunch by Harbor Associates, except on Saturday and Sunday, but I seldom work weekends anyway.

From my first day back in Halifax, I wondered if Cornelia Tell would ever take up her own invitation to go to the pictures with me. And for four years, though I hadn't seen her, we stayed in touch. Letters and the occasional telephone conversation. My letters were all written on hotel stationery. She did visit Halifax a number of times, but did not telephone. Her choice, and her own business. But she'd always write and tell me which movie she'd seen, and then I'd go see it, too. Then I'd write her a letter and ask her what she thought of *The Return of Monte Cristo* or *A Notorious Gentleman* or *Holiday in Mexico*, which starred Walter Pidgeon and had Xavier Cugat and his orchestra in it. Or *The Strange Woman*, with my favorite actress of all time, Hedy Lamarr, who I thought was the second most beautiful woman in the world next to Tilda. All of those movies played at the Casino Theatre. I'd ask Cornelia's opinion of *Nobody Lives Forever* and *The Show-Off*. And I remember a sign out front of the Capital Theatre for *Undercurrent*, starring Robert Taylor and Katharine Hepburn (who grated on my nerves), that read NOT SUITABLE FOR CHILDREN. *The Shocking Miss Pilgrim* with Betty Grable, *Notorious* with Ingrid Bergman and Cary Grant, *No Leave, No Love* with Van Johnson. Believe me, Marlais, when I say that Cornelia Tell was generous with opinions about movies, pages and pages worth, on everything from A to Z.

Cornelia never once apologized for not contacting me on her visits to Halifax, and I thought, Well, when she's ready she will contact me, that's just the way she is. Finally, on the evening of January 8, 1953, she telephoned my room at my most recent hotel—the Glendale, on Hollis Street—and said, "I was thinking how about tomorrow, since it's a Friday and I could get weekend rates?" And so I met her at the Halifax bus station, her bus roughly ten minutes late.

I carried her small suitcase to the Dresden Arms Hotel, at 103 Dresden Street, where I'd arranged a room for her. We had supper at Halloran's restaurant on Sackville Street, and she caught me up on this and that news from Middle Economy. For whatever reason, Marlais, she did not mention you or Tilda at dinner. From ice water to dessert, it was as if we'd read each other's minds, that certain subjects should wait until later in the evening, when we could sit for tea back at her hotel. Toward the end of our meal, she reached into her handbag and took out a piece of paper on which she'd written the schedule of pictures then playing in town.

"Now, my preference would be *49th Parallel*, a war movie," she said. "It originally came out in 1941 in the U.S., but for some reason it's only just got to Nova Scotia. Movies keep the war with us, huh?"

"I've never heard of it," I said.

"Let me warn you in advance—it's got a German U-boat in it."

"I've seen a lot of war pictures, Cornelia."

"I just don't want you to be put off this one and want to walk out. I go to enough movies alone. So I don't want to start out not alone and then suddenly it's the opposite, you know?"

"I wouldn't think of doing that."

49th Parallel was playing at the Casino Theatre, seven blocks from Halloran's, and had showings seven days a week starting at 1 P.M., including one at midnight. We arrived a few minutes early for the 7:15, and when I paid for the tickets, Cornelia said, "Why, thank you, Wyatt. I'd bat my eyes at you if I was thirty years younger." At the concession stand we each purchased a box of buttered popcorn, and Cornelia a box of bonbons, too. The usher escorted us until Cornelia said, "I'll sit right here, on the aisle." I sat next to her. The theater was quite crowded.

There was a Movietone newsreel to start things. This was followed by two Looney Tunes cartoons. One was a Bugs Bunny and Elmer Fudd called *What's Opera, Doc?* in which Elmer sings in Wagnerian tones, "Kill the wabbit! Kill the wabbit!"

Then *49th Parallel* came on screen. Look, it wasn't a great movie by any means, though it had a lot of witty repartee and such, and parts were truly laughable, like how the crew of the German U-boat—*U-37*—all spoke British English. I suppose they couldn't get authentic German actors for those roles, and why offer good money to the devil? But they might at least have required that the actors they did hire try their best to sound German. Maybe they thought even fake German accents were too painful to bear in 1941. Who knows?

Basically, what happens is, *U-37* has wandered up the St. Lawrence River, gets thrown so far off course that it's finally stranded in Hudson's Bay—icebergs all around—where it's sighted, strafed and bombarded by Canadian planes, and finally sunk. Some of the crew is killed, but the captain and others manage to escape and hide out in isolated villages, on the lam, and from there the story contains all sorts of adventures. In the end, good triumphs over evil.

Like I said, I wasn't much taken by *49th Parallel.* I do remember the first ten or so minutes quite vividly, however. *U-37* torpedoes a passenger ship in the St. Lawrence. It takes survivors on deck, the Nazi captain questions a few, and then they are set free, sent off in life rafts. *U-37* slices down into the water and disappears, and soon a rescue plane is seen approaching. Happy result—for those Canadians, anyway. Right then and there I realized that this incident depicted on screen would have had to take place before 1940, or maybe in 1940, because not long after that, U-boats didn't pick up survivors. I'd learned that from a newspaper article on the wall of my uncle's shed.

In the audience during *49th Parallel* there'd been the occasional hissing and booing. And I heard Cornelia laugh and weep and say "Bastards" a few times. On the walk back to her hotel, I discovered she'd already put things into balance. "Well, I won't see that one again," she said. "But I got something from it."

It was only a movie story, so not entirely dedicated to the claims of fact, Marlais—I know that. And there was one particular line of dialogue that was definitely false to history, and to prove it you just have to look at a framed photograph behind the bar at Rigolo's Pub right here in Halifax.

See, when *49th Parallel* begins, the camera zooms in on a map of Canada, and then the St. Lawrence River looms large, and then we see *U-37* cut the surface, sinister as all hell. While it cruises along, the captain tries to work up historical gloating and excitement—of a Nazi sort—in his crew. "You'll be the first of the German forces to set foot on Canadian soil. The first of thousands."

Yet if you study the black-and-white photograph in Rigolo's, you'll see three men in their early twenties standing at the bar having a grand old time, all happy-go-lucky and clinking mugs. They have fishermen's caps on. They are wearing thick fishermen's sweaters and looking directly into the camera. What's more, someone—the photographer, maybe, or the pub owner—has circled the face of the man in the absolute bull's-eye center of the photograph, his big round face, dimples, strong chin and eyes heavy-lidded from drink.

A line runs in ink from the circle down to the lower right-hand corner of the photograph, where these words are written: *Nazi U-boat navigator Wernor Timm, U-69, the Laughing Cow, October 12, 1939.* You'll remember, Marlais, the *Laughing Cow* had sunk the ferry *Caribou*, on which Constance had been a passenger.

I learned from the newspapers that before the successful crackdown on U-boats—before thick-link fences were submerged in the harbor—the German crews used to anchor offshore (some people said near Peggy's Cove) and make their way into Halifax. They went to pubs, movies and restaurants, telling everyone they were Swedes off a Swedish freighter, or Norwegians, or some such lie.

As it happened, this Wernor Timm had stepped out some nights with a Haligonian named Wilma Raymond. People had seen them together, but nobody would ever have known Timm's true identity except for the fact that on their last night together, Timm got drunk and told Wilma everything. He even proposed marriage! She refused him, and as she later said, "He stumbled out of my apartment and just disappeared into the streets."

Wilma Raymond was the niece of the bartender at Rigolo's Pub. She was horrified to discover the photograph her uncle had put up behind the bar. There was Wernor Timm, big as life! She was so ashamed of having consorted with a German U-boat officer it took her another few days to work up the courage to tell her uncle what she knew. Of course by that time the *Laughing Cow* was long gone.

Once he knew the facts, Wilma's uncle wrote Timm's name and rank on the photograph. Soon word got out that a U-boat navigator had come and gone undetected, and this sent a current of anxiety through the city. The photograph was reproduced on the front page of the *Mail*. Pub owners now asked for identification before serving customers, except for those they were already familiar with. The newspaper said that Wilma Raymond left Halifax "to visit relatives in Saskatchewan." I bet she did.

Well, if only the poster slogan "Loose lips sink ships" would have worked in reverse, and the *Laughing Cow* had been ambushed at Peggy's Cove because of what Wernor Timm had revealed to Wilma Raymond, it would not have been in commission three years later, to sink the *Caribou*, and my aunt Constance might still be alive. Those were my thoughts after reading the whole account.

Anyway, there it was, a photograph proving the German military was on Canadian soil in 1939. I was in Rigolo's Pub just last week and saw the photograph again. It's by now an historical document of sorts, you might say.

But you have to look closely, quite closely, to notice who's standing at the far right end of the bar—Hans Mohring. Hans is deep in conversation with a man and a woman, probably students. It would've been his first semester at Dalhousie. Hans is holding a cigarette, and the woman has a cigarette dangling from her mouth.

After the movie, Cornelia and I sat in the small café-restaurant in the Dresden Arms Hotel and had tea, and she ate her last three bonbons from the cinema. "I've brought recent photographs Tilda sent of Marlais," she said. She pushed a manila envelope across the table. I slid the photographs out and there you were, Marlais! All of age seven, sitting at an outdoor table with five other children. There was a birthday cake on the table, and the birthday girl was blowing out the candles. You sat at the right side of the table, all dressed up, with your hair frizzed out like your mother's and a big smile and soulful expression on your face, like you were having a deep thought. The party looked like loads of fun.

In the second photograph you were standing alone with the sea in the background. On your right wrist you wore a bracelet made of paper angels. Maybe each of the girls invited to the party got one.

"You should go to Denmark, Wyatt," Cornelia said. "Why haven't you?"

"I can't afford the travel, but I put money away for Marlais every month. She has her own bank account in Halifax waiting for her. The money's there whenever she needs it, even if she needs it wired to Copenhagen. Tilda knows this."

"Generous, Wyatt, but not as important as visiting."

"It's how life's turned out."

"And you didn't help it turn out the way it did, right?"

"Okay, I have your opinion now, Cornelia. Maybe you'd care to tell me what Tilda includes in her letters to you, generally speaking."

"This and that. Mostly news of Marlais, her school, her friends, what it's like to live with the Mohrings, what it's been like in Denmark after the war, this and that. She writes well, Tilda does, and always has."

"Tilda and I don't exchange letters. She's never sent me one and I've never sent her one."

"If everyone keeps waiting for the other, no letters will ever arrive, eh?"

"That's proven true so far."

"It's very stupid of you both. In fact, it's the goddamned stupidest, most selfish thing I've ever heard two people with a daughter doing."

We sat for a moment looking out onto the

street, and then I said, "Are Marlais and Tilda happy, do you think?"

"Let me put it this way," Cornelia said. "In her letters she refers to intimate things but doesn't describe things intimately. Something like that. As for *happy?* It sure sounds as if Marlais is having everything good offered by a Danish childhood, which isn't a Nova Scotia childhood, but who knows, maybe it's second best in the world. That's not too shabby. And if Marlais is having a wonderful childhood, then it only stands to reason Tilda is happy about that, right?"

"Something else, Cornelia. I haven't written one single letter to my uncle, either. I haven't been to visit him. And the truth? I don't want to visit him."

"I've been only twice. And my visits were three years apart. But do you know what Donald's doing in Dorchester Prison? They've got a wood shop there. And he's making sleds. I don't think toboggans, but definitely sleds, because he gave me one. I brought it back on the bus. It's upstairs from the bakery, on the floor of what formerly was Tilda and Hans's kitchen. Donald asked that I ship it on to Marlais. He seemed to have no sane idea what he was asking—no idea how much Tilda would despise getting that sled from him."

"I'm sure Reverend Witt—is he still reverend?"

"Till he drops dead at the pulpit."

"I'm sure he can find someone who'd like that sled. He doesn't have to say who built it."

"Good idea. I'll suggest it first thing when I get home."

We talked and talked, and I happened to mention the photograph in Rigolo's Pub, and right away Cornelia said she wanted to see it. "I've never stepped inside a pub in Halifax, not once," she said.

We walked to Rigolo's and stood at the bar where we had a clear view of the photograph. I ordered a beer and Cornelia a cognac, which she said she didn't really care for, but thought since she was in a pub she should order something exotic. However, she was so taken aback by the photograph, so disturbed by it, she not only gulped down the first cognac but had a second straightaway.

"Wyatt, I wonder if anyone but you and me recognize Hans Mohring in that photograph," she said. "I mean, knows his actual name. Hundreds must've at least looked at it, eh? Of course, those German sailors are front and center, so who'd really notice which people are in the background. But what's strange is that, as I'm standing here staring at it, I see different Germans. There's the ones who did harm and Hans who didn't. And I imagine all of them are at the bottom of the sea now."

"You know, Cornelia, I read in the *Mail* that the

Laughing Cow was sunk off the coast of France in 1944."

"I heard they built a memorial statue in Port aux Basques and survivors of the *Caribou* meet there every year for a reunion."

Cornelia had three more cognacs. She kept looking at the photograph, trying to keep it in focus. Finally, she said, "Wyatt, I can't be in here one more minute." She was so wobbly we had to take a taxi, even just the short distance to her hotel.

At about eight o'clock the next morning, my telephone rang. When I picked up, Cornelia said, "Me and my headache will meet you downstairs at my hotel for breakfast. How about fifteen minutes?"

It was raining. I threw on a sweater and slacks, put on my raincoat, took my umbrella and hurried over to the Dresden Arms. I found Cornelia at a window-side table. "I ordered scones and coffee," she said. "As for the scones, I'm not optimistic."

"You get breakfast free in this hotel. Don't forget that."

"Believe me, if I don't forget one thing all day, it'll be that."

The waitress brought us each a blueberry scone. The scones had been heated and pats of butter came along on the plates. Cornelia said, "Well, mine looks like a scone."

I took a bite and said, "It's the one hundred fifty-fifth best one I've ever had, Cornelia."

"The first one hundred fifty-four being mine."

"Your arithmetic is correct."

She ate her scone, drank some coffee and said, "You know why I like this scone? Mainly because I didn't have to make it. In fact, you just saw me eat the very first scone I've eaten outside of Middle Economy, which includes ones my grandmother and mother made, and mine. There it is, then. I've still never been to Paris. I've still never been to London. And here I'm of a certain advanced age, and this was my first scone ever in Halifax."

It was Saturday. I walked Cornelia to the 11:05 bus out of the city, the same run on which Tilda had first made the acquaintance of Hans Mohring.

Speaking of birthday parties again, that same evening I'd been invited to a party for Evie Michaels's daughter Ellen's fifth birthday. The party was held at six P.M. at the Michaelses' house on St. Harris Street, not far from Halifax North Common. Evie's husband, William—he's a custodian at Halifax General Hospital—was there, and ten other girls, all Ellen's kindergarten classmates. The girls had gotten gussied up, and Evie had made paper corsages to pin to their dresses. She served peanut butter and jelly sand-wiches followed by a chocolate birthday cake and vanilla ice cream. A balloon floated above each girl's chair, tied to it with string. They all had a great rollicking time. Evie had invited the gaffing crew, and all of us showed up. Ellen got a ton of presents, and each time she opened a box, she tied the ribbon in her hair, so by the end she had them streaming out like fireworks. William had borrowed a camera and took a lot of photographs, mostly of the children, naturally, but a few of the grownups, too. At one point Ellen Michaels got so excited that she stuck her fingers right into her slice of birthday cake and then rubbed frosting all over her face and let their mutt Handy lick it off, and nobody cared. After the cake, Evie set out two metal tubs and the children bobbed for apples. Rules are rules, and they had to clasp their hands behind their backs, so of course got their faces soaked. Evie dried them off with a bath towel. When the children went into the parlor to listen to a fright show on the radio— there were two fright shows on Saturday evenings—the gaffing crew got into the spirit of things. One by one, we bobbed for apples. Evie Michaels said, "Look at this! Us expert gaffers of Halifax Harbor and not one apple's been lifted out of the water!"

The children had all left by eight o'clock. Ellen went to bed by nine, and then Evie got inspired to make a big pot of spaghetti. We could see that she seemed quite happy to provide this meal. It was just spaghetti, butter and sprigs of parsley, and two bottles of red wine, but enough to go around. At the table Sebastian Firth said, "Evie, that was thoughtful of you and Bill to put warm water in those tubs. You don't want children bobbing for apples in freezing water, no sir. That's one childhood memory I have. For some reason, whenever me and my friends bobbed for apples, my mother always put cold water in the tub."

"I suppose she couldn't think of everything," Evie said.

Those apples floated in the tubs until after our late supper. Finally, Evie smoothed out the napkins from the party, lined them up on the dining room table and set the apples on them to dry.

I was the last guest to leave. When I put on my coat, Evie said, "Hey, Wyatt, come look at this." She led me into the parlor. It had bookshelves all around.

She pointed out the set of encyclopedias. "It took a full week, but William and I dried them out individually by the woodstove. A lot of pages stuck together, and you can see that some bindings warped, but my children use them every week for homework. Neighbor kids, too. It's known up and down the block we've got a complete set."

"The effort was worth it, Evie," I said.

"Thank you," she said. "Say, Wyatt, why not take two or three apples back to your hotel?"

Conversations with
Reese Mac Isaac

L IFE WENT ALONG, Marlais. Life just goes
 along. I'm never late for work. Never late,
that's one thing. The other is that every Sunday I
listen to the Cavalcade of Radio programs. I tune
it in from Buffalo. There's *The Jack Benny Hour*
and *Our Miss Brooks* and a detective show,
Dragnet, another one about a gumshoe, *Yours
Truly, Johnny Dollar* and a mystery fright show
called *Lights Out.* These are called nostalgia programs now, but they remain my favorites. Last
but not least, there's *Classical Hour.* Sometimes
on *Classical Hour* they celebrate a composer's
birthday by playing as much of his work as they
can fit into an hour.

What else? Fridays after work, for years now, I
stop by Ballade & Fugue. Randall Webb's store is
now on Argyle Street near City Hall. In 1955 he
married a Dutch-born woman named Helen
Duoma, whom he called his best customer. Helen
once remarked that almost their entire courtship
took place in the store. She works for the
International Refugee Organization, mostly as a
translator. For years she was a colleague of a
woman famously nicknamed "German Sister"—

her real name's Sister Florence Kelly—at Pier 21. Pier 21 is where immigrants are legally processed and welcomed to Canada. German Sister worked with a group called Sisters of Service. Her nickname became a kind of joke, because how did someone with the Irish last name of Kelly come to interpret in the German language? Truth was, Sister Florence Kelly was born and raised in Nova Scotia. She'd become fluent in German in university, is all. Nevertheless, Helen Duoma said that every so often a newly arrived German claimed to recognize exactly which part of Germany that German Sister was raised in, just from her accent.

Helen and Randall have a son now, Talbot. The boy's full birth-certificate name is Talbot Duoma Frederic Webb, the Frederic after Frédéric Chopin, Helen's and Randall's favorite composer. Randall splits his time about equally between his house and the store, so we don't socialize much except in those two places. Helen and Randall always invite me for Canadian Thanksgiving and for Christmas, and that's always pleasant. We spend New Year's Eve together, too, and without fail that's the night Helen and Randall separately ask, "When are you getting married, Wyatt?" And each time, I never know if they'd agreed beforehand to ask it.

Ballade & Fugue is open Fridays and Saturdays until ten P.M., and the other nights until six P.M.

Randall's got plaster busts of the great composers on a shelf along the back wall (no Canadians). I sit on the sofa and listen to various gramophone records as customers come and go. Sometimes I attend the cash register while Randall and Helen have supper in a restaurant, usually at the Rex Hotel. On those occasions Randall always returns to the store within an hour and a half. For my birthday every year they give me a recording. This year, for my forty-third, it was Arcangelo Corelli, Violin Sonata opus 5—my first Corelli—and I went right back to my hotel and listened to it twice through.

However, it's not as if life hasn't offered some recent surprises. For instance, there's a pawnshop on Salter Street just off Hollis. It's called J. P.'s Pawn, the proprietor being J. P. MacPherson, who arrived through Pier 21 from Scotland. I couldn't tell you what the J. P. stands for. I'd passed by this shop more times than I can count. I'd looked in through the window and seen J. P. chatting up a customer. Seen the sign over her counter that reads NO BARGAINING—NO EXCEPTIONS! From what I'd noticed, she was not quite fifty, somewhat thick at the middle, with a shock of reddish hair and a no-nonsense, determined look. Then again, I'd never set foot in her pawnshop until about a year ago. On a freezing Saturday afternoon I was ten steps from her awning, which was sagging under snow—she should have rolled it up—when I saw her wielding a snow shovel out front. Suddenly she slipped and fell hard to the gutter. I stepped right up and said, "Can I help you there?"

"I don't know, can you?" she said.

She allowed me to take her by the elbow and help lift her to her feet. The sleeves of her overcoat were soaked with dirty slush. "Thank you," she said. "As you can see, we've got a lot of fine merchandise in the window." Quick back to business like that. When J. P. MacPherson went into her shop, my eyes immediately fell on a display of five radios, front and center in the window. And I confess, Marlais, that even at my age, I almost burst into tears right there on the public sidewalk. There was an Emerson Snow White model, a Majestic with a Charlie McCarthy decal, an RCA from the San Francisco Expo, an RCA Victor La Siesta and a Stewart Warner set with a decal of the Dionne quintuplets.

Now, I realized that any number of these models had been manufactured. But I went inside and said to J. P. MacPherson, "I'd like to purchase all those radios in the window."

"This far away from Christmas?" she asked.

"They wouldn't be for gifts."

"I can take them out for your inspection, one by one or all at once," she said. "Which do you prefer?"

"All at once," I said.

"Fine."

She lined up the radios on the counter. I looked them over. "By any chance were there more radios brought in by the same person on the same day?" I asked. "Like these—not your everyday radios."

"That's short guesswork, all right," she said. "Yes. As a matter of fact there's more out back. Each and every one of real character. I take it you're a collector of sorts."

"May I see the others, please?"

It took about ten minutes for J. P. to produce twenty-three more radios, which now completely covered the counter.

"I've had these for quite a while," she said. "A number sold quickly. Then never sold, never sold, never sold, so I stuck them in back. I'd just put them on display again last week. Lucky me."

"Lucky both of us," I said.

"The man who originally brought these in, brought in fifty-eight radios altogether," she said. "You don't forget that, I guess."

"I know your sign says no bargaining, so I won't haggle over price," I said. "But I want to suggest a trade."

"What sort?" she asked.

"I'll agree to buy all twenty-eight if you tell me who pawned them in the first place."

She didn't hesitate an instant. She opened a drawer in a metal file cabinet and after a quick search lifted out an invoice. "Are you police?"

"My name is Wyatt Hillyer," I said. "I can give you a telephone number to call to verify that I'm a detritus gaffer for the City of Halifax. Hold the radios for me. I'd give you a down payment right now. How's that?"

"So that's what you people are officially called, detritus gaffers," she said. "I've always wondered. I've seen your crew out in the harbor."

"We're pretty noticeable, I guess."

"Listen," she said, "if you ever find something that you deem pawnable—"

"We officially have to report everything," I said. "Most of what we find is broken or otherwise useless, but not all of it. For instance, we fished out a complete set of encyclopedias."

"No kidding," she said. "Well, you know where my shop is, just in case."

She studied the invoice a moment and said, "These radios were pawned by a Mr. Paulson Lessard, resident at 56 Robie Street, Halifax."

"Thank you," I said. "How about what I've got in my wallet, eighteen dollars, as a down payment?"

"That's a lot of money to carry around," she said. "Just come back Monday and it'll be in one bill of sale, what say?"

"I'm going to take the rare day off work to do just that," I said. "I'll start to feel in ill health when, do you think?"

J. P. laughed a little, like she was pleased to

participate in such harmless chicanery, and said, "Well, Mr. Hillyer, you know your superiors and I don't. But to be convincing, I'd claim you woke to a raging fever about three A.M. Monday morning. *Woke to a raging fever*—be sure to use those exact words. If you're worried about being caught out on the street Monday, I can send my husband, Oliver Tecosky, over to wherever's your address. He'll have the radios and you can give him the money and sign the bill of sale."

"A pawnshop that makes house calls," I said. "That's something."

"Let me write down your address," she said.

"I've been at the Waverly Hotel for six months or so," I said. "Two Seventy-four Barrington."

She wrote down the address. "Let's see, banks open at nine, so how's eleven A.M.?"

"I'll be in the lobby."

"I can tell you're good for the money, Mr. Hillyer," she said.

"And I can tell you're good for a fair price," I said.

"Let me add another item of interest. I'm making one hundred percent profit off these radios, due to the fact that Mr. Lessard's met his Maker."

"How do you know that?"

"I generally believe the obituaries in the *Mail*."

"Not every day a man pawns fifty-eight radios, eh?"

"It was memorable," she said. "You know what else? When Mr. Lessard first brought these radios in, he said he was going to use the money to travel down to New York City to stay in a hotel and go in person to see a live orchestra. The such-and-such orchestra, I can't recall."

Marlais, at that moment I had unforgiving thoughts toward Paulson Lessard, the cunning old bastard. I kept them to myself, though. J. P. didn't have to suffer them.

The following Monday, as promised, I met Oliver Tecosky, nice man, in the lobby, and after a few excursions up and down in the lift, within half an hour every last one of the radios was on my bed. He told me the price, I paid him in full, and he left, the whole time maybe ten words spoken between us. I percolated coffee and the telephone rang. I thought maybe it was Oliver Tecosky, that he'd forgotten a radio, but it happened to be the Waverly's accountant, Frances Banner. She reminded me that I was late three weeks in my rent. "That's not like you, Mr. Hillyer," she said. "Usually—according to my records, you're usually no more than two weeks late."

"Well, I've just put out a lot of money for twenty-eight radios," I said.

"Why on earth?"

"So I'm a bit overdrawn. Which means I can't pay my rent just yet," I said. "But I can put in overtime at work, and that's guaranteed."

"My call was an order from management, Mr. Hillyer," she said.

"So, Mr. Brockman asked you to call me."

"Yes, Mr. Brockman," she said, "the hotel manager."

"Can I speak to him, please?"

"It won't do any good, Mr. Hillyer. I've made inquiries around town, and Mr. Brockman suggests the Homestead Hotel at 6 Duke Street. Their rent is twelve per month more reasonable than ours, if you catch my meaning."

"This isn't good news."

"It could be worse," she said. "Mr. Brockman's not charging you this month's rent."

"That's very decent of him," I said.

"The Homestead has a room reserved under your name. Mr. Brockman took the liberty."

"The fact of why he had to call them couldn't be much of a recommendation for me," I said.

"It's not so undignified as all that, Mr. Hillyer," she said. "You're hardly the first we've made such an arrangement for. And hotels in Halifax try to accommodate each other. Whenever possible."

I needed only two days to move. I was now in room 301 at the Homestead Hotel, which was a bit shabbier than the Waverly, but my room looked out through clean windows onto Duke Street, and there was a closet spacious enough to hold the radios. The bed had a good mattress, and my neighbors on either side, and above and below, were fairly quiet. I'd persuaded two bellmen from the Waverly to help me carry my possessions across town. I bought them each a beer at Rigolo's.

A week later, I'd come back from a long, exhausting day of gaffing in rough weather. Still in my work clothes, I sat at my one table, eating halibut, green beans and carrot sticks off the hot plate and listening to Corelli, the gramophone turned low, when I had the idea to telephone Cornelia. It may be that I wanted to hear a familiar voice, even though there may not be much to say. Just to speak with an old friend. I tapped the receiver buttons half a dozen times and the switchboard operator said, "How may I help you, room 301?"

"I'd like to call a Mrs. Cornelia Tell in Middle Economy," I said. "I have the number right here. Should I read it to you?"

There was a long silence. Maybe the switchboard operator was new on the job, didn't know how to connect a long-distance call. But finally she said, "Wyatt Hillyer, I noticed your name in the hotel registry."

"I beg your pardon?"

"It's your old neighbor Reese," she said. "Reese Mac Isaac."

I can guarantee you, Marlais, that I almost fell off my chair. It wasn't so much that Reese was

274

still living in Halifax. In fact, I thought I'd seen her a few times across some street I was walking on, and once through a restaurant window, but on those occasions I couldn't really be sure. More, it was the fact that she'd described herself as "your old neighbor." As if a whole world of incidents and experiences had been reduced to that.

"You know, I saw you that day," she said. "How many years back? You were standing with two people quite a bit older than you, and I was boarding the *Victoria*, going to New York City. This wasn't long after Katherine and Joe had died and I was being hounded by newspaper reporters and had to get out for a while. I stayed in New York only a short time. Foolish me and all of my foolish ambitions, eh? I actually considered trying to find acting work, but when I consulted the trade papers, there were hundreds of people looking for the same kind of work. You can't imagine. I didn't know how to go about things there. I walked around a lot and sat in my hotel room and came back within a couple of weeks. Job to job to job—and I ended up here at the Homestead about two years ago."

"You've traveled widely in Halifax," I said. "Same as me, hotel to hotel."

"That's right."

"It seems being a switchboard operator suits you," I said.

"I need a job and I know this job," she said. "In that sense it suits me."

"My parents and I saw you in *Widow's Walk*."

"Were you surprised I wasn't nominated for an Academy Award?"

"As it turned out, what surprised me was what you meant to my mother and my father," I said. "*That's* what surprised me."

"It surprised us three as well," she said.

"Yeah, it surprised them both off a bridge."

There was a long silence.

"I'll try and connect your call now, Wyatt," she said.

In about ten minutes Reese Mac Isaac called back and said, "I let it ring thirty times or more, but your Cornelia Tell didn't pick up. Shall I try again later?"

"Maybe tomorrow," I said.

"I'm not supposed to use the switchboard for personal business," she said, "but I'm in my same house, 60 Robie. Just for your information."

"Goodbye, switchboard operator," I said.

"Did you ever know that old Paulson Lessard got a public notice and was fined for disturbing the peace?"

"I'm not on speaking terms with Mr. Lessard," I said.

"Nobody is, since he's dead and buried, Wyatt," she said.

"He pawned off my mother's radios."

"That was unkind."

"It was out-and-out theft."

"Him receiving a fine and citation, it's a small piece of news, I know. I mean, we've been through a war, haven't we? It's a small, small piece of news, but what happened was, when you moved out of town, you apparently had arranged for Paulson Lessard to look after your house. You gave him a key."

"That's true."

"Well, one Sunday night he had all of Katherine's radios blasting music at top volume. More noise than if a ghost walked through a zoo. You see, I'd only just come back from New York and was asleep when it happened. I woke up and looked through my kitchen window, but I didn't see anyone in your house. A neighbor from across the street called the police. I went out on my porch. The neighbor was standing on your front lawn. I wasn't on speaking terms with her. Nobody was on speaking terms with me, really. Except newspaper reporters, and what they printed was unspeakable, all sorts of trash about me and Katherine, me and Joe. I was even offered tabloid money to tell my true story, so to speak."

"The harlot's true story," I said.

"Yes, harlot that I was," she said. "Anyway, a police car arrived and two officers knocked on your door. By this time, maybe ten or a dozen neighbors were on your lawn. I was looking out my kitchen window again. An officer stood on your porch and shined his flashlight in through your dining room window, and that's when I caught a glimpse of Mr. Lessard standing on your dining room table, naked as a jaybird. Not a lovely sight. And he was waving a spatula over his head like he was conducting an orchestra."

"What happened then?"

"They opened the front door and walked in and had a sit-down with Paulson Lessard," Reese said. "He'd wrapped the tablecloth around himself. In the end, he was charged only with disturbing the peace."

"I guess that didn't improve the reputation of my house any," I said.

"I'll say this for him, though," Reese said, "he watered the plants. He kept the lawn clipped and the snow off your driveway. He was old, but he got up on a ladder and washed windows."

"He pawned my mother's radios," I said. "But I got them back."

"From the pawnshop?" Reese said.

"That's right."

"Oh, my, you had to purchase your own heirlooms."

"That's one way to look at it."

"Wyatt, my shift is four to midnight, seven days a week, though Sundays I might shut down the switchboard at ten. Management allows me that. So if you want to avoid me, and why wouldn't you, don't ask me to connect a call during those hours, okay?"

"I might have to move hotels," I said.

"That would work, too," she said.

I heard the switchboard's electric *buzz-buzz-buzz* in the background—Reese had to connect a call but didn't put me on hold. She just rang off.

When I thought about it, it didn't seem all that big a coincidence, Reese Mac Isaac working in the same hotel where I rented a room. Being a switchboard operator had been Reese's one steady employment. Most of the hotels in Halifax had switchboards. If I could change hotels so often, why not Reese? That's how I saw it.

But you know what, Marlais? Unless Lenore Teachout had been on the third-party line at the Homestead, pen and paper in hand, and later provided me with transcripts, it's otherwise impossible for me to remember all of the conversations—dozens—that I had with Reese Mac Isaac over the next six or seven months.

I can assure you, however, that for a long time we never spoke face-to-face. If we saw each other in the lobby, we allowed for only the slightest acknowledgment. Hello, a half-smile, sometimes not even that. A few days would go by, no conversation, then we might talk for upward of an hour, depending on whether other people in the hotel required Reese's services. But there was one conversation I definitely want to tell you about, and here goes.

Simply put, I was sick and tired of not knowing—not knowing and not knowing—very much about the day my parents jumped from those bridges. So one night at about ten P.M. I said, "Reese, did you speak with my mother or my father on the morning before they died?"

I suppose it's to her credit that Reese didn't hesitate to answer. I was grateful for that. "Not that morning, no," she said. "The night before, I did speak with Katherine, but not with Joe. I was going to spend time with Joe the next night, but there wasn't a next night."

"No, there wasn't," I said.

"Wyatt, do you want to know what Katherine and I spoke about?"

"It would allow me to stop tormenting myself wondering."

"Well, Katherine was in a philosophical way. We talked about the impossibility of life. No, that's not quite it. More to the point, we talked about the impossibility of *us*." Reese stopped, seeming to collect herself. Then: "I'm just going to say this, all right, Wyatt?"

"Just say it."

"The impossibility of us having a love. A love for each other. I mean physical, Wyatt. And I mean all other aspects, too. Oh, how we could talk with each other. Especially about theater and movies, I suppose. But about most anything, really. We spoke about—forgive me—her marriage. Your father seldom spoke about the marriage. Then again, he didn't cry wolf, either. If he did say something, he'd already given it some thought. About the thing itself, and if he should tell me. And he never once—not once—directed a harsh word toward Katherine. Joseph was discreet like that.

"As I said, Katherine was in a philosophical mood that night. We spoke about the impossibility of a person fitting a secret life within the life they already have. Wanting desperately to hang on to that secret life, because it's the life that touches you the deepest. Believe me, Wyatt, she suffered real anguish, because her secret life touched her deepest. This can't be easy to hear, but you asked."

"Of course, you had two secret lives, didn't you, Reese," I said.

"Yes, and they had the same address, didn't they," Reese said. "Right next door."

"Three times as lonely, I bet."

"It wasn't mathematics, Wyatt."

"Did you talk a long time with my mother that night?"

"Through two pots of tea and some other things to drink," Reese said. "It was Joe's night to have his typewriter shop open late. So we talked and talked, Katherine and I. It's common wisdom, but a rare actual experience in life, that if you find someone you can truly talk with, you can love that person. We declared certain things to each other. No promises were made, but anguished declarations were stated. And what tears me apart every night of my life is that I'm convinced late that night Katherine confessed everything to Joseph. She was so much at wits' end. What's more, I'm equally convinced that Joseph then confessed everything to Katherine.

"They were two good people in a terrible situation." Reese cried a little, then said, "Sorry."

"No need to apologize," I said.

"Well, there is a need," she said. "But I don't know. I just don't know. I don't know what they said to each other. And the truth is, I heard about the bridges the same way everyone else did. On the radio."

I set down the telephone on its cradle. But Reese rang me right back.

"You asked me a question, Wyatt," she said. "Now I have one to ask you. Am I correct in thinking you hold a poisonous grudge against me? That's my question. Do you hate me because you believe Katherine and Joe jumping off those bridges was somehow my fault?"

"And what would it matter to you if I did hate you?"

"I don't expect sympathy. I don't deserve it. But I've gotten a lot of nasty letters—unsigned, by the way, a lot of them. Good Christian judgments, but they don't sign their letters."

"Sounds bad."

"Just please answer my question."

"I hated you and hated what my parents did. But no longer. Let's leave it at that."

"All right. That's something at least. Thank you."

"Ten thousand Haligonians reading about it. How was I supposed to get any peace about what happened? I still don't know how to find any peace about it."

"In my own small way I was happy for you, Wyatt, that your aunt and uncle took you in. That you didn't get hounded."

"It's not like life didn't have other things in store."

"Yes, I know. I read the newspapers. The murder of that German student was on page two. And there was your uncle's name. There was your name. And I thought, My God, that's Katherine and Joe's boy."

And that was the third-to-last time I spoke with Reese Mac Isaac.

The second-to-last took place on the evening of November 9, 1962. Halifax had recently experienced one of the nastiest storms in memory. It lasted a good three days. Gale-force winds, hail, rain and sleet. There had even been bulletins warning of water spouts—water spouts were bad news, and I recall being told that in 1940, a member of the gaffing crew, Paul Syberg, was a victim of a water spout, which more or less ambushed a tugboat he'd been working on. It whirlpooled, flung him overboard and nearly capsized the tug.

On one of the relatively calm days during the November storm, my crew took the opportunity to get some gaffing done—taking precautions, of course—and Hermione Rexroth and I had been assigned to the waters close by Pier 21. The *Cascania* was tied up at the pier. Hermione commented on just how high up on the *Cascania*'s hull the waves had pasted slick ribbons of kelp.

In her spare time—she wasn't married—Hermione was something of an historian of Pier 21 and of immigration in general. "The harshest thing, to my mind," she had once said to me, "the most shameful? It was a long time before Jewish displaced persons—refugees, orphans, all that—were welcomed to Canada. Here we fought the war, Canada did, but the government wouldn't take in the people who had it worst. Well, the War Orphans Project—what, 1947, thereabouts? That allowed Jews in—if I have my numbers right, between 1947 and 1949, about eleven hundred Jewish orphans and fifteen thousand Jewish refugees were allowed in."

"That's all good deeds there," I said.

"Finally—sure," she said. "But it was late.

Very, very late, Wyatt. Besides, Halifax wasn't all saints in other ways, too. If you go up to the sporting club, corner of Gottingen and Gerrish? You'll find JEWS NOT ALLOWED stenciled by the front gate. Sure, they've since scrubbed it. But look closely—it's legible. Same for the public swimming pool, Northpark and Cornwallis."

"Jesus, look right now at all those people on the gangway," I said.

"All Hungarians, according to the newspaper," Hermione said.

"And listen to the bagpipes," I said. "Rain or shine for how many years now? A piper's always there to greet every ship."

"I'd bet that those Hungarians, for better or worse, have never heard bagpipes before."

I couldn't figure out the reason, but all that day I'd battled a terrible headache, sometimes to the point of blurred vision. And late one afternoon, I threw up my hands to fend off what I thought was a seagull, but it wasn't anything. With that incident, I should've called it a day. Instead, I said, "Hermione, let's take an hour break, all right?" We rowed over and tied up to a tug that had escorted the *Cascania*, climbed the ladder on deck and had hot tea with the four-man crew, fellows we knew well, and it was a blessed reprieve from the biting cold. From the wheelhouse, all of us watched immigrants—suitcases in hand, children alongside, sleet sticking to hats and scarves—move slowly down the gangway. It must've been the headache having its strangest effect of all, plus the sleet somewhat obscuring the view, the steam out of the tug's galley pipe, too—I don't know what all—but, Marlais, I thought I saw your mother moving slowly along the gangway, and a girl of about sixteen, which would've been your age at the time, was huddled against her.

Of course, Marlais, it wasn't you and Tilda. Of course not. It was some kind of mirage, you might say. Hermione noticed my expression and said, "Wyatt, you don't look so well, my friend." I said I thought I'd better see a doctor. I lay down on a cot below deck, covered by a coarse blanket. Believe me, you have to be bone tired to be able to sleep on a tugboat next to an enormous ship, a hundred seagulls complaining by the minute, the tug's engine running. Yet I did sleep. I didn't even wake when the tug tied up at Purdy's Wharf. Hermione had to wake me. She climbed down, got into our boat and rowed it in, and I went directly ashore and walked home. I couldn't shake the mirage out of my head, though. I mean, Marlais, it was the strangest thing.

I was still rooming at the Homestead Hotel, and when I stepped into the lobby, no doubt looking more like a rain-soaked dog than a human being, I didn't glance left or right but instead marched straight to the electric lift and took it up to my room, whereas normally I would've taken the stairs. I soaked in the bathtub, the water as hot as the hotel could possibly make it—tenants had recently complained—and then got dressed in trousers and a shirt that I'd ironed myself. When the telephone rang, it was Reese Mac Isaac. "Wyatt," she said with some alarm, "didn't you even notice? Your friend Cornelia Tell's in the lobby. She's been there at least five hours, Wyatt." I rang off and hurried down the stairs to the lobby. In the corner, on a sofa near an enormous potted plant, Cornelia was asleep under her coat. Her overnight bag was on the floor at her feet.

I lightly shook Cornelia awake. "Oh, Wyatt, thank God you're here," she said. She sat up and took my hands in hers. "Our Tilda died in Denmark, Wyatt. It was sudden and I don't know from what."

"Was she ill?"

"All I know is what the wire said. Tilda passed two days ago and is buried in Copenhagen."

"Wire sent from whom to whom?"

"Sent from your daughter to the post office. Reverend Witt happened to be posting a letter. He signed for it."

Cornelia fell into a kind of exhausted sobbing, then said, "You know, Wyatt, all the time she was growing up—and she half grew up in my bakery, eh?—I'd look at Tilda and think, She'll never leave Nova Scotia, not our Tilda. And now she's permanently in Denmark, of all places. Goes to show what I know, doesn't it? Shows what I know, which is nothing."

I tried to contact you, Marlais. I made every possible effort to get in touch. I hadn't before, but I did then. Cornelia gave me your address—did my wires arrive? Did my letter arrive? They couldn't have sufficed, but did they ever arrive?

In time I learned that Tilda had died on her way back from posting the first payment for the Learn Your Library program in Copenhagen, a six-week course, taught in both Danish and English, for people interested in becoming librarians. Cornelia also told me that, a few weeks before she died, Tilda had been in hospital for an infection of the lining of her heart.

Cornelia took a bus home that same evening.

The next Sunday I attended Harbor Methodist, and while all the other parishioners listened to the sermon, sang hymns and said prayers, I kept my own counsel in the backmost pew and held a private funeral service for your mother. For a moment, I had the startling worry that her obituary might appear only in Danish, in a Copenhagen newspaper. But as it turned out, Cornelia had written one and given it to Reverend Witt, and it appeared in his church's bulletin. It was nicely composed.

At church, I desperately wanted to avoid all the sanctimonious crap—sorry—usually heard at funerals. I began what I thought was a silent prayer, "May Tilda Hillyer rest in peace. She was the best person imaginable. She was beautiful," until I realized that I was mumbling out loud. Several worshipers on either side of me moved farther away.

You were still in the world, Marlais, very much in the world. But otherwise, in every other possible way, life felt disreputable and collapsed. After church, I spent seven straight hours out in the boat, gaffing in Halifax Harbor. The rain had stopped. The wind was manageable. As usual there was a cormorant on each buoy. I took hardly anything into the boat. A lady's hat, the feathers frayed and matted against the silk band. I wondered, had the wind swept it from a Hungarian leaving the *Cascania*? A toy water pistol. A window, its double panes cracked into spider webs, but the frame intact. Around dusk, near Purdy's Wharf, I saw a flock of gray geese descending. They are here year-round. I followed them in.

The last and final time I spoke with Reese Mac Isaac was on the following Sunday morning. No church for me that day. There was a knock on my hotel room door, and when I opened it, there stood Reese, dressed smartly, as always.

"I know, I'm showing my age," she said.

"How can I help you, Reese?"

"Sunday mornings I visit Katherine and Joe's graves. I'm going there now. I thought you might accompany me. Just this once."

My begging off might only have led to her insistence—though maybe I wanted Reese to insist—and what purpose would be served by not going? So we walked to the cemetery together. We stood at my mother's grave a few minutes, my father's the same, and then walked back to the Homestead.

"Except for restaurants and the cinema," Reese said, "any place I visit, I don't stay very long. Come to think of it, maybe I'll be cremated, you know? I don't want to overstay my keep, not even in a cemetery."

Once I was done laughing, I said, "Reese, you sure don't hesitate to think out loud, do you? I'd imagine both my mother and father liked that quality."

Midweek, when I'd got back to my hotel, a hand-delivered letter was waiting for me. No return address. I sat on a couch in the lobby and read it.

Wyatt,

It was kind of you to go to the cemetery with me. My house is now put up for sale. I leave Halifax today by train. I've arranged a room with a distant cousin—said cousin has secured employment for me in the oldest hotel in Vancouver—need I mention what that employment is? So, there should be no concern that I've gone off to Hollywood! I wish for you a good life.

Reese Mac Isaac

A Possible Anodyne

MARLAIS, WELL INTO my twenty-sixth night in a row of writing to you, I realize I've sometimes raced over the years like an ice skater fleeing the devil on a frozen river. That's a phrase from one of Reverend Lundrigan's sermons. (I've attended five in the past six months at Harbor Methodist here in Halifax.) Still, what's been true of all the intervening time between 1948, when I last set eyes on you, and this very moment, 3:20 A.M., April 21, 1967, is that I've savored each and every morsel of knowledge about you I've been given. For example, during the years you attended that small, "progressive" (your mother's word) English-speaking school in Copenhagen, Cornelia Tell provided me with your report cards.

I was grateful to get them. The report cards had substance. Your mother had copied them out and mailed them to Cornelia at the bakery in the first place. I'd rung her up when the first one arrived. "Tilda asked me to forward it to you," Cornelia said. "But I'd probably have sent it without her permission." I read each one dozens of times. I still keep them in a separate envelope. News of how you performed in school was important to me. Yet as anyone but a complete fool knows, no child worth her salt ever reveals her entire character in school, no matter how deep her allegiance to teachers or textbooks, right? So all along I naturally wondered about my daughter's whole self. What did you get worried about? What was your sense of humor like? Everything, everything, everything. I had more selfish curiosities, too. Did your mother ever begin a sentence with "Your father"? You must've asked about me, and when you did, what did Tilda say? Was there sympathy, blame, or what? Did you ever see a photograph of me? I know that Cornelia sent one to you when you were ten. Did you ever receive the official City of Halifax portrait of my gaffing crew, maybe four years ago? I'd drawn a circle around my face.

When I read a report card, if a teacher's comment was in the least critical, I railed against it, though for all I knew it might've been accurate. For instance, I've just taken out a report card from when you were eleven years old: *Marlais Hillyer is intelligent—sometimes there's too much emphasis on words. Very good recall of facts— sometimes a rather snippy tone. Frequently laughs to herself—this puts fellow students off. Bold opinions—"If I started to ride horses, I'd probably stop admiring horses so much." At times offers theatrical, morbid excuses for being lazy—"Mother says if you assign me to sharpen*

*pencils again, she'll swallow poison."
Arithmetic—below standard. Excellent reader but
possessive about it—"I read a lot of books but
you'll never know their titles." Enthralled with
her own contradictions—does poorly in Danish
lessons, yet makes certain her teachers hear her
speaking it quite fluently on the playground.*

After your mother died, you began to write letters to Cornelia, though I imagine you were too
young to remember—do you?—what she looked
like. Or that you licked frosting from an outsized
wooden spoon in her bakery, or that she took you
for walks, or that you and Cornelia spent hours
drawing with crayons. Of course, writing her letters was picking up where your mother left off,
though I'd bet my last nickel you had your own
flair for it, Marlais.

Anyway, you kept Cornelia up to date, and in
turn she kept me up to date about my daughter.
"Secondhand news, sure," Cornelia would say,
"but whose fault is that? Count your blessings it's
news of Marlais at all." This past September I
learned that you'd taken a summer course and
graduated from a two-year degree program in
library science at Trinity College, Dublin.
Graduated at the top of your class! Reading of
that, I was allowed only a distant pride, but it was
pride nonetheless. My goodness—Nova Scotia,
Denmark, Ireland—you've already seen the
world.

Three-thirty, four, four-thirty, five in the morning, still April 11. I've just made coffee. Dawn light touching the window, the glass beaded up from last night's rain. Insomnia—the mind jumps around a bit. Just last week I was walking home with Tom Blackwell and Hermione Rexroth. We'd accomplished ten hours of gaffing in rough waters, eight of those mainly along Queen's Wharf, but also as far out as the mouth of Halifax Harbor. Add to that two hours of overtime across to Dartmouth. After work, it was still raining at a windy slant and so we kept our rain gear on. It was dark out, streetlamps were like frozen pale explosions in the mist, and we were heading to Rigolo's Pub. At one point, Hermione wanted to light a cigarette, and we found ourselves standing in front of a place called Museum Gallery. The window announced PHOTOGRAPHS OF WAR BRIDES.

"Hey, fellas," Hermione said, "let's stop in and take a look."

After a few deep draws, Hermione tossed her cigarette in the gutter and Tom and I followed her into the gallery. It was one big room painted white. There were five floor lamps and three woven rugs, the attempt being to make it like somebody's living room. There was a sizable crowd, people milling about, the women quite gussied up, some of the men wearing tuxedos. Fashion-wise, Hermione, Tom and I certainly stood out. There was a table with a white table-cloth, wine glasses, bottles of wine. "This is a fancy event," Hermione said.

"At least we didn't just gaff in sacks of fertilizer, like last week," Tom said, "or this gallery might've quickly lost some clientele, eh?"

"I didn't know you spoke French," Hermione said to Tom. "Isn't 'clientele' French?"

Tom looked at a wall of photographs. "Here I'm forty-five and still hoping to find a wife," he said. "But the women in these photographs are all taken."

"I bet that's where the word 'brides' comes in," Hermione said, grinning and handing Tom a glass of wine.

There were fifty-five photographs on exhibit. First thing I looked at was a chronological sequence consisting of four photographs, which followed a particular British woman—most of these war brides were from Britain, a smaller number were from France, a few were from Italy and Holland—from the moment she stepped from the gangway of the *Pasteur*, a luxury liner that had been converted into a warship, to her first meeting with her future husband, to their wedding, to being carried over the threshold. The caption to this sequence was "British sweetheart to Canadian wife in less than an hour."

Everyone on our crew had seen thousands of women at the rails of ocean liners—*Aquitania*,

Mauretania, Queen Elizabeth, Queen Mary, Ile de France, Lady Rodney, Pasteur—we'd looked up at them just hours before they became legal brides on paper. We'd seen military personnel escort each woman down the gangway and onto the dock—some had children with them—their baggage carried by soldier escorts, too. It was dignified.

I wandered about and came to a photograph of a woman looking lost and bewildered, with a forced smile if ever I saw one. The caption read, "Pale homesickness will soon give way to rosy blush of love as war bride meets love of her life." When Hermione joined me in front of this photograph, she read the caption and remarked, "Now, you ask me, that woman left the love of her life in—where's she from?"

"Edinburgh, it says."

"Look at her face—I'm convinced of it. She left the love of her life in Edinburgh."

"How can you tell?" I asked.

"I can tell," she said. "I look at that photograph and you know what I wish her? I wish her some kindness and possibly children. Here she's traveled to Canada—seasick at least half the nautical miles, probably—and what's she in for? Imagine stepping off that ship and spying some bloke at the dock only bears a slight resemblance to the photograph he'd sent, and thinking—probably it's like a screaming prayer in the head: Please, God, don't let that be him!"

"You figured all that out from just this one photograph, right?"

"Okay, I suppose I had a predisposition, you
might say."

I liked Hermione a lot. She was good, honest
company. "I'm going to get a carrot stick with
cream cheese, Wyatt. I'll meet you by that big
picture over there," she said.

It was the largest photograph on exhibit. In it, a
doctor posed facing the camera. He stood next to
a woman, about age thirty, who looked humili-
ated and proud in equal measure. She also stared
into the camera. The doctor was holding a stetho-
scope to her chest, though she had on an overcoat. The caption read: "With great care, Dr.
Roald Ivy lovingly treats a French immigrant as
if she is already a Canadian citizen."

Hermione stepped up and said, loudly, "My
God, that's Mona!"

"You know this woman?" I asked. I inspected
the woman's face closely.

"Tom!" Hermione shouted across the room,
drawing lots of attention. "Tom, come over
here!" As Tom walked over, Hermione touched
her friend's face on the photograph. "Tom, this is
Mona d'Ussel! This is my friend Mona d'Ussel!
She's my neighbor," Hermione said, "catty-
corner from me on Bliss Street."

"So you say," Tom said.

I thought Hermione was going to give Tom

every nasty word just for doubting her. But she said, "All right, let's go to her house. Right now."

"What about Rigolo's?" I said.

"Rigolo's is open till one A.M.," Hermione said, buttoning up her rain slicker.

"Looking at this photograph," Tom said, "one thing I know for certain. Dr. Ivy here's a quack. He can't hear her heartbeat through that thick an overcoat."

"I'll take that under consideration," Hermione said. "Next time I'm in the market for a personal physician, it won't be Dr. Ivy."

The rain hadn't let up in the least, but Hermione was determined to show us what was what. She was fuming at Tom, and made me walk between them the whole way to 45 Bliss Street, which was about ten blocks. "This is Mona's house," Hermione said. "As you can see, my own house is over there across the street."

We stepped up onto the front porch and looked in through the living room window. There were at least twenty women in the living room and dining room. It looked festive. There was a gramophone turned up loud, a female voice singing in French. Some of the women were coupled up and dancing.

Hermione knocked on the door. The woman who answered was clearly Mona d'Ussel, except add all the years to her photograph. But there was no doubt it was her. "Okay, I apologize," Tom said.

"Oh, Hermione—hello!" Mona d'Ussel said cheerfully. She seemed a little tipsy. She had on a beautiful dress. Pearl earrings. "I'm so sorry, Hermione, but I cannot invite you and your friends in. I've even sent my husband off to the movies." Her accent was distinct, and she was more than cordial. "You see, it was my turn to have the meeting of our little club, and everyone's about to sit down for a late dinner. Please forgive me."

We heard someone calling Mona back to her party.

"Mona," Hermione said, "I work with these two fellows. Wyatt and Tom, meet Mona d'Ussel."

"Tom, Wyatt, I can't invite you in," Mona said.

"We just saw your photograph in the art gallery, Mona," Hermione said. "The boys here wanted to meet a famous person."

"That doctor—in the photograph?" Mona spit on the porch. "Not a nice man. And now I'm permanently stuck with him. When I learned the photograph existed, I tried to buy it so I could destroy it, you see. But it wasn't for sale. Now that day in my life—my first day in Canada, the day I met my husband—it's no longer mine alone. I might as well be stuffed in a museum."

"I'm sorry I mentioned it, then," Hermione said. "What kind of club is meeting here, may I ask?"

Mona's face brightened a little, though she still seemed upset. "Oh, all of us are French war brides," she said. "The War Brides of Halifax Club. There was a newspaper article about us."

"I missed it," Hermione said.

"Had you seen it," Mona said, "you would have learned that we've met every month for years now. Some of us are no longer with our war husbands—well, that's what they're called in Britain, anyway. Some of us are still with our husbands but wish we weren't. And some of us are still married and satisfied. We've all become great friends."

"Look, I apologize, Mona," Hermione said. "I feel stupid for just dropping in out of the blue like this."

"Out of the blue in the terrible rain, yes?" Mona d'Ussel said.

"Well, goodbye, then," Hermione said.

"You're not French and not a war bride, Hermione," Mona d'Ussel said, still apologizing. "Otherwise—of course!"

She closed the door, and as we stepped off her porch, Hermione said, "Well, I'd much rather be in there than in Rigolo's Pub with you clowns."

(At that moment I wondered, had my mother and Reese Mac Isaac ever danced to French popular songs? One summer night, through the open kitchen window, I'd heard Reese play some.)

"Rigolo's, then?" Tom said.

We started back down Bliss Street, Hermione in the middle. Rain hats on, collars up. "French war bride or not," she said, "I bet I could've fit right in. I'm a good dancer."

We got to Rigolo's Pub between eight-thirty and nine. We'd just found a table when in walks our foreman, Charles Blakemore. Charles is a big man, about six feet five inches tall, with a handlebar mustache. He's been my foreman for twelve years now. He walked right up to our table and said, "I thought I might find you three here."

"Well, here we are, then," Hermione said. "Sit down and share a mug with us, Charles."

"No time," Charles said.

"What, are you late for a different pub?" Tom said.

"You look on edge," Hermione said.

"Any of you want triple overtime?" Charles asked.

"When?" I said.

"Tonight—now."

"In theory, yes, I'd want overtime," Hermione said. "But it's pretty nasty out. What's the deal, anyway? This time of night."

"What the Navy's telling us," Charles said, "is that a German U-boat's floated to the surface. Off Hartlen Point. It's lolling on its side out there."

"Jesus, Mary and Joseph," Hermione said.

"It's all rusted up inside a length of antisubmarine chain," Charles said. "Remember the sort that was laid in the harbor?"

"For the most part it did the job," Tom said.

"Well, it did the job on this U-boat," Charles said. "Already there's any number of gawkers out there in private boats, and the newspapers got wind of it. There's two tugs on their way. They're going to try and tow it in."

"It's got to be one big coffin, though, right?" Tom said.

"Got to be," Charles said.

"So, what's there for us to do?" Hermione said.

"When the thing gained the surface," Charles said, "a section of it burst apart. I don't know, release of pressure or some such thing."

"Is this some sort of rare phenomenon or something?" Tom asked.

"Off the record, the Navy says this has been happening since the war ended. All over the Atlantic, apparently. Off the coast of France. Off the coast of England and such. U-boats popping up, and the Navy said that just last year one showed up in a Norwegian fjord. Some guy pissing off the rail of his trawler under a full moon got a once-in-a-lifetime surprise, eh?"

"Our U-boat, Charles, was sunk when?" Hermione asked. "Is that for the public?"

"Late 1944. It's sat at the bottom of the harbor since late 1944. Probably it filled with gases and buoyed up. But part of the hull blew open, and we're told there's all sorts of things been jettisoned."

"And that's where we come in," Tom said.

"There's items distributing themselves far and wide, some already washed up to Dartmouth, we're told," Charles said. "And that's why they called us, and that's what the triple overtime's about."

"Look, Charlie, say we volunteer," Hermione said. "Tell us straight out, are there bodies?"

"I wasn't told," Charles said.

"There has to be bodies inside the U-boat," Tom said.

"Doesn't mean they've got out into the water," Charles said.

Finally, all three of us said okay, finished our beers, took handfuls of crackers from the basket at our table for a little sustenance, seeing as we hadn't had supper, and followed our foreman to his car, parked not more than a block from Rigolo's. In twenty minutes we were out in the harbor again.

Good Lord, what a spectacle, Marlais. What a spectacle of history. In 1960, the City of Halifax purchased two new tugboats, equipped with all the latest gadgetry and sporting twice as many running lights as the old tugs. They still had truck tires secured all around just below the railing, to protect the tug from blows—that much hadn't changed. When Hermione, Tom and I motored out a ways, we saw that tugs were on either side of the U-boat and eight crewmen were standing on the thing itself, fixing hooks and ropes. By my quick calculation, there were no fewer than fifteen private boats out there, too, including a small cabin cruiser. Harbor police in a launch were warning them with a bullhorn to keep a safe distance. Cameras flashed, mostly from a boat owned and operated by the *Mail*. As we got closer, we could see, through binoculars, at the rail of the closest tugboat, two representatives from the coroner's office, with official identification badges hung around their necks. A uniformed RNC officer and a half-dozen sailors were on deck, too.

Closer yet, we could see patches of the U-boat's original black color, but in general the paint had gone to leprosy and rust. The entire hull was covered with barnacles, the conning tower as well. As we watched, one of the tug's crew crowbarred open the hatch. The hatch cover was now upright, and three men shone flashlights and gazed down into the hole. Their mouths were covered with what looked like surgical masks.

Faded but legible on the bow was *U-99*. The loud, incessant whine of an industrial saw started up as a man in protective gear and wearing goggles attempted to cut the fence. In a few minutes we saw a link break apart and a length of fence fall into the water. When the saw had started up, dozens of gulls scattered, flew off and back, then swirled overhead as if they'd been drawn by a carcass, the likes of which they'd never seen, in Halifax Harbor at least.

When the RCN officer waved us away, we veered off, and just as we got out of range of the tugboat lights and into dark water, we saw a decomposed body, or what shapeless stuff was left of a body, inside a German uniform, contorting and changing shape with the movement of the water. Tom cut the engine and we drifted.

Really, the only thing that looked at all solid was the belt buckle. I'd seen the buckle glint, and now I shined my flashlight on it and—*whoosh!*— in swooped a gull, which nabbed the buckle. The gull tried to rise with it but was pulled back down, and the bird refused to let go. It sort of half fluttered above and half sat on the uniform, lifting it a little, attempting to dislodge the buckle. Eventually the gull abandoned the effort and coursed back up into the black rainy sky.

The three of us had drifted close to the body, and when Tom poked it with his gaffing hook, Hermione said, "If you keep doing that, I'll vomit on your shoes."

Tom pulled in his gaff and said, "Guess what? I vote against attending to these remains. Let's leave them alone."

"Me, too," I said.

"It's unanimous, then," Hermione said.

"Too bad that German sailor in the water there didn't live to see our example just now," Tom said, "of Canada being a country where everyone gets a vote, eh?"

We looked over at the U-boat. All that macabre industry. Sparks spraying off the industrial saw. I felt we were out among some madness or other.

"We should've grabbed some sandwiches or something," I said.

"I didn't think of it, either," Tom said.

We spent another five hours out there—wallets, shoes, plates, not much else. One logbook. One album of family photographs. Many items of clothing. Hour after hour, peering through binoculars, we followed the progress of the salvage crew and then, near dawn, saw *U-99* towed in to Purdy's Wharf. It had taken the entire night, but they'd done it.

"Let's head in, too," Tom said. "We've done enough."

Hermione pointed to the five burlap sacks we'd filled. "Not all that much loot," she said. "Except for triple overtime, it's been a pretty useless night. But we won't tell anyone that, now will we?"

"Next time Charles tells us one of these bastards pops up in our harbor," Tom said, "we should bargain. Immediate retirement at full salary, plus we each get a house in Cape Breton, plus medical for the rest of our lives. Or else the answer's no."

"Let's stick together on that," Hermione said.

"I've never been to Cape Breton," I said. "Is it nice?"

Close to shore, Tom barely maneuvered around a flotilla of sea ducks, peacefully sleeping. And the tugs and U-boat had just passed noisily by. At Purdy's Wharf we stood awhile under a tarpaulin roof set on poles and watched close-up as six RCN itemized and photographed the contents of the burlap sacks. They were very methodical about it.

"I figure it as seven hours' triple overtime," Tom said.

"Seven and a half," Hermione said. "I'm the one wore a wristwatch out there, remember?"

Charles drove up. We got into his car. Hermione was the first to get dropped off at home. When Charles pulled up at the curb, he said, "All of you look like this whole night's been one solid punch in the gut. Today's what?"

"Thursday," Hermione said.

"My decision is, everybody takes the rest of today and Friday off."

"Good Lord, Charlie," Hermione said, "marry me."

"Do I have to tell my wife?"

"That question shows remorse in advance," Hermione said. "Forget it."

"Today and Friday off and full pay accorded," Charles said. "Meantime, I'll arrange a substitute crew, no problem there. If you want, drop by the office, I'll cash out your triple overtime. Otherwise, we'll take care of it Monday morning, first thing."

"See ya, fellas," Hermione said. "I'm off to dreamland. After a whiskey. And not on the rocks, either." She got out of the car.

Bone tired, I slept on and off throughout the day and night and late into Friday morning. Hardly got out of bed at all except for tea, a bowl of oatmeal, bathroom and to listen to the radio. Friday evening I dropped by Ballade & Fugue, and the moment I stepped through the door, I heard the teeth-grating sound of a needle gouging a gramophone record. "Talbot, you dunce!" Randall said. "I told you, if you carry a big stack of records like that, you can't see where you're going."

"Sorry, Pop," Talbot said. He was sixteen now.

Randall laughed. "That's okay. I'm always so happy when you're putting in hours here with me. Besides, that gramophone wasn't long for the world, anyway."

"Pop, try calling it a record player, remember? It's not your old RCA Victor anymore." There was great affection between them.

"Hey, Wyatt," Talbot said. "You're here—it must be Friday, right?"

"Last week I came in both Tuesday and Friday," I said.

"Right, my dad told me that."

"Wyatt, have some coffee and let's listen to Bach's unaccompanied cello suites," Randall said. "They make some people lose the will to live, but they cheer me right up."

"Just what the doctor ordered," I said.

"Listen to this from the liner notes," Randall said. " 'Played as Bach intended they be, Pablo Casals succeeds in not allowing a single note of compromised sadness. A profound accomplishment.' Know what? I didn't know you *could* compromise sadness."

"I guess a lesser cellist could," Talbot said.

While the Bach cello pieces played, customers drifted in and out, a few making purchases. Suzanne, Talbot's girlfriend, dropped by, and Talbot left with her, and by eight o'clock it was just Randall and me. I thought, I've been coming to Randall's store for well over twenty years, subtracting my time in Rockhead, and I often thought about his store even then. There were no other consequences to the evening, I suppose, except that I envied Randall for having such passion and dedication toward his chosen profession, record store owner and classical music expert. He asked me about the U-boat, and I described it as best I could. "Somebody should've blasted some Wagner through loudspeakers off those tugboats," Randall said. "You know, provide a nostalgic sendoff to Hitler's finest. May they rot in peace."

And then we settled into the comfortable banter we'd come to rely on. Randall on the threadbare sofa, me in the chair with the lumpy cushion and broken springs, listening to cello music. Just before he closed up shop, Randall said, "Wyatt, my friend, wonders never cease."

"Don't tell me Ballade and Fugue is making a profit so far this year."

"Not quite that wonderful," he said. "An hour before you got here, one of those RCN who put me in hospital came in and apologized, right in front of my son. You could've knocked me over with a feather. He had his wife with him, and their two daughters. His German wife he'd met in Germany. She bought a few recordings."

Saturday afternoon I walked down to the harbor. *U-99* was elevated in dry dock, on reinforced scaffolding. There was also a grid of beams, specially made to compensate for any possible shift in the bulk of the submarine. Upward of thirty people had come with their cameras, posing with *U-99* in the background or taking pictures of the boat on its own. Trucks had converged from a local television station and the Department of Health, and an RCN jeep and a few other official-looking vehicles were parked nearby. On deck three men stood near the open hatch. They were wearing black frogmen's suits and buckle-up galoshes and had surgical masks over their mouths, a strange combination. One by one they climbed down, hauling in the hose of an industrial vacuum—the truck it was attached to was close by. On the truck's doors it read MONTREAUX REFUSE CONTROL. The City of Halifax often worked with these guys, and I always found them very competent. A fire truck was parked near the stern, and a fireman in full gear was blasting the hull with a pressure hose. Pretty soon the industrial vacuum could be heard rumbling at high throttle.

Though a police cordon had been set up to keep onlookers at a distance, you could get close enough to see everything there was to see, except of course inside *U-99*, and who'd want to see that? I stood with a family of five—mother, father, two daughters and a son—and since each had their own camera, I figured they must be well-to-do. "At our hotel I read in the newspaper they're going to clean this U-boat right up," the son remarked with excitement. He looked to be twelve or thirteen. "Then they're going to move it to the Maritime Museum."

I lingered at *U-99* long enough to realize I never wanted to see it again. The next time I'm in Harbor Methodist, I told myself, I'd fall on my knees and pray not to ever see it again. I knew where the Maritime Museum was. I'd have no difficulty keeping away.

I got a scone and coffee in an open-air café in the historic district and read the *Mail*, which had a two-page article about the salvage of *U-99*, but gave no details about what was found inside. The article did include an official statement from the RCN: "Records show that on December 19, 1944, at approximately 3:15 A.M., Axis attack submarine U-99 was severely damaged under a massive barrage of depth charges, and in all probability drifted or was mistakenly steered with crippled maneuverability into Halifax Harbor, where it was ensnared in antisubmarine fencing and finally sunk to the bottom. Records also indicate that U-99 was one of the last to have carried out attacks in Eastern Maritime Canadian waters."

The following Sunday I went to the ten-fifteen service at Harbor Methodist. I didn't feel particularly inspired, but there I was anyway, on my way to church. Maybe it's a simple equation: if you arrive uninspired, a sermon has a fighting chance to inspire you, but if you're already inspired, a sermon has to work wonders. Approaching the church, I'd seen on the bulletin board that the title of Reverend Lundrigan's sermon was A POSSIBLE ANODYNE. I'd never heard the word "anodyne" before (my thoughts went to Hans Mohring; had he known what it meant?), and when I walked in and sat, as usual, in the back pew, Lundrigan was already holding forth:

"Anodyne—it's not a word recently in good

repute. But, my friends and neighbors, we all need an anodyne, and the definition, according to *Webster's* dictionary, will tell you why." He set a dictionary next to the Bible on the lectern, put on his reading glasses and continued. "One: a medicine that relieves or allays pain. Two: anything that relieves distress or pain; as in, *the music was an anodyne to his grief.* Three: soothing to the mind or feelings." He closed the dictionary but left it on the lectern. "And may I suggest that *God* can be an anodyne. Think of Job—think of others in biblical times who needed God at moments of great distress, facing challenges of immense proportions. But I don't wish to speak about that quite yet, my friends. For as you know, the sea has recently delivered us a disquieting messenger—a messenger in the form of a German submarine. We must look directly at this messenger and say, 'Evil One, we defeated you. We put you in chains and we defeated you. You have come back to try and torment us with bygone fears, but we reject you!' Here, today, on this holy Sunday in Harbor Methodist Church, Halifax, Nova Scotia, we call forth the memory of our best good deeds and how Canada defended its own. Let me now read from Scripture—"

My whole life, Marlais, I've had difficulty coming up with the right word to use in a given situation, but at least I know what the right word would have been once I hear it. After about

314

two more minutes of Reverend Lundrigan's sermon, I left Harbor Methodist and walked home. I took out my *Webster's*, purchased at J. P. MacPherson's pawnshop for a dollar, and studied the definition of "anodyne" again. When I'd bought my *Webster's*, J. P. had said, "This wasn't fished out of the harbor, but some of its pages are frayed, some might be missing. Don't worry, there's more than enough words left to improve the English of the average detritus gaffer like yourself." She meant it nicely.

And so, Marlais, my letter has caught up with the present moment—right now—7:35 A.M. on April 21. My next-door neighbors in the house formerly occupied by Reese Mac Isaac—Marshall and Caryn Phillips—have already left for work. They're both physicians. Through my kitchen window I can see their seventeen-year-old daughter, Elizabeth—Lizzy—sitting alone at their kitchen table having breakfast. She'll catch the school bus at 7:40 at the corner of Robie and Welsford. And like every morning for the past two months, she's playing *Sgt. Pepper's Lonely Hearts Club Band.* Lizzy's got it at full volume on her record player—*I read the news today, oh boy*—and I'm going to open my kitchen window a little to hear it more clearly. I like the Beatles a lot, and wish Marshall and Caryn would've left earlier than usual for work so Lizzy could've played even more of *Sgt. Pepper.* When she heads off for school, I'll put on the Bach cello suites that I bought at Ballade & Fugue. For no good reason, I'm taking the day off work. Since in all these years I've never taken my yearly two-week vacation, I've got hundreds of days saved up.

In yesterday's post there was a letter from Cornelia. I have it here in front of me. I'm going to copy it out for you.

Wyatt,

I haven't mentioned this, because I didn't know how things might turn out. It's been in the works for some time now to try and find a new librarian. First Mrs. Oleander passed, and her successor, Miss Claire, married and went to live in London. Since then, we've had able volunteers, but a professional was badly needed. It was my brainstorm—I admit—to approach Marlais Hillyer for the position. After all, I knew her credentials, and she'd written that she was not having the best of luck with gainful employment in Denmark. Plus which, she has a house in the village. Of course, it's her house by rights.

So as of today, I'm freely privileged to inform you that Marlais is our new librarian! Even by the high standards set by Mrs. Oleander and Miss Claire, there's much confidence in this decision. I know because I heard this confidence expressed more than once in my bakery. Naturally, when Marlais requested that Chester and Delia Waterford, who were the most recent tenants in Donald and Constance and Tilda's house, find a new place to live, they understood right off, and now they live in Advocate. That went smoothly. Marlais arrives tomorrow.

I'm soon to be seventy-five. You'd look at me, though, and be fooled into thinking I wasn't a day over seventy. I suppose I'll have to bake my own birthday cake. I must confess, my fingers still feel youthful when I'm baking, seldom times else. And of course I'm pleased that my bakery continues and that I can still manage the stairs up to my room.

Wyatt, dear, I pray you're in good health and in as good spirits as can be expected. After you've read this letter, I'd think a visit from you was in order.

Don't forget: now and then, life can be improved upon.

Your old friend,
Cornelia Tell

And now I know where to send my stack of pages: Marlais Hillyer, Cove Road, Middle Economy, Nova Scotia, Canada. I'll post it this morning.

Given my absence, Marlais, I have few expectations, and may deserve fewer. But I won't bring loathsome sentiment into the bargain here, as I'm fully aware that my life has been all failure and delinquency toward my daughter, who deserved far better. But let me say this: I wish to see you and talk with you. My coming to Middle Economy, to the library or to your house, may not be quite the right thing, not just yet, if ever. I must tell you, however, I've consulted a road map and there's even possibilities on it, too. For instance, do you know what restaurant's still in business? The one overlooking the Tidal Bore in Truro, and we could meet there.

Selfish, but at least directly put—I know you could be my anodyne, all three definitions, in fact. And while you may have no need of this whatsoever, might I not be an anodyne of some sort—any sort—for you as well, Marlais?

Is *In a German Pension* still on the shelf there? Before returning it weeks and weeks overdue, Tilda Hillyer, against all library etiquette, underlined the sentences that moved her most deeply in each story. I had this thought, that you might locate the collection and page through it, so you can know which sentences.

Center Point Publishing
600 Brooks Road • PO Box 1
Thorndike ME 04986-0001 USA

(207) 568-3717

US & Canada:
1 800 929-9108
www.centerpointlargeprint.com